The Wrath *of the* Divine Scepter

The Wrath *of the* Divine Scepter

SAMUEL NDAWULA

ARPress
45 Dan Road Suite 36
Canton MA 02021

Hotline: 1(800) 220-7660
Fax: 1(855) 752-6001

Ordering Information:
Quantity sales. Special discounts are available on quantity purchases by corporations, associations, and others. For details, contact the publisher at the address above.

Printed in the United States of America.

ISBN-13:   Softcover   979-8-89356-980-3
                 eBook   979-8-89356-981-0

Library of Congress Control Number: 2024910295

Chapter One

THE NOISE WAS unbearable. I could not take it anymore, so I forced myself to sit up in bed and glared at my century's old alarm clock as it blared. Reaching over, I tapped the silver-tipped stop—button on top of the clock, almost knocking the thing off the bedside table. The alarm stopped, but I winced as the sharp pain on one side of my head hit home again, reminding me of the headache that comes around every time I am suddenly aroused from a deep sleep and always hangs around for about five to ten minutes before slowly fading away. I fell back on to the bed and closed my eyes for a moment. I wanted to go back to sleep, but I knew that was not to be.

You see, I go through this routine every morning. Unbelievably so, but yes, it is customary of me that every night, unable to trust myself to wake up in time, I set the alarm clock for six o'clock in the morning. Not only does the old alarm clock wake me up in the morning, but it also reminds me that I have to do a regular two-way three-mile jog every morning, bath, brush, and get ready for work. This, also, is an eight-year plus old, basically daily habit, with the exception being only on Sunday when I do the jogging, but instead of heading to work, I try church. I say try church because sometimes, if not most times, I am so tired, because of an extra night at work or party attendance.

Gathering up my wits, I finally and slowly got out of bed, wincing up, and made my way to the bathroom. My bladder was so full I felt like it was about to burst. After the welcome relief, I stared at myself in the bathroom mirror. Yap, it is me, alright. A five-foot-eleven, one hundred and ninety pounds, boldly headed (by choice), brown-skinned male with round eyes, sharp nose, strong chin and pronounced jaws lines, a naturally grinning mouth topped by a scaled-down mustache that eventually turns bushy all over the area under my lower lip. Someone by the names of Kiron Day, but commonly known to all friends and foes alike, as "Day." At this moment, I think I resembled a sewer rat, but with my experience, ten minutes would be enough to make me look reasonably human again. But that is after jogging. So I slapped on my sweat pants and a sleeveless t-shirt with the word "cobra" on the back, grabbed my jogging shoes from their usual dwelling place near the pile of dirty laundry in a small closet near the bathroom and put them on. I was ready to go. The Sony run-man digital music player was already preset with the repeated theme from the rocky movie "eye of the tiger," ready to play, so I clipped the Walkman to the waistline of my pants, placed the headset over my head and without bothering to lock the door, I hit the road.

Cool and breezy, this morning, I thought. Yet it could quickly turn out to be one of those Texas summer mornings that would eventually change into sudden dangerously crazy temperatures in the wee hours of the afternoon, a mixture of heavy humid conditions and temperatures running between the upper nineties and one hundred something. I pressed the start button on the player, and inspiring words of "eye of the tiger" started streaming into my ears.

My concentration started sharpening immediately, my muscles tensing as they received their early morning toning.

On the other hand, I knew how it felt if I missed out on any of these exercises. I was so used to doing it that missing one jog routine would not only create physical pain but also hurt me emotionally.

The routine jog reminded me of those days with the covert cobra military unit, when we did those special weekend training camps with the specials from navy seals and army ranger's units, occasionally interlaced with marine core people. This was camp, unlike any other, unique, and fun. At that time, I belonged to the U.S cobra unit, the unit that gets sent to crazy places to do equally crazy things in very many crazy ways. The camps were designed to test whether we still can function under intense pressure at any given moment, to taste our survival capabilities, and improve on our skill sets. Not only did they keep us fit for duty, but we also got to exchange ideas with other special forces and to get to know each other better. This was important because we frequently shared joint ventures which required us to be pretty much on the same footing in terms of survival habits. During these camps, breakfast consisted of a quick six to twelve-mile jog at precisely five in the morning, cold breakfast cereal you have to eat in sixty seconds, followed by press-ups and other toning exercises to burn up those calories.

I had joined the military right out of high school at the urging of my mother, who thought it was a good idea for me to try it out since I seemed to be less challenged in my life. According to life, "those days," I was kind of bored. I was in trouble on the streets of my neighborhood, always fighting someone I thought had wronged me. Although I am the laid-back dude, still trying to mind my own business, I deemed it imperative to deal severely with those in the neighborhood who dared to mess with my little sister or me. And that was because I thought I could do so. At age six, my mother had enlisted me for martial arts training with Master Wong and his equally masterful wife, Wang. The couple, both very skilled, old school Chinese martial arts experts, also had jobs training the local Dallas Fort Worth FBI unit, where my mom worked as secretary to the section's chief. The couple also had contracts with different national government security units to supplement combat training schedules and camps.

The school was their own side business.

By the time I was fifteen, I had gained special fighting skills equivalent to a black belt in both bare and "tool" handed martial arts combat. Because each instructor had different skills sets to teach, I was able to benefit from both within pretty much the same time, but also because the couple had taken a special interest in me, taking me in as their adopted kid, their special student, having known me for so long from such a young, tender age. After this period, and by the time I was eighteen, I was fit to be one of their associate instructors, instructing new students old and young alike. I became so good at it that Wong and Wang prided in me as their golden child, a product of their effort, and took the extra effort to thoroughly skill me to their best, sending me for special sessions with other trusted masters outside the country. I even made several trips with them to their native china just to experience the originality of the art.

With such empowerment, especially for a youthful being, patience for those who knowingly crossed my little sister or me. Because of this, my mom was constantly contacted on issues involving my sometimes, but not all the time, uncontrolled actions, or reactions. Some people even mentioned to her that I was becoming a danger to the community. So, to get away from an increasingly wary and aggravated community that was increasingly making my mother's life very difficult, I agreed to join the army and leave the neighborhood. It did not take long for my Special Forces instructors to realize how skilled I was, and they immediately sent me to their special covert operations unit, which categorized me as a "cobra." There I stayed for five years before being discharged for beating up an abusive and arrogant senior officer. I was in the right, but the command did not want to instigate a rebellion among its men and women, so I was simply discharged.

Once again, I returned home, only to find that my mom's feelings about me being restless and unruly had not changed at all, and she wanted me out of her life again. The discharge from the military seemed to be the last straw to break the camel's back. She sent me to my grandmother, who lived in another town, about fifty plus miles from her house. After that, I stayed with my grandma until I found my current job by responding to a mysterious ad in a newspaper. The job turned out to be the kind of job that would fit my intuition, adventurous. Less than a year later, I was able to move out of grandma's house and into my apartment. Two years later, and at 25 years old, I am still with the same company, still living in the same place, and have never looked back.

As I jogged, I became aware of the change in the breeze pattern around me, which signaled that someone, or something, is getting close to me. I could not hear them because of the blaring music in my ears, but thanks to "cobra commando" training, motion and environmental imbalance of the slightest nature were one of those other senses installed in me. I slightly turned to see Karen Moss, one of the neighbors that lived in an apartment in the block next to mine, steadily catching up with me. I grinned at her. She winked at me and then ran past me and ahead. I continued jogging at my current speed, knowing that I would catch up with her later when she stopped to catch her wind. She is one of the two people I closely associated within the apartment neighborhood, the other one being an older man who was my next-door neighbor. A single mom living with her little boy and a cop by profession, she always comes to my place to share a glass of wine and or talk, and I to hers.

And her little son, David, liked me a lot. I caught up with her at my third mile, her upper body bent down, hand on knees, panting for breath. I smacked her cute behind, but she didn't barge. She was used to it. I jogged ahead for another ten minutes, then turned around and started back. The return jog is always faster because I am eager to be done with it. I rushed past Karen quickly and without a word as she steadily picked up the pace on her return jog. She increased speed, caught up with me, and together we made it back to the apartment complex. I waved at her, and we split. She rushed off toward her block as I ran up to my apartment and entered my place. I shut the player off, threw the headset off my head. It was time to catch my breath.

The phone rang.

"Hey, hi," It was Karen.

"Hey, hi," I replied, repeating the familiar greeting she always passed on to me every morning after the jog.

"See you this evening?" she asked.

"Sure, why not?" I replied. "Is David coming over with you?"

"No, not today; He will be with his dad".

"Ok. I will see you later then." I said.

"Later." She concluded.

As I proceeded to take my shoes off, I noticed that the message light on the phone set was flashing red repeatedly. I had erased all old messages last night, and so it was easy to know that this one just came in this morning. I walked over to the kitchen – living room divided counter and pressed the play message button.

"Hi Day, this is Jim. Call me back as soon as you get this message. If I am not at home, call me on the cell."

That is Jim Holmbeck, my work department manager. To get a call from him, this early meant something big is up, usually a hot job. As I reached for the phone, my beeper went off. I could hear it from where it lay in my bedroom, still attached to the pants I wore last night. For a moment, I stared at the phone and in the bedroom. I decided to check the pager first before I called. The pager going off meant that something critical was up from two different parts of my life: either for work or from my folks. Only these people had the pager number. I had told my family only to use it if there was an emergency. My sister, however, always abused this privilege by blowing off the pager with flash messages, now and then, even when she had nothing significant to say except to hear from me. This time, though, it was Jim's number again. He needed to talk to me. I picked up the phone and dialed his cell number directly from my memory. Five seconds later, he picked up.

"Day, I need you to meet me at the office as soon as possible today," he said.

"Everything alright, boss? "I asked.

"Everything is alright, but something has come up, and I need to talk to you," he said. "Can you make it in thirty minutes or less?"

"I will be there in twenty or less," I said.

"Great. See you in twenty then."

The line went dead. I hung up too, threw my shoes off, and hit the shower. Five minutes later, I was done and quickly dressed up. I gulped down a glass of cold milk and a banana and was ready to roll. It was Saturday morning, so traffic on the freeway was not bad at all. I managed to pull up outside my workplace building in Irving right on time. Jim Holmbeck was pulling up too. He did not say much except "hi" as he got out of the car and led the way into the building. This was unlike Jim, though. Normally, this unusually cool guy stopped to say hello and jokingly commented on your current appearance or complimented you on being able to come to work that day. Born of Chinese parents, but adopted and raised by an American couple, **Jim Holmbeck** maintained a simple profile while running one of the most sensitive jobs at one of the most profitable private firms in the state of Texas. He is the chief of field operations at **Eden Communications**, or **EdenCom**, a private investigative and communications firm attached to such big names as the United Nations exceptional archives division and the world research council. The thing is, EdenCom is not the usual small-time paparazzi operation. Its operations are much more sophisticated and on a bigger scale. The company specializes in getting first-class information from areas of interest for its clients. Usually, that means areas that are not readily available or easily accessible to the client themselves by reasonable means.

Soft-spoken and humble, Jim was well known for respecting not only his superiors but his subordinates too. At the same time, he was always cautious that his job was done right and took his work very seriously. He, therefore, turned out to also be a strict and demanding boss to work for. But he also made sure that once if the job was done well, the person responsible was rewarded well. If the opposite happened, the line between maintaining this person at the department or even with the company becomes very thin, all depending on the circumstances. He was also said to be a lenient boss, but not very tolerant, just because his boss gave him no slack for that. That is how he maintained his team. The field operations department is the heart of the company and took a massive chunk out of its functioning budget. So, he was not fulfilling the promise to the client in the best way possible, also meant loss of a lot of money to the company. So, a lot of responsibility is vested in the director of the department.

"Sit down, Day," he said when we entered his office, a simple one desk, one computer, one phone, two chairs set up.

I sat down in one of the chairs by the side of his desk, facing him but slightly to his right. He adjusted his chair, so he was facing me directly.

"Murphy just called me this morning and told me there is a big job coming up," he said. "You know Murphy. Part of him works on instinct, and now he feels that this job is a big thing and wants someone on it immediately. He wants me to find the right agent to go on this because he wants it done right. I am lining you up as my number one choice. This means that if you have anything lined up in your life after the next twenty-four hours that is not a matter of emergency, please do cancel all because, after that, you are most likely going to be on assignment. If you do have emergency situations to deal with that time frame, stuff that has to be taken care of and can't wait, let me know so that I can arrange for my number two choice to come in for a briefing."

"I have nothing critical on my upcoming agenda, boss, except for an appointment this evening with someone," I said. "That means I will take the job."

"Great. Murphy asked me to call him back immediately once I get an agent lined up for the job," Jim said, sounding relieved. "I am supposed to meet him for a department briefing in two hours. But he said the earlier, the better. When he called me, he was on his way to his office. That means he is here now. Since I have you lined up for the job, I will call him to set up the briefing now. Are you o.k. with that?"

"Anything you say, boss," I said, grinning.

"That is why I dig you, man," he said, laughing. He picked up the phone and dialed a number. He held on for about a minute before it was answered. "Sir, I do have an agent lined up as you requested. Yes, that fast sir…thank you for the compliment…in thirty minutes in the private conference room. That will do." Jim hung up and looked at me. "He could not believe I had already lined up an agent. He said he hopes that my efficiency also means I got him the best. We meet with him for the briefing in thirty minutes."

"Do you have any idea of what the assignment is about?" I asked.

"Not a clue, but when he calls me like this, then something big with an equally big, well-paying client is up for the show," Jim said. "It is most likely going to be an overseas job. What remains for me to find out is the job's actual nature so I can start preparing for it. He said he wants me to find an agent who is capable of handling a special project if I am to quote his very words."

The thirty minutes went by fast, and I spent this time with Jim in his office. We talked about family and sports. The man is an intense soccer lover, and so am I. At twenty-five minutes, we left his office and took the elevator to the fifth floor, where the private conference room is located. I had been there once, two years ago, when I came back from an assignment that had Mr. Murphy furious (assignment china). At the same time, it had also turned out successful on my side, and that was how I had won Jim's favorable side. I had stuck to my guns during this assignment and, in doing so, had done the job right, pleasing my boss. Since then, I am still in Jim's good books.

Outside the conference room, Jim knocked lightly on the door.

"Come in, Jim, "the big, raspy voice that sounded like someone just recovering from a nasty heavy cough came from within. Jim pushed the door open and then stood aside to let me in. I stepped into the well illuminated, wall to wall red-carpeted, room. It was fully loaded with video conferencing capabilities of all kinds, comfortable-looking leather-backed chairs, and a big polished oak conference room table. An array of accessible refreshment units was also visible, ranging from a big coffee pot to a hot plate and refrigerator. Jim came in behind me and closed the door.

Harold Murphy stood about six foot five tall, a medium-sized man with a clean shaved head that had that bright shiny look one could be convinced from just one look that the man probably has his head waxed and buffed. His trademark eyes, sharp as an eagle's, were strangely complemented by a sharp nose, thick lips, high cheekbones, and a narrowing forehead.

Humorous tales circulating about this man and the strange aura of myth surrounding him said he was thought to be the human reincarnation of the bird itself. His eyes had that piercing stare, he rarely smiled, and he moved with ease and confidence, always standing straight up and erect. It was said that while he is a good listener, Harold Murphy's intelligence was unprecedented amongst his peers and very demanding of his managers. I also heard that he has a hell of a temper if ever triggered into one. He was famous for throwing his hands up in the air and raising his voice in a snarling way, and at that point, if you were the source of his annoyance, it was better to listen until he finished venting. One single word before that, someone had lamented, and your days at EdenCom would be over. With Harold Murphy, having to be in his good books was subject to what was at hand in that period. That means that if you are good at one time, and then messed up later, the previous episode of goodness would be forgotten. So, to be in his good books, one had to stay current, doing well in every project allocated to you.

He now waved us to a set of chairs with a single hand gesture, and then took one himself, facing us. He put on his glasses and looked at me. I thought he was glaring at me, but it was something to do with these spectacles of his. "Kiron, Good to see you again," he said.

"Good to see you too, sir," I replied. I was surprised he remembered my name. I had only met the man twice, and that was on my hiring confirmation day at least two years ago, and for a mere fifteen or fewer minutes three months ago.

"You guys can help yourselves with stuff from the fridge and shelves," he said. "There is coffee and some cookies made by my mom. They are pretty good; I can tell you that. Whatever you can lay your hands on."

"I will make some coffee," Jim said before I had a chance to intervene.

"I already made some for myself, and I left some for you guys," Murphy said.

"Actually, the cups are all set up so we can get going as soon as possible."

Jim poured us some coffee and brought both cups over to the table. He also carried over some cookies. Murphy was right, and they tasted perfect. We now faced the "eagle" and waited for him to deliver. He picked up a set of papers from a thin folder in front of him and passed them over to Jim. "I received these late last night from the U.N. secretariat. It is one of those strange special projects that they want us to handle for their archive's division. After reading through, I faxed back an acceptance. The thing is, the nature of this one is extraordinary, and for some reason, I felt the urge to take it on for its curiosity simply. It also requires immediate action on our part."

"Ethiopia?" Jim asked as he took a glance at the first paper.

"Yes, Ethiopia, "Murphy confirmed. "Here are the facts. A young Ethiopian native who happens to be the son of a local priest seven months ago reportedly had a dream. The dream was about a stick. Now, according to the boy, the stick in the dream belonged to biblical Moses. The boy claimed that an angel appeared to him in this dream and instructed the boy to get the stick and take it to a certain mountain from where Moses would pick it up. The boy described the place to his father, who then went on to this place to investigate. The father found a stick, wrapped in pieces of old sheepskins in the exact location the boy told him. According to the boy, the stick was supposed to be in seven pieces, and once found, was supposed to be left in the same sheepskin wrappers for seven months for the pieces to join into one full rod. This too, was found to be true as described by the boy to his father. The father was apparently so shaken by these findings; he went straight to the head priest and reported the matter. The head priest came to look for himself, and once he laid eyes on the sheepskins and its contents, he officially took charge."

"And what became of the boy?" Jim asked.

"He was immediately declared a living saint, placed in a special house, and given all, he asked for at once," Murphy answered." I hear that included a play station. All priests, the dad inclusive, were ordered to revere him and pray through him. One thing, though. The boy had also told his father that the angel's orders were to be strictly followed, or all sorts of the trouble of great magnitude would engulf the land. He said the nation of Ethiopia would be doomed, if not the entire world if the instructions about returning the stick were not strictly followed in the seven months after being discovered, and after the seven pieces rejuvenated into a full rod. That was seven months ago. Today, the whereabouts of the stick is unknown, but we do at least know that the head priest took it. So, there is our head start. What is also known is that the boy is guarded by Ethiopian special police with automatic rifles. Thousands of local's throngs to this place to see and pray to him. What our client wants us to find out is what this is all about, but most important of all, to track down the whereabouts of the stick itself. The boy is part of the assignment puzzle, although he is less relevant at this stage."

"Why don't they directly contact the head priest?" Jim asked.

"Well, right now, there is no trace of the head priest or even the boy's father," Murphy replied." They have both vanished from the public eye. I have put that on our concern list too. Find the head priest, and most likely, we shall catch a glimpse of the stick."

"But time is up," I said. "You said that this happened seven months ago, and that is the time it takes the broken pieces of the stick to rebuild back into one full stick so Moses can pick it up. Isn't it too late for us to intervene?"

Both men looked at me. The "eagle" smiled. I thought his mouth had grown a few inches extra outwards, into beak.

"Precisely," he said. "The seven months are up, and further reports from reliable placed sources state that of recent the boy has become very restless, has stopped playing his games, eats very little and refuses to see or pray with anyone. A British reporter, who is affiliated with the U.N.

and on the scene at the house where the boy is, reported that the boy had demanded to see his father, and that when the father was ushered into his presence, the boy had warned his dad that the time was very close and if the instructions from the angel is not carried out as ordered; the resulting doom would spread to the rest of the world. To be precise, we are in the seventh month now.

Anything could happen anytime now. And that is why our client wants us to go in there and look this up quickly. So, Gentlemen, we have to act fast."

The "eagle" stood up and started pacing the room. "Here is the deal. I want an agent sent to Ethiopia quickly. Go down there, dig up all you can, and use all means possible to document: Audio, visual, satellite relay, telephoto, whatever and get this material back to us. Our main objective is to try to find the high priest and his accomplices and get as close to the stick as possible. We need to get some tangible results for the client. We need to get as close to the facts as possible and come up with some substantial evidence concerning these events. That is what they want from us. One thing to note, though, is that the client has also warned me that they are not the only ones interested in this case. Sources have it that other parties are getting involved, specifically the Israeli military intelligence, Egyptians, and wealthy Arabs. Even our government is presumed to be picking up interest in this. The warning here is that it can turn out to be a dangerous and volatile assignment. There is no telling how many players are now involved. The prize is big, and people are willing to kill for it. So, you have orders to tread carefully. Watch your back all the time and be on the alert for trouble. If it gets too rough for you to handle, keep what you have and quickly get the hell out of there! Is that Understood?"

"Yes sir, we understand," Jim said quickly, but then turned to me and said. "But it must be seriously hot before you abandon the project, right Day? I mean, try to get us something worth the effort, something good. Our client must get something tangible. That is why I believe this kind of assignment is right for you."

"Sure, I will do my best," I said.

"Great," Jim said and turned around again to face his boss, who was staring at both of us, hands in pockets. "We are ready, Sir. Just give us the details, and we shall roll."

"How fast can he leave?" Murphy asked.

"Give us about forty-eight hours," Jim replied.

"That will work," Murphy said. "Kiron, I am going to go over this material in detail with Jim, who will prepare you for everything.

Meanwhile, I suggest you hung around the building until we are done because I want Jim to get you briefed on the basics before you leave this building today."

I nodded affirmation and left the room. I wondered around the place. It was mostly empty of people, being the weekend, save for a few workers who were most likely finishing up work with deadlines. Only workers in critical departments like Jim have no typical weekends off. Jim's job required him to be on call twenty-four hours, seven days a week, in case an assignment showed up on the operations radar, just like this one which popped up from nowhere, and hence the call was made. But I was surprised to hear that the person most on call twenty-four hours is the owner himself, Harold Murphy. Even in his private time, after all his employees have left for the day, Murphy can still be found alone in the private conference room, working on something, or watching CNN on the ninety-two-inch screen T.V. He also has several telephone lines directly linked to his cell phone and travels around in a Chevy suburban that has satellite communication capability installed inside, together with all sorts of communication equipment. In short, the big SUV is like some sort of mobile communications station. Murphy made sure to stay in constant touch with the world as it revolved around. The man worked hard, and Jim had once told me that this dedication and hard work had gotten the company to such prosperity, turning it into a multi-million-dollar private communication outfit.

Armed with a master's in communications technology specializing in internal security, Murphy had worked for the defense department's satellite transmissions department. The U.S. national security agency had used him to head its national communications technology network. He quit the job when the political establishment in Washington started to sort of make his official position a public and political stunt. He preferred working in the shadows, does not like politics, and understands control of communications systems better than messing with human minds, Jim said. Murphy then went into consulting, working for such big gigs such as individual governments, local states, and big conglomerates that specialized in his trade. That was how he found out about Eden communications, by then a small outfit that used sophisticated technology to investigate issues too hard for anyone to handle, but at a local level. It was a kind of small, spy tech firm. The owner was calling it quits and trying to sell off the company to pay off his private gambling debts. Murphy was fascinated by what the company did and had the vision to take it even further. With his expertise, he would be able to streamline its operations into perfection. He scraped up some money and bought it. With his network of contacts in the intelligence and communications world, he was able to get better jobs for the company.

Now in its twelfth year, EdenCom has a high reputation as one of the best global infiltration's firms in the world. The consulting services, which Murphy now linked together with an investigation function, were raking in money for the company. I also heard from reliable sources that Murphy had been involved in some big global deals that raked the company a hefty share. Now there was a rumor that Murphy was planning to retire, and that one of his two twin daughters was being trained to take over.

Murphy has a son born out of wedlock, and who had, unfortunately, turned out to be a mess. His compulsive gambling habits, trouble making episodes, and over-drinking practices had put a heavy toll on Murphy's shoulders. Most of the time, the young man had to be escorted off the company premises by company security after trying to harass his dad, often complaining that Murphy only cared about the girls. Murphy was rumored to be so disgusted and disappointed in his son that he had once denounced him as not his own. It was also said that this was the sole reason he was still working as hard as he did, for fear that the company would end up in the wrong hands. His daughter, an I.T. major like her father, was still so young to wrestle with company politics, not to mention her brother. The two young people thoroughly disliked each other, with the brother accusing the father of favoritism and the sister accusing the brother of being a worthless loser. It was also rumored that she had once mentioned to someone that when she takes over as head of the firm, she will make sure this problem of a worthless, overbearing relative is taken care of permanently. This twin had the same fires as her father, often unyielding, with a lot of wits and very intelligent.

Her twin sister, on the other hand, was the opposite. She was not interested in the business but instead had a knack for the humanitarian side.

She was the only person who seemed to have some control over the brother. She was studying to be a doctor and had plans to open her clinic. The only time this twin showed up at the company was during company anniversary celebrations, chatting with her father once a while, or when she wanted some quick money for a school project. Both twins were said to be beautiful young women, born of an Egyptian mother who their father had met during his tours of duty. She had unfortunately died giving birth to them. Their grandmother then raised the twins, Murphy's mom, who was proud to share the same upbringing with the two girls as she had done with their father. No wonder they were said to have the same demeanor and attitude as their father, the difference being that they are female.

My first encounter with Harold Murphy was instead a twisted string of indirect events.

On my first day of the interview, I arrived early enough to be on time. I was part of a group of people waiting in line for an elevator.

This older lady was standing next to me with two plastic bags full of stuff, and she looked like she was straining to hold on. So, like my mom had taught us always to try to be helpful whenever the occasion arises, I offered to help carry one of the bags for her. She declined the help, and another one of those senior members of the community that firmly believed that she still had all the ability to do everything by herself and certainly did not need any help, thank you! I did not insist on either.

The elevator arrived. Now, it was one of those early morning times when everyone was rushing to get to their allocated work areas on time, as strictly mandated by the owner of the company, and so the rush for the elevator was massive. I managed to secure one of the last corners near the elevator doors and right in front of the control panel, but the older lady became the casualty.

Someone with a more extensive, extended elbow advanced the long-awaited loss of control of the bags she was holding, and she found herself letting go.

The bags hit the floor, and the stuff spread out on the floor.

Nothing scary or personally embarrassing, but the items were littered all over the floor outside the elevator. The elevator doors started closing, leaving the old lady standing out there and looking dumbfounded. I realized that the nut who had elbowed her was not thinking of backing up to help pick her stuff up. So, I quickly and automatically volunteered. I immediately hit the stop button with my big thumb, and the door rolled back open. Everyone in the elevator looked at me, wondering what I was doing, perhaps thinking I was crazy. But no, I was not. I was going to do what I had been taught to do by my grandma, and that is to try to do the right thing, given the right time. At this time, I was required to step out of the elevator and help what appeared to be a distressed old lady. I stepped out of the elevator and approached her.

"Lady, please let me help you pick this stuff up," I said. But this time I did not wait for her to re-engage that stubborn, independent attitude. As the elevator doors started closing behind me, I started picking up the items on the floor.

"Young man, the elevator is leaving you behind," she cautioned with a look of concern on her face as she watched me quickly gather her stuff. "You ought to be on your way before you get delayed."

"I can see that, but so are you," I said. "I am just glad that I can help you with this, and it only takes a couple of minutes of my time to do so. I am also surprised that the person who bumped his elbow into your stuff did not even have the thought to stay behind and correct the situation."

I finished collecting the items and bagging them up again. Lucky enough for her, the bags were still intact. I handed her one of the bags and retained one. "And I will help carry this for you to your destination, mom. And please, this time, allow me to do so." I said to her conclusively.

"Yes, this time, I will let you," she said, smiling brightly. I could tell she was pleased by my persistence to help. "You must be one of those rare young people of today's generation. I am surely thankful for your help."

"My pleasure," I responded dutifully. We waited quietly for the next elevator, which showed up in the next five minutes or so. There was no rush for this one, so we could get on it without being bashed. I asked her what floor she was going to and pressed that floor number's button.

"And you may be one of those wacky vendors or a new employee," she said, smiling and without looking at me. "I have never seen your face around here before."

Wacky vendor? That sounded funny to me, and I laughed. "No, Mom, I am no wacky vendor. I have a job prospect with this company, and today I am having my first interview for the job. You are right; you have never seen my face around here before because this is my first day here."

"A job seeker, oh my dear," she said. "I think management would make good use of people of your nature around here. I am curious; for what department are you looking forward to work under?"

I told her that I did not know yet, that I had responded to an anonymous Ad, and was invited for an interview. The elevator arrived on the fifth floor, where she was going. We stepped out together, and she led the way without saying another word. Surprisingly, she had a robust and quick stride for an older lady, and I found myself having to readjust to keep up.

We arrived at what appeared to be a walled glass section of desks and computers outside another closed in a suite of offices. A young woman was sitting behind one of the desks, and she looked up as we walked in. Smiling widely, she stood up quickly and came around her desk and took the bag from the old lady. She smiled at me briefly, and then that smile disappeared even before she fully turned her face away from me. One of those fake smiles projected to replace the words "good morning" or the simple term "hi." I always wondered why people bothered to fake the smile when it was not really meant to be. But she smiled brightly again at the old lady and, after uttering a good soft morning to her, disappeared with the bag of stuff inside the inner office. I watched as she swung her hips gaily left and right and out of the vicinity and could not help but to note that she has both very good shape and a very pretty face to match with it. I also thought she looks like one of those girls with a very expensive taste and a zest for very expensive things.

"You may place that bag on that table next to the computer," the old lady said. "Gina will take care of it from here."

I did as I was told. She extended her hand out, and I was shaking the dainty hand when Gina returned.

"Thank you very much, young man, for being so helpful," the older lady said, "And for being so nice at it. Good luck with your job prospects."

With that and a bright smile on her face, she joined Gina into the inner office.

I acknowledged, said goodbye, and smiled at Gina as she picked up the bag with a lot of ease and grace. There came a fake smile again. Then she was gone, disappearing back into that inner office, leaving behind a memory of gracefulness and a whiff of perfume that made me feel hugging her for eternity.

But after I left that office, Gina instantly ceased to be anything but an admirable object in my memory. I also remembered that this floor is also my destination in the building. I checked the piece of paper from my pocket, bearing summarized details to make sure. The fifth floor was room 405; I quickly found it because it was not too far from the glassed-in office. It did not have walled glass cubicles outside its entrance like Gina's place, but just two doors with numbers on them. I knocked, was asked to come in, and so I did. An older looking lady was seated behind a desk with a computer on it. I introduced myself and then gave her the piece of paper that was emailed to me, inviting me for the interview. She asked me to take a seat and wait.

Meanwhile, she took the paper from me and entered an adjoining office, closing the door behind her. She came out of the office about a minute later and quietly resumed her seat behind the computer, which completely obscured her from me. Ten minutes later, a man came out of the office and came over to me. Shaking my hand, he asked me to join him in his office, one of those luxurious four-walled enclosures with controlled climate, wall to wall carpet, and the whole modern office technology set up. The man sat behind a high, leather-backed office chair, offering me one of the other comfortable chairs he was facing.

It was to be one of those interviews that I dreaded.

A multitude of questions followed after the man took his time examining the data, he had on me, plus the brief resume I had given him. The questions ranged from explaining what I was precisely doing prior to the interview date to why I think I should be the right person to work for this company. Do I agree with a strict drug and background check? Have I ever experimented with drugs and alcohol abuse before and been arrested and convicted of a felony? Given the job, what good things will I bring to the company? And so forth!

A printed-out questionnaire followed and was given to me to fill out. While I penned it, he left the office briefly. When he came back, he started doing something on his computer. I was done in about ten minutes and handed it back to him. After briefly glancing at it, he nodded his head and then told me that the interview was over and that he was going to review, and compare, my results with other applicants, together with his colleagues, and if they found me suitable for the job I will receive a call. I thanked him, although I did not want to do it.

Judging from his attitude, I felt that this guy did not really want to give me the job and had already made up his mind why I had no clue.

I was getting up to leave when the telephone on his desk rang, a series of fancy but precise sound blips. He picked up the receiver, listened without saying a word, and then hung up. He strangely looked at me and then said, "Uh, Mr. Day, don't leave yet. I just received a call telling me that someone else also wants to talk to you about this job prospect."

I sat down again and waited. About five minutes later, there was a light knock on the door, and when it opened, the elderly secretary's head popped in. "Mr. Boyd, Mr. Murphy, is on his way to your office. As I speak right now, he is next door talking to someone."

"Murphy himself?" the man asked, sounding edgy. "I just received a call from his office a few minutes ago. Gina told me Murphy was sending Jim Holmbeck to hold a second interview with this guy. She did not tell me the man himself is coming."

"Well, I just came to give you a tip-off," the secretary said with a smile. She seemed to be getting a kick out of her boss's anxiety, which was clearly showing. "I think I can hear some people outside my door. He is here. Have fun."

Her head disappeared, and she closed the door softly behind her. I watched as Mr. Boyd readjusted his tie and sat up erect in his chair. Two minutes later, the door opened, and there was no knocking this time. A tall man walked in, his right hand in his pocket, and left side holding a small paper folder. Mr. Boyd stood up immediately.

"How are you doing, Boyd?" the newcomer said, his voice deep throated as he had just come out of a severe coughing illness. The man projected a lot of confidence and authority.

"Very well, thank you, sir," the office incumbent answered, "It is rather a surprise to see you out here this early, sir. What can I do for you?" Boyd sounded genuinely surprised.

Mr. Murphy smiled. "Surprised? Well, get used to the fact that you should expect me anytime and without warning," he said. "Anyway,

I wonder if a young man came through here for an interview a few minutes ago. I do not know him very well, but I want to meet him."

Boyd looked at me and then said. "This must be him, Mr. Murphy, sir. He was about to leave when Gina called me…"

"That will do, Boyd. No need to explain," Mr. Murphy cut in. "I will take over from here with him if you don't mind. Send his paperwork to my office, and I will review it from there." He now looked over at me. It looked like a minute, or so ago, I had not existed at all in this room. The intensity of those piercing eyes behind the horn-rimmed spectacles was overwhelming. "What are your names, young man?"

"Kiron Day, sir," I answered, getting up. The guy was tall. I found myself looking upwards.

"Quite an unusual name, your last name," he said. "Come with me to my office Day. Thank you, Boyd. That is all I needed." With that, Mr. Murphy turned around and strolled out of Mr. Boyd's office, with me at his heels. Boyd said something, but I didn't catch it, because it was some kind of mumbling. I don't think Murphy got it either, because he didn't acknowledge back.

We ended up back to that office suite with the attached glass-walled cubicle where I had gone first. And there was pretty Gina again, sitting behind her desk. She looked up and smiled. This time, the smile lingered around longer than the other two I had experienced. I smiled back as we walked right past her and entered the inner office. This was a much bigger room than Mr. Boyd's, carefully designed to accommodate a lot of stuff elegantly. It had sofa seats all around it and a glass desk facing the arrangement. Behind this table was another leather-backed chair with its black leather shining brightly from the morning sunshine rays coming through the big window behind it. Two chairs were facing this chair on the other side of this desk. I was offered one while Mr. Murphy claimed his throne. His desk had nothing much on it except a laptop computer, printer, and telephone, a multiple pen holder, and framed photos of some people. I immediately noticed one particular photo amongst the whole set. It was the picture of the old lady I had helped earlier.

Murphy cleared his throat and said, "I gather you want to work for this company. What kind of job do you have in mind?"

"I did not have a chance to figure out what this company is all about because the Ad was anonymous, so I don't know what's available," I replied. "But I bet you; I can try anything."

"So, you just applied blindly?" he asked. "That's very unusual too. I am curious, what prompted you to try us out even though you knew nothing about us?"

"Keen Sense of adventure, sir," I replied flat out.

"Hmmm," he said, slightly raising his eyebrows. "What kind of background do you have, Kiron?"

"Military, plus a lot of martial arts, sir."

"Still active? Are you in the reserves?"

"No, sir. I am ex-military."

Opening the paper folder he had come with, he picked up a pen and jotted down some stuff on the paper inside.

"Ok, let us try that out," he said. "Take this to my secretary right outside my office and tell her to take you with this folder to Jim Holmbeck. He will tell you what to do next."

He closed the paper folder up and tossed it over at me.

"Thank you very much, sir," I said as I stood up. To my surprise, he stood up too and offered his hand, which I shook. The firm iron grip was very notable.

"I appreciate you are helping out an old lady the way you did," he said. "She was so impressed she insisted I hire you without question. To quote her words, "hire you without much ado." She told me you had nothing to do with her bags spilling over. Some jerk did that, but you volunteered to help, even if you knew you would be late. Now, as much as I don't encourage the late coming of any sort; I am pleased that you went out of your way to help an old lady that you knew nothing about. This old lady happens to be my mother, and she means a lot to me. If it were not for her, I would not be where I am in life today. So, young man, keep up the good spirit."

He winked at me and then resumed his seat again, a sign that he was done.

I didn't know what to say. I just smiled like an idiot, mumbled something, and then left the big office. Once I close the door softly behind me, I stood there for a moment, trying to get myself together, not believing the way things were happening. I looked at the paper folder in my hands and then quickly opened it to take a peek at what was inside. His notes on the paper were below a summarized profile of my data, probably from the material I had given to the person who had called me about two weeks ago to provide me with a preliminary interview before granting me an interview date. His scribble read:

Jim. Fix this guy up in the field office and put him on payroll immediately. Skip probation and put him on entry-level one with a pre-professional pay code. Call me if you have any questions. He had signed "Murphy" underneath this paragraph.

I was in. I had a job. I finally had a job. I couldn't wait to tell my grandmother about it, because in my whole life, she is the only one person who always believed in me without question, and always encouraged me to follow my instinct and to believe in myself. She is my sole motivator. And wait until she hears about the bizarre way, I got the job. She would be wide-eyed with surprise, and I could now hear her calling out to the lord.

And so that was my first encounter with Harold Murphy, owner and founder of Eden communications ltd, now a multimillion-dollar, privately owned and run company with global tentacles and connections and one of the most influential organizations in the state of Texas.

And it was also the first time, on this day, that I met Jim Holmbeck. But that was not bizarre, so I am not going to talk much about it. I now proceeded to tell Gina to take me to Jim. I approached her desk and waited for her to finish up with what she was doing on the computer. She finally looked up. Big, brown eyes with a shiny twinkle in each stared up at me questioningly.

"Yes, sir. How may I help you?" She asked.

"He wants you to take me to Jim Holmbeck," I said.

"Sure, come with me," she said. Her voice was soft with a country-western teenager tone in it. She gracefully rose from her seat. Slightly taller than me, I figured out that the high heeled shoes were the extra inches above me. I also now noticed that she lacked that skinny, sickly physical outlook of today's so-called supermodels. Just lightweight lean. She also had probably spent a considerable amount of money on the perfume she was wearing because she smelled terrific. The makeup on her face was balanced to an almost natural look, while her long black hair was carefully tied into one long silky ponytail that went all the way down to the base of her spine. This girl was gorgeous.

I followed her to the elevator, and we stepped in together. There was nobody else in it. I stood next to her as we rode the elevator, and for a moment, I did not know what to say. When I spoke, words just came flat out from nowhere.

"You are lovely, Gina."

She showed surprise, perhaps because of my boldness when addressing her directly by her name. "Thank you," she said, not looking at me. "So…did you get hired?"

"I think so," I replied.

"I think so too," she said, still not looking at me. The doors to the elevator opened when it came to a stop at the floor of our destination, and we stepped out. A group of people was waiting outside for it. They greeted her and then entered the elevator. "What manager are you going to be?"

"Manager? I don't think I am going to be Manager of anything," I said. I did not understand why she thought I am to be a manager. I didn't know I looked like one right now in my black slacks, blue long-sleeved dress shirt, and black Italian Giuseppe all leather dress shoes. Maybe I did, by her standards. "All I know is that I am going to be fixed up with the field office."

"Entry-level?" she asked.

"Yes, I believe." I came with my immediate reply.

"You are going to be a field agent, then," she said. "But you must be exceptional to receive what I call the royal treatment. Mr. Murphy does not deal with the hiring process at all except with senior management level positions like department heads. In your case, he came down to get you himself. If you are not a relative of some sort, you must be one lucky guy."

We came to a door labeled director of operations. Gina knocked lightly on the door and then pushed it open. A lady was sitting behind a desk outside another entry, just like the Boyd office. "Melanie, this guy is here to see Jim. Mr. Murphy asked me to bring him over immediately."

"He already called and spoke to Jim about it," Melanie said. "Jim is waiting for him right now."

"Now then, he is all yours," Gina told Melanie. Turning to me, she switched on "that smile" again and said, "Well, it was nice meeting you, Mr...."

"Kiron. Kiron Day," I cut in.

She laughed, which sounded more of a giggle." Alright, alright, Kiron. It was nice meeting you and good luck with your new job."

"Thanks, Gina," I said. To my surprise, she touched my arm lightly, smiled again, and then gracefully swiveled her way out of the room. And just as she walked out of the door, she turned around, smiled at me again, and then was gone. Now I believed that this last smile was genuine.

I turned around and looked at Melanie. A middle-aged lady in a beautiful clean white blouse and black skirt, black medium soled shoes, and decent makeup. She had apparent glasses, probably for reading, seating at the end of her nose, and stared at me through them with keen, intelligent eyes of an elderly school headmistress running an all-girls' school, the kind that you don't get by that easily. Why? She has been there and done that.

"Hi, Melanie," I said.

"Did you and Gina already know each other from somewhere or did you just meet today?" she asked, ignoring my greeting and leaning forward over her desk, her head slightly cocked to the left in a questioning stance. But that did not bother me a bit.

"First time meeting," I replied.

"I think she has fallen for you," she said flatly. "I have never seen her behave this way towards a stranger. But she is a nice girl; she is worth a try. And she is single, very hard working and neat as a freak. I highly recommend her."

"Thank you. I will look into it," I said.

She uncorked her head back into position and stared at me wryly like she did not believe I was taking her seriously. "Well, I will let Jim know you are here. Please have a seat."

I did. A few minutes later, Jim Holmbeck took me into his office and, without asking me any questions, quickly processed my employment authorization at EdenCom. From that moment, I officially became a company employee in the most bizarre way I have never known.

But Harold Murphy seemed to suffer from a bad memory, at least as far as my case was concerned. The next time we met along the corridors within the building, it was like he had never seen me before. Then we ran into each other in the parking lot. I made every effort to greet him while trying to let him know that we had met before and that he had hired me. I was disappointed when he flatly responded by asking me how the job was going and then driving away before I could even give him a full answer. I soon came to realize that the man was so work-driven that to him, every event is a timed process to be completed. Thus, by hiring me (he had most likely been pressed by his mother to do so), he had merely accomplished an event, getting it off his schedule and creating space for the next pressing matter. Once done, I was history.

So, this day, as I walked the corridors of the fifth floor, those memories came flashing back. By the way, I had decided not to pursue Gina because when I tried, I realized she was extremely high maintenance. I did not have the cash for daily lunches and dinners, and neither was I interested in babysitting her Chihuahua. I did that once, and I almost kicked the dog because it could not stop barking and more so tried to bite me. But recently, I learned that she had finally gotten engaged and even set a wedding date next week. One of the company's senior accounting executives had fallen for the long gig. She was also now pregnant. She was now on vacation, preparing for her wedding.

In her place now was Julieta, a much more down to earth and easy-going, less exotic, and less eccentric beauty from Mexico. I went over to the walled glass cubicle and asked her if I could use her phone. With a smile, she moved it to where I could easily access it. I dialed Karen Moss's cell phone number.

"This is Karen." She answered, crisp and clear.

"Hey, Hi," I said, using her habitual greeting style." What are you doing?"

"Cruising around the city, police business, "she replied.

"Listen, I was summoned to Eden's this morning by my boss, and something has come up," I said. "I am being set up for a field job, and right now, I am waiting for him to finish summing it up with his boss so that he can fill me in with the final details."

"Are you traveling?" she asked.

"I believe so. To Africa, I am told," I replied.

"When?"

"Within forty-eight hours, I am told."

"Knock it off, Kiron. That is too soon. Tell me you are kidding," she said. I could tell that had set her off.

"Unfortunately, I am not, Karen, "I said. "But we still have time for this evening. Did you have something planned out, or do I have to improvise?"

"Why is this always happening to me?" she said, sounding distant suddenly. "I had plans for a weekend getaway with you in mind. Every time I tried to do something with someone like you, it gets knocked off by the very person I want to be with. Sometimes God is unfair."

"I am sorry, babe." It was all I could say.

"Well, my sister and her friends are going out tonight at this place in Dallas, and she wants me to go with her," she said. "Her lousy boyfriend is coming along with her, and I bet you all her college cronies are. It is one big group coming from Houston. I refused, because college kids bore me like hell, but then she had mom involved. Mom called me and asked me to tag along. My sister had been partying a lot lately, and my mother is worried that her brat will get into trouble. So, I accepted. And I have this fun part for you."

"Hit me," I said.

"She wanted to hook me up with one of her fellow students, a male criminal justice major who had told her he would very much want to hook up with a real-life cop to experience justice first class. Now, I must be some booger head to fall for that kind of immature stunt." Karen said.

"You mean you did not accept the offer"?

"Of course not. I told her I had someone else in mind."

"This isn't me. So, may I ask who that person is going to be? Just curious," I said. I was toying with her now. Of course, I knew I was the fill-in guy. She didn't buy it either. She was too smart and too down to earth for that.

"Kiron are you coming with us or not?" she asked, sounding impatient already.

"With you, yes. I do not know about 'us', "I replied.

"You are so pig-headed," she said. "I will see you this evening then, around six, ok?"

"Sure. Don't be late," I said, and then hung up just as she did.

The relationship I have with Karen is one of those unique, free-lance things. We kept each other company, did each other favors, and talked about our problems. Occasionally, we slept together, depending on when one or both of us are in extreme need for that kind of thing. It is one of those relationships where no one exactly claimed the other as their permanent partner or lover. She occasionally went out with other guys, mostly from her department, and I took some girls out too. Let us say we are just 'very good friends.' For example, Karen would never come over to my place without calling me first and rarely asked questions about my personal life. I acted the same way, yet we spent a lot of time together. I hope you get the idea.

I thanked Julieta and left. I went back to Jim's office and sat down, burying myself in a copy of Time magazine's most recent issue. Fifteen minutes later, Jim came back to his office and shut the door behind him, locking it. He then proceeded to fill me in.

"You will be flying to Addis Ababa, Ethiopia, within seventy-two hours or less from now," he said, "within this time frame, all necessary operation issues will be arranged, including your travel and stay in that country. Due to the nature of the assignment, we have arranged for your equipment to be part of your secured luggage. You will have a UN tagged visa while in Ethiopia, and you must have your UN credentials with you all the time. Your co-operative is a native Ethiopian female by the names of Salieya Menankala. She is our head contracted liaison in the region. She has been with us for a little over two years. She knows the region very well, she is fluent in most of the native dialects, and those are some of the reasons why we put her on this assignment. I will give you more data for you to read about her. We have already contacted her to get things going, and she is already doing that. Mr. Murphy is supposed to hold a video conference with her and me tonight to brief her on all the fundamentals of the assignment. Once there, you must keep in touch with us as frequently as possible. We are also processing an international firearm permit for you, although we do sincerely hope that you won't need to use one during the assignment. We don't want our name tarnished with nasty firearm endangerment codes, making it difficult for us to get one the next time we need it. Any questions so far?"

"Who will be in charge of the assignment?" I asked. "The last time I was on assignment, my co-operative had superiority over me, and that almost ruined everything because I wasn't allowed even to suggest anything. I don't want to be a dummy again."

"You guys have shared responsibility," he answered after hesitating for about fifteen seconds. "But you have more say in what to do and as you deem fit. She has leeway in things like the best way to travel, what directions to take, and what place to go to further the assignment. She does not influence the whole operation. In other words, you decide what to do given the circumstances and have the final say in the assignment's real business. Is that good enough?"

"Fair enough," I answered.

"Please be nice to her. She is a sweet girl who knows her stuff very well and does her job as instructed," Jim said. "I know you had a bad experience on the previous assignment with your co-worker, but I am sure this one will be different. You guys will have to work together to make this work."

"Got ya, boss."

"Good. Now get your stuff ready and perhaps take a long nap. I predict that this assignment will be intensive, even engaging, and you may not get much sleep once you get fully involved," Jim said. "Monday morning will be your final briefing, and I think we should be able to fly you out that evening or early the next day."

I wished Jim a good day and left. I felt sorry for the poor fellow, because every time Murphy got on to him like this, it meant that he was going to be completely tied up for the next several days, just working on the project, and maybe another somewhere. This meant sometimes taking the work home.

Sometimes I wondered if he even had a life. He spent most of his free time with his little two-year-old son. His wife, a nurse at one of the major hospitals in the area, equally worked hard, and the short time they had together was considered valuable, according to him. He had jokingly told me one time that it was a miracle they had got some time set aside to make a baby, but that he ended up being compensated very well.

I drove back home after stopping by a grocery store to pick up a few items. I like cooking most of my meals from scratch and just occasionally eating out. This way, like my grandmother, always told me, one has greater control of or say as to what ingredients went into your food. Whenever my grandmother engaged me in such dietary theories, I was also busy helping her prepare meals from scratch. This was rather intriguing to me. I saw a whole new creation comes to the dinner table from scratch. That is how I got into the habit of preparing my meals. I like doing it. This meal, though, was quickly assembled and consumed.

Next, I cleaned up the house a little bit and then rechecked my travel bag. As part of the job requirement, a field agent working for Eden Communications Company had to have a "quick travel kit" always at hand because most assignments showed up unannounced. Everyone had been drilled as part of the job training as to what to include in the kit. You could add your stuff as needed, the official one serving as a guideline. I always have mine ready and intact, checking it once in a while for upgrades. After that, I took a nap for about three hours before waking up again and then feeling a little bit under the weather. I took a cold shower and felt much better. A phone call from my sister killed some time, and then other people called wondering what I was doing this Saturday night. I have a date, I told them. Some people wanted to come and hung around at my place, but I declined due to conflict of interest. I felt it would not be nice for Karen to go around and find herself rivaled by another one of her kind. So, I decided to read the material that Jim had given to me concerning the assignment.

There was some printed material about Ethiopia, and about my co-operative Salieya Menankala. Two years older than me, which made her twenty-seven, Menankala was a native Ethiopian, the fourth daughter of an Ethiopian news broadcaster and a Jordanian businesswoman. She possessed a mass communications degree earned from one of the top universities in East Africa and was now working on her masters in linguistics, which EdenCom was helping finance. Fluent in English, Arabic, French, Spanish, Hebrew, Chinese stuff, and a host of Ethiopian dialects, she was officially a member of the international linguistics achievements club, quite powerful and distinct in her way, I thought. She was listed in the manual as "driven by ambition", loves tennis, a very down to earth person but also very a very charming person. After reading the summary on her, I felt like I was ready to meet charming Salieya Menankala in person.

Around eight o'clock I pulled out a black, sleeveless leather outfit with matching trousers complemented by a white collarless shirt, from my carefully selected wardrobe and endorsed it with flat-soled leather shoes. Adding on my beloved military-style beret completed the semi stealth look. Karen showed up about thirty minutes later, dressed "almost to kill" in black, a tight leather outfit complemented by leathered Lady Giuliana - Gasso ankle-high boots. Her hair, now loose, looked silky and black and covered her shoulders. Karen Moss was born of Puerto Rican parents, with high cheekbones and big round eyes that sparkled with a twinkle in the center.

Moss was her ex-husband's name, the father of her little boy. They were now legally separated, the divorce in the works. Very pretty and confident of herself, she sometimes went on the wild side of life and, most of the time, displayed a tough, no-nonsense attitude when on duty as a cop.

This attitude was what kept her on the Fort Worth police force, and she was not far from becoming a lieutenant.

Now she looked me over and grinned. "You look like Mariachi at a wedding party," she said, flopping herself on to the sofa.

"The last time I wore something like this, you said I looked like a displaced drug lord," I said. "Now I look like Mariachi? What's next, woman?

I hope that pretty much sums me up for now because Mariachi is about to walk out of his pad in the company of a very hot girl."

She laughed a short-lived, soft, girlish giggle. "You are so sweet, Mi. Amigo," she said. "Just kidding, though. You look cool, big boy. You always look way cooler, though, without any cloth on. Happy now, big boy?"

I joined her on the sofa, and we embraced and then kissed her long and hard. I sensed the hunger rising and decided this was not the right time for it. This kind of fire needed a lot of time to be quenched. Her sister was about to show up anytime, and that would undermine this intention. So, I pulled back from her.

"Ok, I am ready. Let's beat it." I said.

She stood up and quickly straightened herself up. "Mine or yours?" She asked. She meant the car.

"Your preference," I said. She had a one-month-old, fully loaded jeep Cherokee sport with one hundred miles on it. Compared to my ten years old Honda pilot, hers was a much better ride.

"Let's use yours then since we have been using more of mine lately," she said. Then without warning, she wrapped her arms around me again and planted her lips on mine. They lingered there for about a full minute before she moved them to my neck, clinging on me tightly. Her rosy perfume was so naturally overpowering I felt myself doing the same and did not want to let go. "Kiron, I am glad you agreed to come with me to my sister's thing on such short notice."

"Well, you are always there for me, too," I said.

"I am going to miss you when you are gone for that assignment," she said. "I can feel it already. I don't know why, but I hate being so much alone these days."

"I am going to miss you too."

"Any idea of when you're coming back?"

"No, I am not sure when," I replied, "Most likely in a couple of weeks or so."

She disengaged herself and looked straight into my eyes. The twin twinkles darted to and fro. "Do be careful, Kiron. I want you back in one piece. Can I drive you to the airport, or at least ride with you?"

"I will be careful. I don't know about giving me a ride to the airport because agents are usually transported by a company car for the assignment. But I will ask Jim, my boss, he might agree to it. I will let you know. Now let's go see what your sister has for us," I said, picking up her small purse with a big silver chain. I linked my arm around her arm, and we walked out of the house. I disengaged myself briefly so I could lock the door, something I was getting used to doing because she insisted that I must. For some reason, I always forgot to do so. Maybe it was because of the days in military camps, where everything else was in the open. We spent most of our field training in tents at night and outside during the day.

"Hey, Kiron, you look swell!" Someone shouted from the parking lot the moment we stepped out of the house.

That was Karen's sister, Emily. Two vehicles loaded with people were parked in the parking lot outside my block. I could see the red dots glowing from the lit cigarettes. College kids ready for a night out.

"You didn't tell me they were outside," I quickly said to Karen as Emily got out of one of the cars and made her way towards me. She was as tall as her sister, moderately chubby. Karen worked out at the police gym, Emily didn't. If it were not for this physical difference, the two could easily pass for identical twins. "Thank God you didn't invite them into my apartment. I could have been youth raided. Hello, Emily. How have you been doing lately?"

"Great, great," She said, giving me a squishy hug, followed by a five-second vigorous back rub with the palm of her hand, and Sounding happy as usual. "Thanks for coming along. Big Sis here told me she had someone special coming along with her, and I guessed it would be you. The rest of the guys over there are all my school mates. You guys follow us. It's a straight shot into Dallas."

"Just don't drive like a bat coming out of hell and expect us to keep up," Karen said to her sister. "We lose you; we turn back."

"Got it, big sis," Emily replied, smiled briefly at me, and then ran back to car.

We got into Karen's car and followed Emily and her entourage into downtown Dallas. We ended up outside a private club at a party organized by one of Emily's wealthy friend's family. It was a birthday bash for this friend and her twin brother. We soon found ourselves bored, so Karen and I wandered away back to the car where, at her initiative, we did some more smooching. For some reason, Karen was having a 'high romantic fever of extremely high temperatures' this

Saturday night. We were still gazing into each other's eyes when there was a tap on one of the windows. It was Emily. I rolled down the glass.

"Hey guys, we are now heading out for the real thing," she said. "It's not far from here. Just follow behind my car. And sis, don't forget to straighten up your top. Otherwise, it will be pretty obvious that you have been smooching and the guys might start making fun of it." Emily then did her high-pitched giggle. She loved teasing her sister.

"They better mind their own business," Karen said, sitting up straight in the car seat.

"And if they don't, what are you going to do? Shoot them?" Emily asked sarcastically. For some reason, she always got that way with her sister and without warning. It happened more often in my presence too.

That drew one hell of angry verbal rhetoric from Karen, but the younger sister was already scampering away, giggling loudly.

"Chill out, woman, she is only teasing," I said.

The next thing I knew was keys being tossed at me. They landed on my chest with a thud. I guess that was one way of telling me to shut up too and drive. Both sisters had a fiery side, and right now, it was clear to me she was on that side of the fence.

"She's so wicked. Does she always have to mention something about my job to gratify her so-called teasing?" She snapped at me. "And why in the world are you always standing in for that little devil? You and my mother just doesn't get it. I am really fed up with this abuse, and one of these days, that little devil will get a serious whooping."

I was very aware that the two girls never really had a flourishing, harmonious relationship. Nine years apart, they had a lot, not in common between them. Yet Karen always tried to be very protective of her little sister, making sure that Emily did not get involved in any trouble. Emily, being the youngest in a family of four, was spoilt rotten by her family. I could not understand why she liked being the over annoying kid sister to Karen, even if Karen always displayed patience and tried her best to be supportive of her teenage life. Karen had been pushed to the edge already, but her mother kept urging her to be understanding and to always be there for her baby sister. She believed that I, like her mother, did not realize that Emily goes too far. What she didn't understand was that I just hated to see her "lose it". Karen can be a beast when angry.

Anyway, we followed Emily to another location in downtown Dallas, to a place on Elms street. The street, lined with numerous night clubs, was now throbbing with all kinds of music. The one we went too was club El Chico. It was packed to the brim, even this early. We paid the entrance fee, got in and everyone spread out.

"You guys have fun," Emily said to us as her boyfriend, a bold headed Tex-Mex kid with a round, chubby face, and a buildup of muscle, started tagging at her arm. It was a statement that was directed at me only. Emily knew it that with Karen around, the fun was not going to be maximized. She hated her sister watching over her even if she were already twenty-one and could legally do whatever she wanted. Karen would tell their mother of her awkward acts, and then things would change for the worse. Since she was still in college and therefore entirely dependent on her parents, the one thing Emily did not want to do is to annoy them, more especially her mother. But she made sure that Karen knows that she wasn't always wanted around. Neither did Karen want to, but her mother always called on her help, to be there, knowing that it could keep Emily in line. And Karen had pulled Emily out of several nasty incidents that would have landed her in some terrible trouble had their parents known. She had not mentioned anything about all that to them. For that, Emily should have been grateful, but as I said before, baby sister wasn't getting it yet. Now Karen grabbed at her sister's arm and pulled her back. It was like playing tag between the boyfriend and the sister.

"Emily, you're going to play it safe, right?" Karen demanded. "I don't have my uniform on and neither did I carry my gun. I don't want to get involved in any reckless issues tonight, understand?"

"Alright, mother hen, I will!" Emily replied, shrugging herself free. The two women then glared at each other like two sworn enemies with no vengeance to spare. Karen let go of her arm and then suddenly flipped her middle finger off at her sister, an upward thrust right into her face. Now that was new in Karen's world. I had never seen her do something like that and never seen her show so much resentment in her face. It was clear that she had now reached the peak of her tormented tolerance and had broken free of it. She wasn't taking it anymore.

Now I saw Emily lose some, if not all, of her composure, and for a moment, she stared down at the floor, a grim look on her face. When she looked up, she still had that blank, serious look on her face. She then quickly said something to her boyfriend, broke her arm free from his grip, and took a step or two towards her sister. For a moment, at least for those few seconds, I believed we were going to witness a sisterly wrangle. Of course, Emily would get her butt whooped, but this was the wrong time and place for that. We would probably end up being thrown out of the club, both women embarrassed, and the night would be over for everyone. The thin red line between the two sisters was about to snap. But instead of this happening, Emily reached out with wide-open arms and hugged her big sister tightly.

"I am glad you are here with me, Karen," she said, now looking into her sister's face with that big hearty smile she always showed when she saw me, "And I am sorry if I made you angry, sorry that I make you angry a lot of times. But I love you dearly, big sis, because you, out of the whole family, are always there for me. I promise you that I will never do so again, and I will play it safe tonight. Are we ok now?

That was one of the most touching scenarios I had ever witnessed in my life and between the two women. It was then that I realized that Emily was finally changing into a grown-up, mature person. I saw Karen blush, a visibly relenting show of relief, but also surprise, transforming her face instantly with a smile from ear to ear. She patted her sister heartedly on the back.

"You go, girl, and have some fun," she said.

Emily kissed her sister on one cheek, winked at me and then the two young people disappeared into the crowd on the floor.

"Well, talk about making up," I said, turning around to face her. "And since when did you learn to finger flip people off? I have never seen you do that before.

"Yeah, talk about attitude change. It's high time she did that," Karen said. She ignored my comments on the finger flipping. We were standing very close to each other now, and I could feel her fresh breath in my face. Instead, she put her arms around my neck and dragged me through the maze of heated bodies on the dance floor. We didn't stop until close to the center, and just in up in right timing for a hot reggae tone beat.

She guided me into it. One hell of a dancer, she started slowly swinging her waist and hips like there was no bone in there. The sexy way she did it instantly turned me on. I felt the frenzy build up in me and found myself adapting to the movements involuntarily, automatically, like I was under some witchy spell. Around us, linked up couples were catching up to the intoxicating big beat with a not too slow, yet grinding rhythm. Bodies were getting very close together. Karen's hands were all over me, pulling me closer to her so close that I could feel her heartbeat. Her torso started rubbing against mine, slowly but hard. She went up and down, spun around, and felt her buttocks rubbing me in a flip, up and down motion. Then she was back again fronting me, her forehead stuck to mine, eyes staring into mine, her body shaking from head to toe. She was leading me into every beat and turn of the music. Before I knew it, I was into the real mood of the evening and did not care a bit about how frisky the dancing was or what was going on around us.

We got off the dance floor to take a breather, stood on the side, watched others do it, and then hit the floor again. The next breather came, and Karen went looking for drinks. She came back with two bottles, one a cold beer and the other near-frozen ginger ale soda. She handed the ginger ale to me. I am no alcohol enthusiast, and she respected that, insisting that it was a good thing to have one of us sober. Not that she ever got drunk, she never went beyond one beer on a night like this. I was also always the designated driver when going back home.

The night went smoothly well until way after midnight when things were at the peak. Karen and I were resting on the side when we heard the noise coming from somewhere on our far left. Karen became immediately concerned.

"Hold on to this. I will be right back," she said, handing her bottle to me and took off immediately in the direction of the uproar. I found myself a free corner and stuck myself in the shadows, right below a ceiling fan. It was becoming muggy in here, and the music was beginning to sound deafening to me. I was sure glad to be directly under the swishing blades. About two minutes later she was back, not looking very happy. "Kiron come with me. Something bad is about to happen out there, and I think Emily and her boyfriend are involved."

I followed at her heels, once again pushing through the tightly packed dance floor, filled with sweating, leather-clad, and partially clothed bodies. The only way I managed to know where I was going was because she was holding on tight to my hand and leading me through the crowd. We finally made it to the problem in approximately one minute, and as she said, it was escalating into a bigger problem every second. Two groups of people were angrily confronting each other. If I were to define the situation, I would say that the so-called elite group, which consisted of most of our company from Emily's school, was confronting these guys who seemed to have come

from the meaner side of the streets. Even their attire was different. Dressed in sleeveless leather jackets, pants, and iron-clad shoes, these guys traded Fu Manchu beards and bold heads. Thick fake gold chains hung around their necks, and some had pin-spiked finger gloves on. To sum it up, there was nothing neat about these guys. One among them looked meaner than the rest. I think this was the ringleader.

"Alright, break it up, boys. What's going on here?" a big growling voice intervened. It was the club bouncer easing his way through.

"Fu Manchu here came up from nowhere and started pawing my girl, man," one of the 'elites' said, pointing the finger at the street side ringleader. "I told him to back off, and now I am being confronted by his cronies."

"Hey, I just wanted to dance with the bitch, that's all," the street man said. "It's supposed to be free, ye? Out there, it says free lady's night, man. Then Mr. Freak here started getting worked up over nothing, calling me this Fu Manchu shit."

"Alright, you guys take your arguments outside," the bouncer, an over six-foot hunk of muscle in a light checked shirt, leather sleeveless jacket, and black trousers said. He wasn't willing to get into it now. Hell, the night was nearly over, and I don't think he was thinking about going into overtime. To my surprise, the bouncer turned around and left.

But the disagreement was by no means over yet. The 'elite 'group was beginning to disband when the mean street man called out again.

"Hey, bitch, I said I want to dance with you, so you aren't walking away from me," he said. "And don't make me come for you, because you won't like it if I do. So, you better get your pretty ass over here now."

To which the girl's boyfriend, turning around angrily, snapped back. "Come and get her, if you can, you piece of shit."

That was it. Fu Manchu strolled over and grabbed the girl's wrist. As she screamed at him to let go and started twisting and pulling, trying to free herself, her boyfriend lashed out by throwing a straight punch at the street man's face. Mean and more experienced than his adversary, the street hood ducked, grabbed at the flying wrist, and twisted. Down went the other guy, screaming in pain as his wrist got bent around with brute strength. In no time, the other members of the 'elite' group jumped on to the street man, prompting the rest of the street hood to pitch in.

"I said break it up!" the bouncer was back, clearly much taller than the stocky, solidly built street fellas and the well-fed, not so fit college group. He jumped right into the middle of the mix and pushed them apart with one heave. "Any more of this bull shit, and I will be forced to break some bones. You want to tear yourselves up, move your asses out of my club to the outside," he growled.

"Why don't you mind your own business, asshole?" someone from the street side said.

The bouncer heard that alright. He turned around and confronted the street men. I also noticed they had a few girls with them. These girls were a show of tank topped upper bodies, mini leather skirts and boots, nose, lips, ears, and belly piercing. So why in the world was one of them getting over the edge with another club patron's woman? That is a question I would try to figure out the answer much later. There was no time for answers right now.

"This is my damn business, buster," the bouncer growled. "And if you have any problem with that, then be a man and show yourself. Then I will show you that I exactly mean that." He started strolling towards the street group. As he did so, he stripped off his jacket and tossed it up into the air.

"This doesn't look good," Karen said. "I better get Emily out of here." She started moving to the other side.

"You stay back there," the bouncer said to her, pointing a finger. But Karen ignored him and continued. At the same time, I saw something gleaming in the hands of one of the street guys. It was a knife. Now I realized how serious this was going to become. Then in the next few seconds, more gleaming things showed up with the rest of the gang. Someone, somewhere, was going to end up seriously hurt. The bouncer continued strolling towards the street gang. Suddenly, someone jumped forward with a knife, and not at the other group, but the bouncer. Karen was right behind him, determined to get Emily, who was standing to the far left, watching everything with horror written on her face. Her boyfriend had left her to defend his friend. The club muscleman saw it coming and leaped backward, and in doing so, knocked Karen right off her feet with his body, sending her sprawling into the other group. Sparing a second, the bouncer turned around to see if Karen was alright.

"Sorry Mom, I didn't mean to do that to you," he said, as an angry Karen tried to get up from the floor. Emily rushed out to her sister's side. It was all the time the street boys needed, or so they thought. Two more gleaming knives lashed out, all aimed at the club's muscle man.

"Watch out, man!" I yelled as loud as I could. The muscle man immediately turned around and managed to parry off the knife blow aimed at his ribs, but the other attacker sunk the toxic metal into the flesh of his muscled arm. Then I saw yet another gleaming knife coming towards the same target. I realized that the bouncer was being attacked from all directions and would soon be overwhelmed.

Not fair, I thought. I had to think fast. In seconds, I threw the bottle of beer that I was holding for Karen at the street man closest to the bouncer, also attacking with a knife, with all the strength I could summon. The bottle smashed into the side of this guy's face with a thud and exploded. The man fell back, reeling from side to bottom as he did so. He hit the floor with his knees with an accompanying, louder than usual shrieking "aaaah" cry from his mouth. At the same time, the club muscleman landed a hard fist into the man who had knifed him in the arm. Bummm! That street guy went down, losing his grip on the knife. I didn't think he was going to get up again soon.

I rushed to Karen's side. She looked dazed. "Baby, are you alright?" I asked with sincere concern. Emily was on the other side, holding her arm and trying to help her up.

"Back off, I am ok!" she said ruthlessly. Too late, I realized. Karen, the cop had now kicked in! But all around us, the chaos had broken out again. Bottles and everything else that could be thrown was flying across the room in all directions and at everyone anywhere.

"Stay down, stay down," I shouted out, fearing that the two women could be hit by one the airborne objects. Then Emily saw what I was seeing. Paco, her boyfriend, had been hit by something and was bleeding from a gash on his head. In a moment, Emily was up and running towards him.

"Oh crap! Kiron, please go after her," Karen said immediately, and I could sense immediate urgency in her voice.

"Are you alright?" I asked again, ignoring her request.

"Yes, I am fine! Just go get her!" she shouted, staring at me with overstretched eyes. Now I sensed panic and hysteria in her voice.

I got off my knee and made my way through the mess of flying objects, to where Emily was kneeling before Paco, trying to stop his cut-up forehead from bleeding.

Half his face was blotted with blood and tissue, and the front of his shirt was all soaked with it. It was flowing from a deep gash between his eyes, right above the nose bridge, and it looked nasty.

"Oh, man! We better get you out of here and to a hospital fast!" I said.

"That freaking piece of shit hit me with something, "he mumbled.

I put my arm around him while Emily grabbed the other side of his body. His heavyset body was tough to haul upwards, but we managed to get him to his feet. We started for the exit, which also proved to be the primary destination for most of the other club patrons. We didn't get far.

"Yo, Chico, that's the punk that threw the bottle at you!" someone shouted from somewhere on my right. I stopped and turned to look, almost throwing the other two off-balance. I found myself staring into one of the meanest. looking, red-eyed, bleeding face on the planet. The last time I saw something similar to that was when I came face to face with a full-grown female baboon, with its young one clinging to its back, during a military training expedition in the South African jungle. What had saved my life that day was the South African unit commando on my side. He had whispered into my ear not to move, or a make any sound, at any cost. The animal would have interpreted that as a provocative signal for attack and would have attacked immediately. After a wait that seemed like an eternity, the animal finally walked off, followed by a dozen other female counterparts that suddenly appeared from nowhere all around us. Now I knew why the commando had kept me down. It was certainly possible to shred this mother baboon's throat quickly using the double-edged combat knife pulled from its sheath on my hip. It was virtually impossible to do the same to a dozen or more equally ferocious, pissed off baboons. They would have jumped on us and tore our bodies to shreds in no time. I appeared to be in a similar situation right now, except there were no piggy-backed babies here. The mean-looking tough was flanked by two other mean-looking, street honchos.

Now check me out: here I was being confronted by three mean-looking, angry, and bloodthirsty gang men armed with gleaming knives, and all I had on my side was a girl and her bleeding, well-fed crony. That was not fair, I told myself. Once again, I felt the urge to act fast, especially when I realized what I had done.

I had messed up the gang leader's face with that beer bottle! And boy was he mad, and without another word, he started strolling towards us, chest heaving up and down slowly, not oblivious of what was going on around him anymore. I took my hand from around Paco and making sure he was stable on his feet, quickly told Emily to pull him to the side and as far away from me as possible while I confronted my adversaries. As I let go, someone grabbed Parco's freed side and quickly pulled him away without a word. A second glance revealed that Karen had come to the rescue. I was now left alone to deal with this dangerous situation.

"Alright guys, everything is cool, please back off," I said, loud enough to make sure they were hearing me. I raised my hands in front of me. It was a classic street brawl, POW style surrender, a sign that I didn't want any trouble. At the same time, I was readying myself for the attack.

But they did not back off. In one quick swoop, Fu Manchu lashed out at me, slashing at my belly with his gleaming knife. But his flying wrist was met with my flying foot. I wasn't about to let that deadly piece of metal come near my body. The force behind the kick sent the knife flying out of his hands and into the air. I have no idea where it ended up, and I am sure he didn't either. He pulled back, clutching his hand, a look of shock and surprise on his face, not being able to understand, perhaps, how fast the kick had come and from nowhere. I was back on my two feet in no time and faced the other two street men.

Whap! I sent in another kick, which targeted the neck, and went down to another gang member. For some reason, the third man did not have the knife anymore and decided to fist it out. He rushed in, and I slammed him with an upper right into his face, stopping his mad rush. Before he had time to figure out what had happened, I stepped in closer and slammed him with three more rapid punches, knocking out both his eyes and renewing the assault on his nose. He reeled downwards and hit the floor.

I turned around to survey the situation. Fu Manchu was coming up, shaking his wrist. I had probably dislocated it with that flying kick. I saw him reach into his pocket with his other hand, and instinct told me that this time he was going for a gun. There was no time to waste. I rushed him, bumping into him with an extended elbow and rammed a hammer fist into his neck. As he staggered, I got a tight grip on his hand as it came out of the pocket. I was right. It was a gun. I twisted hard on that wrist. He managed to put his hand around my neck to stay on his feet, and that grip was strong, almost cutting off my breath. I pulled and heaved, forcing us to tumble backward and hitting the floor with a thud. I fell on top of him, pinning him down, and maintaining a grip on the gun tottering wrist. In one strong move, I swung the gun upwards and away from me, and then forced it downwards, slamming it hard into the floor. The gun went off. It was a loud bang, not new to me, but I had not heard for a few years. That ensured even more panic on the floor. Everyone was scrambling to get out of the club. As Fu Manchu tried to get up, I back elbowed him in the face and fell back. I rolled over the gun holding hand, flattening it to the floor, and managed to pull the gun out of his fingers. In a moment, I had the safety on, disabling the gun.

Then the next thing I knew, uniformed figures were everywhere. Police surrounded me, and they all had their guns drawn. Not pointed at Fu Manchu, but at me.

"Drop that weapon, right now!" someone shouted.

I dropped the gun on to the floor and went down on my knees, putting my hands behind my head. Before I knew it, about five or more guys suddenly crushed into me all at once, like those other guys tackle the other team in American football, knocking me down, and pinning me hard onto the floor, my arms getting twisted painfully to force them behind my back. A pair of handcuffs was put in place around my wrists. I looked over to see the same thing going on with the street gang man.

Someone quickly read us our rights, while someone else was calling for an ambulance and more backup. I was suddenly yanked off the floor onto my feet and led outside to a police car. Everything seemed to be happening so fast now I barely had time to say anything. I was bundled into the back of a police car, and the door slammed shut behind me. I decided to stay calm and wait, figuring out that there was nothing else for me to do at this moment. I wondered about Karen and Emily. I hope they got out of all this, alright, I told myself. Five minutes later, a police officer jumped in behind the wheel and drove away from the place.

"Look, man, you guys got the wrong person," I said. "I am a good person here. I intervened to stop a bad thing from happening. The other guy pulled out the gun and was about to shoot when I took it away. Someone had to stop him before your squad arrived."

"Tell that to the judge, or your attorney," the policeman said.

"I have witnesses who can testify to that," I added, ignoring his advice.

But the police officer simply ignored me too. I realized I was wasting my breath, so I settled back and relaxed. Things would probably work themselves out later. We arrived at the police station ten minutes later. I was pulled out of the car and led inside. A few minutes later, the booking process began. That seemed to take forever. When it was done, I was thrown into a temporary jail cell or, to sound more official, a holding cell. I heard the booking person telling an officer that the real jail cells were full to the brim. Even the holding cell was filled with people of all kinds. This must have been one hell of a night for the Dallas police department, I concluded. I sat down on the floor next to some other guy who appeared to have the same outlook on current events like myself. He seemed to have made himself as comfortable as he can. So, I did the same.

I must have fallen asleep, for someone woke me up by pushing on my shoulder. "Hey man, is your name, Day?"

I acknowledged by shaking my head in affirmation. The cell door opened, and I was led out into this little room with a huge glass window and a telephone. It was freezing in there. They must have had the temperature controls at near zero.

It was Karen, now fully dressed in her police uniform. She had tears in her eyes. "Oh, baby, I am so sorry," she said. "It is my fault that I dragged you into all this. I should have left you to do your stuff while I took care of Emily."

"I will be alright," I said. "The only problem is that I have to wait in here for the morning to happen before I can gain access to an attorney and or talk to a judge. What time is it? There is no clock around here, and they took my watch. How is Emily doing?"

"It's 5 in the morning. Emily is in the hospital with Paco," she replied. "The whole thing pretty much freaked her out, and she now swears she will never go back to any club again. A couple of her other friends suffered minor injuries. But you messed up those street boys, Kiron. Everyone is still wondering how you did it and so fast. You were the talk of the day once everything had calm down. Emily asked me to tell you that she is so grateful for your protection."

"Your car; they have the keys locked up somewhere in this place with the rest of my stuff," I said.

"I went back home and picked up a spare," she said. "One of the guys drove me back to the crime site . . . well, I mean the club, and that is what I drove to come up here. Listen, I have friends here, and I asked them to look out for you. I also explained to them what happened. They told me that we must wait for an arraigning judge, and maybe you would be letting go. So yes, you are right. For now, you must sit tight and wait. Is there anything you want me to do for you?"

"Yeah. Stay here with me tonight. It's cold in here," I said.

"Baby, I wish I can, but you very well know that I can't," she said, smiling through the wet eyes. By the way, I had never seen Karen in this state before. Seeing me incarcerated like this was affecting her deeply. "But I promise you a wonderful night as soon as all this is over."

"This is what I need you to do for me," I said. "I want you to immediately, or as soon as possible, contact my boss, Jim Holmbeck, and explain to him what had happened. You are being a police officer will make things clearer and more understandable to him, and he will listen. I trust he would believe if I told him, but you never know, he may not, and by Monday, I would be jobless."

Karen whipped out a notebook and pen. I gave her both his cell phone and house numbers. On the other hand, none of my family was to know about this yet. Karen agreed to my instructions, insisting too that everything was going to be okay. She then said goodbye and left. I was led back to the holding cell, and once again, I fell asleep in my corner.

It was sometime later that someone woke me up again and told me that breakfast was coming in. I ate some of it and then gave the rest away. I then sat up in my corner and listened to the other occupants talk about what happened to them. Some were laughing about these things, too as if being in this place was fun. But I wasn't feeling that way at all. I wanted to go home, take a shower, and sleep in my bed. I still felt angry because I was in jail, yet I wasn't the culprit.

Then someone decided to use the toilet. The toilet area was separated from the rest of the room by a small wooden partition or wall, high enough to cover the user's head and low enough to leave your ankles in the open. This guy was taking a shit. Everyone suddenly went quiet, very quiet, as the nasty, foul smell hit our nostrils. Moreover, there was not enough ventilation since the only opening was the jail cell door. So now you can imagine. Not to mention that all kinds of noises were coming from his rare side. I could hardly breathe. Everyone was covering their nose tightly with their hands.

I fell asleep again and woke up still, not knowing how much I had slept. In a jail cell, there was no sense of time because there was no clock anywhere in sight, and there were no windows to tell if it is night or day, and of course, your watch is confiscated upon being booked. You had to ask a jail staff member what time it is. I was still listening to this guy talking about how he had been arrested three times for driving while intoxicated and this time caught "in possession" of some bad stuff when the door opened and my name was called out. I was led back to the cold, visiting room, and window.

This time it was Jim Holmbeck. "Your friend Karen explained to me what happened," he said. "How are you doing so far?"

I told him I just wanted to get out of this place as soon as possible.

"I am going to see what I can do today," he said. "Seat tight, and don't worry too much. Everything will be fine. Do you want me to call your folks about all this?"

I told him not to, just as I had asked Karen to do so. I can imagine my mom's reaction when she hears about my being in jail. To her, everything seemed to be my fault. She would probably tell her informer that I damn right deserved what I got, and she hopes I learn my lessons from it. My baby sister would be deeply concerned; she would want to know what can be done to help me out. As a child still under adult supervision, she would be limited to her mother's involvement. Now when it comes to my grandma, she would probably set up a tent outside the jail station and never budge until her grandson is released. That is how much she loved me. Nonetheless, I still preferred that none of them got to know about this.

Jim left. A few hours later, Karen and Emily showed up, and we talked for a few minutes. Paco, Emily's boyfriend, was doing fine and had been discharged from the hospital, and they were both getting ready to drive back to college in Austin. She promised to stay in touch. Today the two girls were going to church with their parents. Karen said she was coming back as soon as church was over. Her friends here would let her see me again. I was taken back to the holding cell again, back to my corner.

The bad smell from someone's bowel movement had cleared up. But then, someone else used the toilet again, probably an aftermath of the breakfast. Once again, the room went quiet, like no one wanted to breathe the foul odor through the mouth. The culprit for this one finished quickly, came out from behind the shield, and stared back at the rest of us with a blank look. Like me, he had decided to keep things to himself and had barely said a word since joining our little group. He flopped back down on to the cold plastic mattress on the floor and fell asleep again.

Some lunch was brought in, and everyone ate in silence. I once again took note of the time, having done so when I got visited. It was eleven-thirty, Sunday morning. Someone mentioned that decent food was always served on Sunday. He probably had been here before, twice, or more. About a couple of hours later, the jail door opened, and this time jail warden himself stepped in. Once again, my names were called. I got up immediately and followed the man and one of his guards out of the cell.

"You must be a very popular guy out there," the warden said to me.

"Why so?" I asked.

"According to my jail's datasheet, in less than twenty-four hours of your stay here, you have had more people wanting to see you than anybody else in the cell," he said. "If it weren't for this particular one being kind of different from the rest, I wouldn't have let anyone see you again for the next forty-eight hours because, in your case, you have already exhausted your visitation privileges for that period."

"But I am here for the wrong reasons," I lamented. "You have the wrong person in your jail, warden. I was trying to help, and I have enough witnesses to prove that."

"You and your attorney will have to tell that to the judge," the warden said. "My job is to keep you locked up in here until they figure out what they are going to do with you, son. But I can tell you this: the judge down here is a fair man. If you are innocent, he will let you go. However, if you are not, he can be very mean. Either way, you will be just fine and dandy at the end of the whole thing. But now your attorney is here to see you. There is a chance that you are probably going home."

Now I was surprised. "My attorney? I haven't spoken to or arranged for one yet," I said.

"If you haven't, then well, someone set up one for you and a damn good one too," the warden said. "He is one of the best, not only in Texas but also nationally. That means he is damn expensive too. So, whoever hauled his ass out of bed on a Sunday morning to come out here must be heavily loaded at the bank or in his pocket too."

Jim. Jim Holmbeck must be behind all this, I told myself. EdenCom could afford to hire such a lawyer for its staff if necessary. More especially if that member of staff were about to go on an important, money-making field assignment. This time I wasn't even taken to the cold visitation room. I was taken to the warden's office, by the warden himself. Seated on one of the chairs, a briefcase between his knees, was a man who seemed to be in his late fifties. He was dressed professionally in a dark tie and suit, and a big cowboy hat on his head. He stood up as we walked in, a big smile on his face. He shook my hand.

"I am Jean Van Sickle, and I am going to represent you in court," he said.

"Van Sickle, the Texas tough lawyer who calls himself the iron tough protector," I asked, genuinely showing interest. "I see your advertisements all the time on prime-time TV channels."

"Yap, it's him, son," the warden said. "And it's quite a privilege to have him set foot in my little jail. Normally, highly talented and educated people like this don't show up in jails for their clients. They send their junior partners or legal assistants. So, this is indeed a surprise and a delight to us."

The "protector" opened his briefcase and pulled out some sheets of paper. He handed them to the warden. "These orders are from the judge who overseas in this area. I just spoke to him about letting my client get out of jail today. Lucky for me, and lucky for you, son, he was in his chambers working. Now, if you don't mind, warden, I would like my client to be released immediately. I will take over everything from here."

The warden, a chubby guy who looked like he was in his late fifties too with a bald head in the middle and gray-haired sides, quickly looked over the papers. I bet it was routine for him to do so, and he probably knew what the judge's signature looked like having probably gone over so many documents with the same signature on them. And it appeared like that was all he needed. He tucked the papers away in one of his desk drawers and locked it up. Opening another drawer, he pulled out a set of documents and put them on top of the desk in front of me. He pointed to three spaces and asked me to initial and sign. I did that quickly. While I was doing this, he picked up the phone and barked an order to someone to get my stuff out and ready. After I signed, he took those papers and tucked them away in the same drawer he had locked the ones from the attorney.

"You are now free to go," he said to me. "Let me hope this is the last time I see you in my jail. I tend to treat repeat offenders with less mercy than the first ones."

I said I promise it would be the last time. I shook hands with 'the protector' and left the warden's office. I was going to give Jim a big hug when I get to see him again, I decided. About Five minutes later, I had my stuff back, and after signing a few more documents, I walked out of the building and into the bright Sunday sunlight. It felt so good. There was no one waiting for me outside, so I sat down somewhere close by and waited. My cell phone was dead, needed charging.

About twenty or so minutes later, as I was beginning to wonder if I should look for a phone to call for transport help, a gleaming, black Chevy Tahoe with tinted windows pulled up in front of me. It was one of those new ones on the market. The front passenger window rolled down, and a familiar face appeared. It was Pam Smith, Jim's assistant.

"Hope in, Day. We are giving you a ride," She said, smiling.

I didn't see why not. Jim had probably asked her to come to get me and take me home. Good old Jim. He always takes care of his people, I thought gratefully. I got into the back seat, and the car immediately sped away from the jailhouse parking lot.

"You guys need directions to my place?" I asked after a few minutes. Pam was looking at a set of papers that she had pulled out of a briefcase on her lap. The driver had not said anything.

"We are not taking you home, Day," she said. "We have instructions from Jim to take you straight to the airport. You are boarding a flight to Addis Ababa, Ethiopia, in about thirty minutes from now. That will give me enough time to go over a few issues with you concerning the assignment."

I reacted immediately. "You can't be serious. I need to go home. I need more time to set myself up: bath, shave and brush my teeth. My handy pack is at my apartment. There are people I need to call and let them know I am leaving the country. A whole bunch of things I need to take care of. So, I can't just leave right now."

"Oh, we have a handy pack set up for you already, and if you need to call your folks, you can do so right now. Call them from this phone," she said, tossing a cell phone unit into my lap. "And as far as this arrangement is concerned, you have to call Jim on that. I was also told that if you do object to this transition, we then pull you off the assignment, and pull the attorney off your case. That means you go back to jail and wait for the case to be settled. I wouldn't advise you to do that, though, because I am not sure there will be a job for you by the time you come out. Now, if you think that what I am telling you is far-fetched, you are free to talk to Jim about it yourself. Like I said earlier, I am acting on his instructions. It's all up to you now."

I didn't like this thing at all. Do these people think they own me? No, they don't, I told myself. To wit, I am simply an employee who happened to be mixed up in something that wasn't even my fault. As far as I was concerned, they are supposed to be understanding, at least. I still had at least more than twenty-four hours before takeoff time for the assignment according to the original plan. I couldn't see myself missing that one great night that Karen had promised to me as makeup for dragging me into a nasty evening, even if that night didn't have a date yet. I was tired and felt like a pig coming out of a dirty sty. I needed a hot birth, fresh cloth, and something to eat that I consider homely. Then there is this taping project that I was supposed to help my sister finish up, a presentation due on Tuesday morning. I had promised to do it tonight. And then, of course, the mandatory Sunday night dinner with my grandma.

Yet again, I considered my options. The notion of going back to jail if the attorney is pulled off the case wasn't exactly what I wanted to happen to me. Seeing me back there in that corner with all the stinking going on and the fact that I had just told the warden I will never be back to his jail wasn't exactly a happy vision either. And then, most of all, coming out of the whole mess and finding myself with no job was one thing that gave me the jitters. I didn't want to go looking again. It was never a pleasant experience. On top of this one, my daily living expenses, however minimum I would try to make them be, we're not going to wait for me. I had bills to pay. There was so much at stake for me to walk off this deal. There would always be another time with Karen. It wasn't a priority yet.

Helping my sister was a priority to me, but I figured she would understand if I explained what was going on. One of her friends would have to help her out. Perhaps ask Karen, do it for her. Karen owed me that much. And my grandmother? She would just send me to my new adventure, as she always called the events in my life. I didn't have to worry about her. I would also bath later, brush later, and sleep on the plane. And as for the feeling like a pig coming out of a stinky sty, well, at least this pig was going to make money and maintain a job to pay its living expenses.

We were now driving into DFW airport.

"So, what will it be, Day?" Pam asked over her shoulder.

"I guess I have to take it," I said, shrugging my shoulders and sounding like I was no longer affected by the action anymore. I wanted to look like I wasn't exactly yielding to their threats but doing them a favor, too by taking the assignment at this very time. "But I have to make some calls now and fast."

"Well, make it snappy. We are running out of time as per your departure flight," she said. I didn't precisely like Pam Smith very much. Unlike her boss, Jim, she never seemed to care much about anyone except her work and or herself. In the organization, she was known to be rude and complicated. Very few people in the field operations department liked her. But, on the other hand, the former attorney proved to be very intelligent, effective, and efficient when it came to her job. She had proved to be the exact complementary component needed to complete the puzzle in the field operations department when it came to the slow talking, easy going Jim Holmbeck. If Jim wanted to deliver some nasty news or actions, Pam was always his mouthpiece. He never was the person to deal with any fired-up issues. She did all the dirty work for him. Rumor had it that together these two had made and saved, the company so much money more than any other department. They were said to be indispensable. Pam seemed to have that very feeling in her consciousness, which was probably the reason she could afford to be so arrogant and self-righteous.

Using the mobile phone, she had tossed at me, I managed to get in touch with my sister's voicemail. She was at church. Good thing too, because I didn't want to listen to the whining about letting her down. But I had to listen to the self-anointing, outgoing message on the machine.

"Hi. If you are calling just because you want to sell crap to me, please save your energy for something else and hang up. Now! If it is one of my girls, tell me what's up, and I will call you back as soon as I may. That includes you, mom, and you too, grandma. If it is any of you guys, including my brother, just leave me a message and then leave me alone."

I did precisely that, promising to call her back as soon possible and then hung up.

Then I called my grandmother's house to tell her that I won't be able to make it for dinner and, briefly, why. She too, was at church, so I had to listen to another strange, outgoing message: "in the looooord's name I am sure glad you called. I am away from the telephone temporarily, so please kindly leave me a message and I will do all I can to return your call in a timely manner. May the looooord be wid (with) you."

I left her a brief message too.

Next, I called my Mom's number. She too was supposed to be at church at this time, with or without my sister.

"Hello?" the crisp and official tone of her voice was unmistakable, always the same when responding to an official call at work or a personal one at home.

"Mom, I thought you were at church. Are you alright?" I asked, genuinely concerned.

"What do you want, Kiron?"

"I just wanted to let you know that I am going to be out of the country on work-related business," I said. "I may not be back for a couple of weeks."

"Ok." And the line went dead.

I hang up on my side too. That was my mom. I never seemed to be in her good book at all at any given time. Yet she will sit down all day and listen to my sister's whining. I was used to it anyway.

I decided to call Karen later. She had no answering machine at home, and her cell phone was always fully turned off, voice mail and all, when at church. I handed the phone back to Pam. "Ok, let's do it," I said. We were parked outside the airline's departure terminal.

"Alright, Pete, take a hike. This is confidential," she told the driver, who immediately got out of the car and wandered away from us, out of ear range. It was standard, routine company policy for non-operations department employees not to have any knowledge of an ongoing assignment. It would be grounds for termination, and perhaps legal means would be pursued if any such employee breached this agreement. Pam joined me in the back seat and quickly but carefully went over a bunch of stuff type-listed on two pieces of paper. It was like a neat grocery list, and all she had to do was briefly elaborate on each line. It included what I was expected to do once I got "into the field," how to conduct business, and an estimated schedule; contact numbers and spending codes to enable a field agent have cash at hand and also keep in touch with the company by any means were also included. There was, though, the third piece of paper that came from nowhere. On it was a worded agreement that I have voluntarily accepted the assignment and was to abide by all company rules and regulations, the company won't be responsible for acts of misconduct and or unrelated to company business, meaning that if that happened, I was on my own. And, that a supervisor had clearly explained every necessary detail to me. She had me sign it. Next, she gave me the flight document, which included an official travel document with UN clearance and five hundred dollars in cash to take care of what the company referred to as "initial basic expenditures cash."

"Well, good luck and don't let us down, Kiron," she said, not smiling. "Jim and I have tremendous faith in your abilities, which is why we chose you over everybody else for this assignment. We believe you can deliver."

She offered her hand, and I shook it. It was warm but also had a firm grip on it. We both got out of the car, and she beckoned to the driver to come back. In less than two or so minutes after that, I was standing alone outside the departure terminal, with nothing else left to do except board a flight to Africa. This was my first time to travel to this continent by myself. A sense of excitement crept up inside me. It was a sensation that always hit me when I sensed unknown challenges ahead. I called them adventures into the unknown. It was this daring fearlessness and relentless restlessness that so much frustrated my mother. She simply got tired of worrying about me. She had, in other words, given up on me and finally told me so when she learned of the fact that I had been discharged from my army unit. She feared that I was always up to something or doing things that normal people wouldn't ever think of doing. She believed that I am very careless with my life, and that danger was my middle name. In other words, as a single mom, she proclaimed that she couldn't keep up with me and my adventures, small or big, and as a result, she had sort off given up caring about me or what I did in any way, time, place. Instead, she now lavished all her attention to my sister. This had affected me emotionally to a certain extent, finding myself suddenly in exclusion from the very person that was supposed to be taking care of me.

But not for long, because I discovered that I had a special place in my grandmother's heart. My grandmother was the only relative I knew that my mother had kept a positive relationship with my father's side. The old lady was a mix of South American Aztec, Mexican, and Spanish blood in her. My dad's father was an Irish veteran who met my grandmother while on tour of duty as a marine. My grandmother had solely raised two twin boys, both dead now because grandpa was always away on military duty or drinking with his buddies to chill out his post-war frustrations. Both her twin sons, one of them my father, had died at war, fighting for the country. Now, she claimed I was the reincarnation of both her twin boys and therefore loved me dearly. She loved my sister too, but she had these special feelings for me.

She was the only one who fully believed in me and thus kept me going. When my Mom complained to her about my recklessness, grandma simply told her that it was the Aztec blood function, and she should leave me alone; I will be alright. When my Mom, a black American and an ex- U.S army soldier herself, complained that I seemed to be ignoring my African American heritage from which she came, grandma said it was Mom's fault that she had not put in enough effort to install the importance of maternal heritage in me. It was my mother's duty to teach me about it, and she had not fully done that. I guess as a single mother, she didn't get enough time to champion the cause. As a result, neither I nor my sister ever fully got the full dose of our black, African American side or Dad's Irish part of it. We simply knew that we were a strange mix of black American, Spanish, and or south American Indian and Caucasian blood. It somehow helped to explain the pale brownness, the black freckles, curly hair, and other features we possessed.

So, I found myself most of the time in my world, created by and suited for me. I simply believed I am who I am, and surely didn't give a damn if anybody felt any different. It is also my genuine belief that the structure of my nature has nothing to do with how I feel today or how I felt yesterday. To me, life is simply an ongoing adventure.

Chapter Two

THE FLIGHT TO Ethiopia was on time, and once I was on board the plane, I immediately fell asleep. I had to switch planes at Denmark's Copenhagen airport, and for that matter, I had to wake up. Once I settled down again on the new flight, I asked for an extra pillow and went to sleep back. Halfway this second phase, I woke up and stayed that way until the pilot announced we were arriving at Addis Ababa airport. It was then that I realized that I have been in transit for over seventeen hours. The big plane circled the airport a few times and then made its landing.

Though small, compared to its American behemoth counterparts, the airport was fairly busy, with small vehicles running around here and there. The airport staff was hospitable, welcoming every passenger to Ethiopia professionally and kindly. At customs, I was, of course, asked what my business was in Ethiopia. I showed them my U.N credentials. They wanted me to be more specific, though, so I told them I was meeting another person so we can film a documentary about a historic Ethiopian event. They agreed to that after evaluation of my other credentials. My equipment? Oh, it was following me on another plane, a cargo plane. The delay was minimal, as everything was in order, and in no time, I officially entered Ethiopia.

As I stood there in the arrival lobby, I watched people say goodbye to those leaving the country and others rushing to welcome those coming in. They all had something in common; tears were involved in both camps. I had no one to welcome me, but that was how it was arranged. Salieya Menankala was supposed to meet me later at the hotel. I was still wondering whether to hail an airport taxi to take me to the hotel when a skinny, tall brown man, dressed neatly in white, khaki pants and long-sleeved shirt walked into the lobby holding a sizeable square cardboard sign that read "Mr. Kiron from EdenCom" written on it in thick marker ink. I slowly made my way towards him. He looked my way as I approached him, and then quickly looked away. He looked back at me, and when he realized I was still approaching him, a nervous look crept upon his face.

"Hello, can I help you?" he asked. It was evident that the man was suspicious, most likely of the way I was dressed and looked.

He didn't think I was the person he was supposed to pick up. He was probably used to picking up people in suits and ties or some other clean, casual attire, and a lot of luggage, and I was the opposite. Remember, I was still in my party gear, just got out jail, and just got out of a long nap. I still looked like I was coming out of a pigsty.

"Hello, I am Kiron from EdenCom," I said, offering my hand.

He didn't shake it at first. He stared at me, looking me over from head to toe.

"Can I see some credentials, please?" he instantly demanded.

"Sure," I said. I opened the small folder bag that Pam had given me and pulled out my passport. Inside was an employee I.D card that was designed for travel purposes. I handed it to him, and he perused it intensively before handling it back to me. "You are supposed to take me to the Hilton Addis Ababa."

A dramatic change came over the man. The nervousness vanished and was replaced by a complete smile showing perfect lined, white teeth. The man loosened up like we had been buddies for ages. "I am sorry, sir, for acting like this, but you know these days we have to be very careful with everyone we see or meet out here," He said. He now offered me his hand, and I shook it.

"I am Iyad, and I am the driver from the Hilton. I am here to take you back to the hotel. Do you have any luggage?"

"Not right now, Iyad," I replied, amused by the sudden change. "My luggage is arriving later on another plane. It is in the form of equipment, so I just couldn't carry it with me now. It will be sent to the hotel when it arrives in a few hours."

"Excellent then, sir. Please come with me," he said and led the way out of the lobby. Outside, a gleaming white Mercedes Benz sedan was parked near the cab, in a space labeled 'reserved for hotel Hilton'. Iyad opened a rear passenger door for me, and I stepped into, and sat down in a fully luxurious interior, all leather and carpet. I was surprised how roomy the interior of the car was. A center console had a telephone set on it and a set of glasses with matching bottles. The environment inside the car was much more refreshing compared to the dusty dry air of the airport. Iyad closed the door gently behind me and then ran around and got in behind the wheel.

"You have some soft drinks ready for you if you are thirsty, sir," he said. "And if you care to be entertained, we have everything set to your convenience." He pressed a button, and the console moved towards the center of the back seat, then folded out to create a wider countertop. A small nine-inch screen emerged as the console divided itself into two to reveal buttons and switches. The screen was a TV, the buttons for the radio. There was also a set of headphones hanging on the back of the seat. A red blinking light indicated where I was supposed to plug them in. For the drinks, there was a choice of soft ones, mostly sprite, Pepsi, and coca-cola classic, and bottled water. I opened a sprite and drank from the bottle.

"Thanks, man," I said as I fell back into the luxurious leather seat's full comfort. The air conditioner was running, and in a moment, I felt different and completely relaxed from the muggy air outside. As we drove out of the airport, I found that I didn't need the music, because

I was taking in every detail of my new surroundings and already loved it. The car itself moved without any noise, just smoothly like we were riding the wind.

Later, I also found out that Iyad was a fascinating guy. He had that jolly, talkative side of him. I asked him to stop calling me sir, and instead, just call me Kiron. That put him more at ease, and we were able to talk more freely. He went on to tell me that he had worked for the Hilton for twenty five years, starting as a janitor and then working his way through several job positions. Then when he realized that he was getting too old for what he called on the job politics, he decided to apply for and tuck himself away into a shuttle limo driver job. So now driving has been his job for the last ten years. He had seven children and two wives. Of the seven children, all but one had finished school and moved out of their parent's house. He now had one daughter at home who was finishing up university. It was quite expensive to take a child through a university, he told me, revealing that his savings were almost exhausted because of this issue. But the Hilton had been kind to him, he told me, because working for the Hotel he had gained money to raise his seven children and take care of household needs.

He asked me where I was coming from and what I did for a living. Of course, I told him I was from the United States and that I did documentary journalism for the UN. I was in Ethiopia to do a fact-finding documentary on Ethiopian religious culture in general.

About thirty minutes later, we arrived at the Hilton. It was a sprawling complex with several stories somewhere in the center of Addis Ababa. Iyad walked me in, cleared up everything I had to do to check-in for me, and then took me to my room, which was on the third floor. He was a popular man here, and everyone greeted him with joy and respect. I gave him one hundred dollars in cash out of my initial benefits money, and his eyes widened. I asked him what was wrong.

"You sure you want to give me all this money, Kiron?" he asked. "I am asking because this is a lot of money here in Ethiopia. When I exchange this money for the local currency, it will be three times my monthly salary. This is a very big tip, Mr. Kiron."

I told him that I was sure and that it was not only for thanking him for giving me a pleasant ride from the airport, but also my small contribution towards his daughter's education, because I didn't know what else to tell him. He thanked me heartily, shaking my hand with both of his, and then left, one of the happiest older men on this planet.

Once he was gone, I once again turned my attention to my surroundings. The hotel suite was modern and spacious, just like the ones found anywhere in the more developed world. I had everything I needed in this one suite. First, I had to go "potty." I had not visited the toilet since I left the States. What a relief! Then I filled up the big bathtub with hot soapy water and dipped myself into it. This, too, just like Iyad's breezy Mercedes ride, was very relaxing. I spent about half an hour in the tub before I rinsed myself up and then put on one of the hotel's comfortable cotton bathrobes. The clock on the wall told me it was coming to midnight here, which kind of led me to believe that it was time to go to bed. But I also needed to eat something. There was a room service notice on the living room table, and I ordered something. They even had hamburgers on the menu. Great, but I ordered spaghetti with lots of meatballs instead, and a bottle of wine. Fifteen minutes later, room service delivered my order, and I started devouring my order like a maniac. The person who had prepared this meal had done an excellent job because it tasted so good.

After eating all the food on the tray, I sat back on the comfortable sofa and turned on the TV. The local channel came on first with the main television news showing a wealthy sheik from one of the emirates, who had just arrived in the country. He had a big entourage with him and was also being met by another big escort of Ethiopian officials in dark business suits. The report said the Sheik was here to discuss business prospects in Ethiopia with government officials. The hotel had a cable channel, so I tuned in to that. I happened to catch a U.S basketball game, and I watched it for some time before I suddenly started yawning in ten-second intervals. I then switched off the TV and just fell asleep on the couch. Considered it jet lag.

The ringing of the phone woke me up from my deep sleep. As usual, the throbbing headache did not spare me, and I was still grimacing in my half-asleep stupor when I reached for the phone receiver and scooped it up.

"Hello?"

"Kiron, Jim here," the caller said. The laid-back resonance was unmistakable in his voice. "Just calling to see how you are holding up. Is everything ok?"

"Everything's alright, boss," I replied.

"Great," he said. "Has Miss **Menankala** made contacted you?"

"Not yet, boss,"

"She will," he said, sounding very confident. "When she does, call me up immediately. I want to talk to her about the assignment."

"I will, boss,"

"Oh, by the way, Kiron, I am sorry that we had to rush you out of the country," he said. "We could not risk having you messed up again somewhere else so the best thing to do was to get you on a plane as quickly as possible and on your way to the assignment. I hope you do understand."

I pondered the issue for a moment. Yes, I was not happy at all at the way I was hustled, but right now wasn't the time to say so. I was out here already, so it now made no difference anymore. I would deal with the issue of mistreatment after the assignment, I decided.

"I understand, boss," I said.

After that, he said bye and hung up. This time I went to bed, and once I got inside the warm, cozy comfort of the linen, I fell asleep again and immediately.

It was the bright sunlight streaming through the slightly drawn white satin curtains enclosing the big bedroom suite window and the persistent ringing of the phone that woke me up again. I slowly rolled myself over to the other side of the bed and picked up the phone receiver.

"Hello?" I said, my voice sounding hoarse and deep.

"Good morning. May I please speak to Mr. Kiron Day?" the caller requested, definitely a female from the tone of her voice. It had that fresh girlish rhythm and relaxed resonance in it.

"This is Day," I replied.

"Hello, Mr. Day, this is Salieya Menankala," the caller said. "I am sorry if I woke you up from your sleep. Mr. Jim Holmbeck asked me to call you this morning."

"Yes, I have been expecting your call," I said. "And it is ok for you to wake me up. I think it is about time I did so. When are you coming over?"

"I can make it over there in about one hour. Is that ok with you?"

"Sure deal. I will be up and ready then,"

"See you in one hour then," she concluded and hung up.

I hung up my side, and getting off the bed, I made my way to the shower. I blew cold water over my entire body, and it was very refreshing. It was after I had dried myself up that I remembered I had no cloth. The first thing I was going to ask her to do was to take me to a cloth store and then go buy me a host of other stuff like toothbrush and shaving gear. The hotel provided its guest with some brand-new mouth cleaning gear, so that was taken care of. I put on my crumpled cloth and then ordered some breakfast. Sausage and eggs, black tea with toast, did the trick. While I consumed breakfast, I surfed through the cable TV channels and found nothing interesting. BET was available, so I watched that.

Just a minute after my estimated time of her arrival, the guest desk downstairs called me to tell me that a young lady by the name of Menankala was here to see me. I told them to send her up. In a moment, there was a gentle knock on the door. I got up, went up to the door, and opened it. I immediately froze all my body actions at that moment. Right before me stood this bombshell of a beauty. Not only was her skin so bronze, it glowed, but the body shape was stunning. Her height matched mine perfectly, so I was able to gaze straight into big brown eyes that were so inviting.

She was so inviting that one could easily be tempted to wish that they were also so wanting. Yes, they had that instant, romantic, sexy look that suggested she was ready to go to bed whenever you were ready. Her black hair was short and neatly balanced into a crew outlook, with a perfect shiny glow. Salieya Menankala was the kind of woman that would turn every male head around wherever she went. Right now, she was dressed in black khaki trousers, neatly pressed, and a white t-shirt neatly tucked in. Flat leather-soled lady's boots graced her feet. Around her neck hung a gold necklace from which a cross dangled. It was probably twenty-five-plus carat gold. It glowed and perfectly matched with her bronze skin.

"Well, Mr. Day, are you going to let me in, or are you going just to stand there and look me over?" she asked, a smile on her face.

Ha! I was busted, I told myself.

I quickly stood aside to let her pass. "I am very sorry, miss. It's just one of those guy things," I said, not knowing what else to say.

She stepped into the room, and I closed the door behind her. She had two leather carry-all bags which she placed on the carpeted floor near the living room couch. Then she gracefully walked over to one of the other two living room sofa chairs and sat down.

"It's alright," she said. "I don't like it at all, but I am now used to it anyway."

"Used to what?" I asked.

"Men are staring at me like that," she said.

"You mean looking you all over?" I asked.

"Yes. Like the way you just did." She answered, nodding her head and still smiling dazzlingly.

"I guess you have what they want to look at," I said, but sensed that this conversation was going to hit a dead end. She saved the day by changing the subject.

"Is this the best room they can give you?" she asked.

"I don't know," I replied. "It was all prearranged by someone in operations."

"They should have done better than this," she said. "You need maximum comfort and rest before taking off on this trip. You may not see anything close to what you people down there call normal living for some time. We are going to travel deep into the country and hills. I can deal with it because my grandparents lived deep down in the village areas and I spent part of my life with them. But most of all, it's my people, my country. I don't know about you."

"We shall see," I said. I didn't want to indicate my military background, which had emphasized rugged inhuman conditions of survival and or zero luxury for six months. We, the participants who graduated from this training step, had ended up referring to it as grueling fun. It was so rugged I didn't think it existed anywhere in the average human life trend. That is why I wasn't so concerned about my upcoming changes. I would deal with them on the spot, basically adapting to the prevailing situation.

"Is the equipment here yet?" she asked.

I told her it wasn't here yet. I picked up the phone and dialed the operator. I asked for a private line to the U.S.A and was quickly hooked up. I dialed the contact number given to me by Jim and waited. He was on in ten seconds.

"What's up, Day?" he asked.

"She is here, Jim," I said.

"Great. Let me talk to her."

I handed the phone to her and wandered off to the mini kitchenette. The refrigerator had a sprite, coke, and Pepsi in it, plus some locally manufactured beverages. I pulled out a sprite and kicked the door shut. Then I wondered off to the patio as I sipped it. The view over part of downtown Addis Ababa was awesome. The sun, coming through a blanket of snow-white fog, made it look glorious. Ten minutes later, Salieya joined me on the patio.

"Enjoying the early morning view?" she asked.

"Yes. Not bad at all," I replied. "It's amazing how news reports can easily distort facts because from what you see on TV, it is hard to believe that a beautiful, peaceful environment exists in Africa. The media shows shacks for houses, ancient vehicles, or bicycles and donkey pulled carts, sick people in refugee camps or looters and gun-wielding people burning or destroying stuff."

"Peaceful people exist, harmoniously, here and all over the continent, pretty much like any other community in the world. It's only a particular group of crazy people who make and impose their bad decisions on others, mostly by force, that makes the state of affairs in our countries volatile, and this, in turn, will destabilize the peaceful momentum," She lamented.

"Well said," I said. "But first, I need to get me some decent clothing, shoes, and cologne. I am sure there is a place nearby that we can buy some stuff, right?"

"Oh yes, I know just the right place," she replied. "We can go now if you are ready."

I said I was ready, so we left the hotel suite and took the elevator downstairs. The lobby area was quiet, and the desk clerk waved at us as we walked by. Outside in the visitor's parking lot was Salieya's car, a gleaming, black Range Rover. The big car had external onboard twin sport lights, thick protective bumpers and thick, well-rimmed tires and a lot of other stuff just on the outside. In short, one look at this vehicle would tell you it was specially equipped for out–in-the-field projects.

"Nice piece of equipment you have here," I said as I got into the passenger seat and closed the heavy door after me. An all-black leather interior, I noted. "It makes you feel like you are ready for any adventure out there."

"1998 Range Rover V8 with turbo engine capability," she said without holding back. "Lots of power; I bought it from my dad after he retired. The car was given to him by BBC world service for use on field trips when he covered news for them on special projects in intercontinental Africa. When he retired, they let him keep it. But since he wasn't going on field trips anymore, he let me have it on a simple payment plan. I had a rebuilt engine installed plus new shocks and other stuff. The interior is original. I have used this car to both tow and push stuff. I have taken this car into places no other ordinary car I know of in this country could have gone. And it has always come back in one piece. I hope it survives this one. I have also been renting it to people doing field expeditions in Ethiopia, and that way, I made some money to fund my education. I am now billing EdenCom for its use on this trip."

"Brilliant girl," I said, as she started the engine and let it idle for a few minutes with brief roaring sound spasms initiated from the accelerator. "Looks and sounds good to me, like brand new. You must have done a good job re-fixing it."

"Thanks," She said. She drove the big car out of the parking lot with ease, and in a moment, we were out of the hotel's gates and on to the main road. The big car rode so smoothly and easy you could hardly hear the engine noise. I found myself falling in love with it instantly. Salieya drove the big car with speed and swift maneuverability through the crowded Addis Ababa streets, minding every turn and stop. She probably prided in, and enjoyed driving, the car so much. It reminded me of the first car I had, a Jeep Cherokee Laredo. We were probably linked together for life until, one day, the engine broke down mechanically and never recovered, ending up in the junkyard after I sold it to some dude who posed as the perfect mechanic but who instead ultimately led to its doom.

We didn't talk much while she drove, obviously minding her driving while I visually took in as many details of my current surroundings as possible.

"Here we are," She said as we pulled up outside a huge building that looked newer than the rest. It was a shopping arcade in the middle of downtown Addis Ababa, obviously for those with lots of money. "They have lots of imported stuff, and most diplomats and other foreigners shop from here. I hope they have what you want or need."

She cut the engine and then waited for me to get out of the car before she got out and made sure the car was locked correctly. Together we went up the broad steps and entered the arcade. The interior was all much like the modern departmental store types like those back home in the U.S. Glass walled shops with all kinds of outfits, make up for women, shoes, luggage, and handbags, and so on. Some shops even quoted their prices in U.S dollars. "Do you shop for your clothes from here?" I asked as I checked out the different clothing in one shop.

"No, not at all," she said. "This is too expensive for me. I am a simple homegrown girl with simple, inexpensive tastes, and I try to keep it that way. I brought you here because I assumed you wanted world-class stuff, and they have it all here. You have to look and select what you want."

"Then pay," I added.

"Definitely," she agreed, laughing softly.

They had world-class stuff here indeed, good stuff but at the double the price we buy them back home. Nevertheless, I got everything I needed: two pairs of khaki cargo pants with belts, designer military-style cargo jacket, t-shirts, underwear, and a pair of leather steel-toed, all-weather, outdoor boots, dental gear, wash towels and even a pair of sunglasses. I also spotted a military-style beret and picked that one up too. A pair of leather, tear, and pierce proof gloves and carry all hand luggage bag completed my purchase. I paid using the company's credit card, which always surprised me with its powerful shopper's worldwide advantage. We left the arcade, and Salieya took me shopping for food and water. We went to a central food market not too far away from the cloth arcade, and here we bought mostly dry, easy to cook, and ready to eat food and bottled water. Two hours later, we returned to the hotel.

The hotel clerk at the reception desk in the lobby handed me an invoiced message, which stated that the gear for the project had arrived. I had to call a specific number to let them know when to deliver it. I called that number and asked them to give it to my room in a couple of hours.

Back in my hotel suite, we ordered lunch. I ordered a meaty stew mix, while Salieya ordered an Ethiopian vegetable mix. It was a mixture of different foods, mostly vegetables, and I got to taste it. It was great. We ate quietly, Salieya citing that she's starving. I sipped some wine while she had water. She didn't like any alcohol, she said. After the meal, we stood on the balcony, and she told me about Ethiopia, and herself.

She had most of her elementary education in the remote area of the village where she grew up with her grandparents. Her father, who was always away from home on his journalism assignments around the country and all over the continent, had explained to her that it was important for her to get properly rooted in her cultural background, and the best way to do it was with her grandparents. But after the elementary part of it was over, the rest of her education was here in the city, Addis Ababa, where she stayed with her father and stepmother and three other siblings. Her mother, a businesswoman from Dubai, had met with her father while he was attending journalism school in England. The relationship didn't last very long, but she was the product of that short union. Her mother went back to the emirates, leaving her behind with her father. The, however, stayed in touch with her ex-boyfriend and, therefore, her daughter, and sent travel tickets to Salieya to travel to and visit with her in the emirates. There, Salieya said, she got a taste of her mother's heritage, Arab culture. I asked Salieya as to why she didn't stay with her mother in Dubai. Great love for Ethiopia, she said. Much of her early childhood was spent here, which pretty much shaped her life up to where she was now and who she is. She didn't really wish to live anywhere else but wished to travel and see the rest of the world.

The equipment arrived in two hours as promised. All brand-new gear, all in one box. It consisted of a Panasonic laptop; the hard-shelled type specifically designed for outdoor activity with the capability to instantly transmit visual information via satellite, and equipped with a solar battery. It came with a bunch of accessories that would render it useless to the field agent if missing—also two cannon point and shoot cameras and a pair of binoculars with night vision capability.

But perhaps the most exciting part of this was the accessories themselves. Wireless visual aids that worked like an extra pair of eyes, complemented by wireless, unidirectional, high fidelity microphones as tiny as a matchstick. Both types of equipment were designed for eavesdropping purposes, and the person that's being eavesdropped on us is supposed to have the least idea that his activities are being recorded. But the fascinating thing about this is that this equipment will instantly transmit these images back to a remote station, which is the laptop computer, which in turn immediately sends the data back to the supercomputer at the communications center at EdenCom. This computer will then convert these images back to normal, and Jim and his team would see them like on a standard TV. The optical transmitters, too, have night vision capability. These transmitters came in the form of thick sunglasses, which the user puts on and can adjust zoom out and in just by touching a tiny little knob on the side of the lens's holder with a fingertip. Now the photo cameras were sent over as decoys. The real deal was the shades.

Salieya had never seen stuff like this before and was amazed when they explained everything to her. She watched me tear open the plastic covers and quickly assemble the equipment. The laptop had already been charged up by the tech team before shipping and was ready for use, with or without the main power supply. Salieya's eyes widened as she watched me test the visual aids. Everything that I focused on showed up on the laptop screen. I told her the shades to transmit these images from any location in this country to the laptop at any location in this country. "Just as you see them now."

There was a portable transmission mast or special high-powered antenna, which I had to carefully unpack and then test to make sure it worked properly. This was to aide in the satellite transmission. One of the techs at EdenCom had told me that it was so powerful that it was capable of transmitting material over forty thousand feet into space and about half that much below sea level. In contrast, the agent can generally transmit through it for an unlimited range of areas on land. The other equipment included a satellite phone, which helped us stay in touch with EdenCom all the time. I typed in a bunch of codes on the computer and messed around with some programs to get the entire hardware package software all linked together. Thirty minutes later, it was all done. The rest was lighting aides and SOS accessories in case we got stranded and needed emergency help.

After that, I placed all the equipment in two easy carry bags, lined with trauma and water-proof material. From the outside, it looked like hiker material destined for a polar camp.

"Am glad it can all fit in just two bags," Salieya said. "I have more stuff in the car that was sent to me from headquarters. I had sent them my list of stuff that we could need for the trip apart from the food."

"We are all set up now," I said. "What time did you say we have to be on the move?"

"Around three in the morning," she replied. "Would you be interested in going out? Just for a short time tonight. We can have some coffee and cake outside a café, in the open air. Anything to get us out of this prison."

"Sure, why not," I said. "What time would that be?"

"Ok, let's say six in the evening, "she replied. "Probably for an hour or so. Say, be back by seven, sleep till two and then get going at three."

"Fair deal," I said. "See you at six then."

She came right on time, but the evening plans changed a little bit. She took me to the national museum first, which turned out to be a fascinating place. It was full of priceless artifacts that dated back several civilizations. Ethiopia has a rich history, and every exhibited item in this museum had a clear, detailed story or elaboration, written in English, in front of it.

I also found out that evening that Salieya was a perfect company, charming, bubbly, and straightforward going. After the museum, she took me to a little quiet café place on the outskirts of the city that closed late and catered for after-hours customers. We had freshly baked cake and hot cocoa outside the café, enjoying the cool breeze that helped lighten up the dusty the air. Salieya told me more about Ethiopia, how it was rumored to be the final resting place of the Ark of the Covenant, carried by Israelites on their way to the Promised Land. She asked me about myself, and I told her not so much, preferring to keep my background in check. I told her I had just left the military when I joined EdenCom but didn't mention my special force training before and during the service. I told her, briefly, all I knew about the Dallas-Fort Worth area, and the story of the Alamo. She was taken up by all this and said she hoped to visit the U.S pretty soon, to see for herself. We agreed that she would let me know in advance as to when she will be coming to Texas so I can prepare myself to show her around. I also told her, though briefly, about my family, too, without spotting my mom's misunderstandings of me.

It was about nine-thirty at night when we returned to the hotel. "I have a room reserved for me on the floor below yours," She said. "I am going in to take birth and then go straight to bed the same. We do have a long day tomorrow."

I told her I was going to do the same. I walked her to her suite, thanked her for the evening, and then headed back to mine. When I got back in, I found a voice mail on my hotel phone, from Jim. I called him up on his cell phone and told him we were leaving early the next day. He didn't sound pleased. He told me he had expected us to be out of the hotel and on our way to our assignment as soon as we got the equipment. Time, he claimed, was not on our side. I told him that I believe it was going to be alright, and that he had to put a little trust in Salieya's programming of things. He said he expects us to get moving as soon as possible.

After talking to Jim, I got in touch with my grandmother. She was so happy to hear from me. She wanted me to be very careful, as usual and wished me the best of luck on my assignment. She promised to pray for me but also wanted me to get down to my knees and pray to God for guidance and protection during this assignment. I promised her that I won't forget to do that. I then tried Karen, but both phones had no answer, and the voice mail been turned off. This didn't bother me very much. I figured out she was still brooding over my leaving and would get over it in a matter of time.

I then tried on my new cloth. They fitted well. I like buggy outfits, though not so buggy. The trend on the streets, where the pants are intentionally so buggy, they fell off the butt, and the wearer had to cling on to them to avoid being suddenly naked was not my style. Some of these guys' pants hung so low it is hard to believe they had not accidentally defecated in them, and that irritates the heck out of me. I wanted mine snug and neat, held in place with a belt, and not having to drag my feet while moving around. In short, dressing buggy meant to ease and comfort for me, not criminalizing peer pressure or underwear show off.

Lastly, I got down to my knees and prayed for the project to go well, just as I had promised grandma. Praying was something forcefully enforced by mom into the deep consciousness of her little family. She firmly believed in the power of God and the power of prayer. Was I trying to run away from mom to avoid the trend? Sorry, grandma was that way too. She made us do the same thing before going to bed and every morning when we got up. Then there was church every Sunday. Both my mom and grandma didn't care about what religious denomination or faction you followed. They believed in the good being done and faith and trust in God. I was now used to doing it, convinced that my destiny was in God's hands, and found it very hard to start the day without a prayer in place. This assignment was no exception.

After that, I got into bed and set the timer on my wristwatch to two o'clock in the morning, an hour before Salieya's schedule. That one hour would be good enough for a cold shower and all other strange things we all do when we get up in the morning. The moment I put my head on that pillow, I blacked out like a well-fed, been-playing-all day, toddler.

Salieya showed up twenty-five minutes to three and showed surprise at finding me awake, dressed up, and ready. I had ordered an extra cup of coffee for her and we quietly sipped it up, with a couple of chocolate chip cookies each. Five to three I called Jim to let him know we were heading out. He was glad to hear that and wanted to talk to Salieya. While she did that, I made sure nothing essential was left behind. By three o'clock sharp, we walked out of the suite and headed downstairs.

The lobby was full of people, to our surprise, and a lot of activity was going on this early in the morning. There was a group of noisy guys holding bay inside the breakfast cafeteria. On our way past the café, I looked at a group of people in the bar zone of the cafe, talking loudly and drinking local beer. I instantly recognized the military type. They were five of them, all with hand luggage, looking like they just got off a plane. The language they were using was not English, and that made me remember what Murphy had told me, about other parties interested in this particular assignment, which included Israelis and Egyptians. I hoped this wasn't the case. During my military training with a group of Israeli commandos, I learned that they always did things their way, the Israeli or never, whichever made them a tight, unyielding bunch. That would make it tough for the two of us to engage such a group if we happened to cross paths during the process of the assignment.

Salieya had to check us out at the reception desk, while I held on to the bags. They were the base for this assignment. After that, she suggested she go reload our coffee cups while I loaded our bags into the car. Five minutes later I had everything inside the car and so having nothing else to do, I locked it up and strolled back into the hotel lobby. Once I got inside the lobby, I checked out the hotel cafe to locate Salieya's whereabouts.

It was then that I noticed that one of the noisy guys was trying to engage her into a loud conversation, which she was trying to ignore. I stood at the entrance of the cafeteria, right outside the wooden swing doors, and watched. The man was stooping over her while she filled up the second cup of coffee and was talking instead loudly. The fact that she was ignoring him seemed to be annoying him. He looked to be the bullying, intimidating kind that would stop at nothing to get his way. I decided to go to help her get out of it. As I moved towards the cafeteria, Salieya finished loading the coffee cup and, after firmly placing the lid on it, turned around and started walking away. The man didn't appear to like that and went after her, now visibly getting anxious or even angry. He was yelling at her. The other guys in his posse were cheering him on, laughing loudly. Other guests in the cafeteria just looked on, wondering what was going on. The situation was escalating into a confrontation. Salieya moved quickly, but he hangs on to her, right on her heels. It was now evident that she was both scared and irritated. Her eyes looked straight ahead, careful not to look back at her aggressor. In her haste to get away from the man, she dashed right passed me without noticing that I was very close to her.

Suddenly, he reached out and was about to grab her wrist when I grabbed his arm and pulled back. Unaware of my intervention Salieya didn't stop, and in a moment, she was out of the cafeteria and gone.

The man now turned around and angrily glared at me. He was slightly taller and bigger than me, with a bald head and broad shoulders, looking lean all over. From the way he poised, he was military.

"Just let her be, man," I said, staring straight back into his stone-cold eyes. For a moment, he said nothing, eyeing me over. Then he tried to pull his hand free from my grasp, but I held on tight. At the bar, all now went quiet.

"I beg your pardon?" he said in a light mid-eastern accent that I instantly recognized from those days of training in the Middle East. He was Israeli or Arab.

"I said just let her be," I repeated.

In one big shrug, he tore himself free from my grip, forcing me to take a few unprecedented steps forward, but that was ok because now Salieya was safely out of harm's way. The problem was now officially in my hands. He now confronted me, still looking furious.

"My friend, do you realize that what you just did could have instantly cost you your life?" he asked.

"No, not at all," I replied. "You are just telling me about it right now. But the woman you are harassing is a colleague of mine, and I hate to see this kind of thing happen to my friends, especially if that friend happens to be a harmless individual."

"Well, I will demonstrate to you what I mean, right now," he said, and I saw his arm go upwards fast. His fist came towards me quickly, but I was ready. With both my hand, I blocked and grabbed it, twisted it and turned, then forcefully shoved him to one side. He was as solid as an oak, yet he staggered, almost losing balance. I maintained my position.

"Care to try again?" I asked, watching his every move. From the corner of my eye, I could see his buddies' jump of their stools and started slowly moving towards us. As for the man, he was now visibly outraged, but his eyes now had a doubting look in them. He was probably surprised that I had easily pushed him aside. He braced himself again, fists now both raised. Without moving, I readied myself for the assault.

"Mukash, stop this nonsense!" A voice barked from somewhere behind me. It was from one of his buddies. But the man continued to move towards me; fists still raised, a look of anguish still on his face, like he was about to fight for his own life. This man, I realized, was typical out of control bully who always fought his way to get what he wants, the type that gets beyond the reasonable control of their mental faculties when even slightly angered; the merciless type that would shoot down somebody dead and then continue shooting until the entire gun magazine was void of all its rounds.

"Mukash, I said stop, right now!" the same voice, still from behind me, repeated, now sternly. "I oversee this mission, and you will abide by my orders, or I will have you sent home. Do you understand?"

The talker now came up and stood between the angry fellow and me. His eyes were fixed on him, not me.

"He has saved you," **Mukash** said, his chest rising and falling slowly." Just don't cross my path again, little man, because the next time you do so I will kill you, whether he is there or not."

"I am sure we shall meet again, and then you will have another shot at your murderous intentions," I said back to him. He eyed me angrily,

He was contemplating going ahead and doing it, but instead, he strolled off out of the cafe, banging the doors behind him.

The man who had intervened now turned to me. He smiled wryly and then offered his hand. I shook it. "I sincerely apologize for, and I am embarrassed by **Mukash's** behavior. Please forward my apologies to your wife. She is over there, waiting for you."

I looked up to see Salieya standing at the entrance of the cafeteria, staring at me, a blank look on her face. I nodded at the man and then slowly made my way towards her. I put my arm around hers and walked her out of the building, taking my time doing so. I knew that all eyes in the cafeteria were on us now, and so this was my way of telling everybody to back off my buddy. Once outside, though, I stepped up my pace till we got to the car.

"Come on, let's get out of here now," I said. I led her around to the driver's door and made sure she was in first before I proceeded to get into the car myself. She started the car, and in a moment, we left the hotel parking lot and onto the public road.

"What was going on in there?" She asked. "It looked like you were about getting into a fight."

"Yes, that's right,» I replied. "That man was harassing you, and when I tried to stop him, he decided it was time to fight with me. Lucky enough, his boss was there to intervene, hence saving both of us a lot of trouble."

"Oh! You mean you were trying to protect me from him?" she asked, her voice registering surprise. "But that is so nice of you. You risked being trampled on by some big man for my sake. I owe you my gratitude. Thank you."

"Precisely, and you are very welcome, Salieya" I said. "Naturally, I hate being bullied and I don't do bullying. So, when the victim is a friend of mine, I will try to stop the culprit. Big people, though, at least for most of them, it is all but mostly a lot of steam. That guy also had a big mouth. By the way, you are being a linguistic major, do you have an idea what their language is?"

"Hebrew," she replied instantly. "I studied it for a year and then decided to switch to Latin. I can decipher most of the words, but don't speak it very well."

"That's what I feared." I said.

"Feared what?" she asked, looking puzzled.

"The Israelis may be mixed up in all this," I replied. "I was told during my briefing on this assignment that other external parties could be involved, including but not necessarily, Israeli intelligence or military. The guys in the cafeteria looked and acted military alright, but I just didn't know from where. Now I think I have a clue."

"You are saying that they may be onto the same issue as our assignment?" She asked.

"Most likely, unless you want to say that your country has very strong ties with Israelis, Hamas or the Palestinian liberation organization," I replied. "I don't see any other reason that could bring their military or intelligence here. It's got to be something very strategically important to their community or sects. If they are involved in this, it means we have to oversee our backs and or all the time. There is no telling what's out there now. The Egyptians, I was told, are already aware of this event, and so is the government of the United States, which inevitably brings the Europeans into the picture too. There is also the issue of private parties getting involved. And because the prize is big, we could easily run into a fully-fledged vendetta of some kind, one that could turn the place into a killing field."

"You are now beginning to scare me," she said, looking worried. "I wish it just doesn't happen that way. I am not used to things like that. I am used to normal assignments involving normal folks, not governments and warring factions or groups."

"It will be ok," I said in reassurance.

We drove quietly through the dark, and the bright lights of the city quickly faded behind us. We lost the paved, tarmac road surface to the rugged, dusty ones. An occasional car drove past us going in the opposite direction, and we also occasionally overtook one. Despite the darkness, the car's powerful headlights provided intense illumination, and Salieya drove with the confidence of a person who had mastered the terrain and knew very well how to navigate around the place. Sensing that perhaps I was getting bored, she turned on the radio. The music was just unlike our own back home; the instruments very clear and singled out to where you can tell which one was which. It had minimal vocal input, so the mixture of drums, flutes, bangles, shackles, and an occasional guitar, plus lots of clapping and stamping, provided a musical interlude such as I have never experienced before. Perhaps the organization and careful balance of all the involved factors made it worth the listener's concentration. The rhythm was enchanting, almost erotic, when combined with the harmonizing voices. The car's music system, too, was perfect, providing sounds in their original form. I found myself listening to intensively.

"That's very cool music," I said. "It's very captivating, the melody and rhythms. You have to make a copy for me to take back with me to the States. I think my sister would be delighted with it too. She loves stuff like this. What is it all about?"

"Traditional Ethiopian Christian," she replied. "This country has a strong Christian background, and religion is a central piece of society. This music is from one of the best traditional Christian singing groups in the country and is also regionally recognized. What you are listening to now is old stuff, though. Now they have also added new modern instruments to their music that makes better listening for a more global audience. You don't even have to understand what they are saying. The instruments themselves are enough to arouse your musical intellect and interest. I used to sing in one of the famous choirs in Addis Ababa but had to drop out because of the school workload."

"Maybe you should have continued with it on a part-time basis," I said, remembering my fascination with martial arts, where I ended up dedicating a lot of, if not most of, my time learning it. I put in all I could, full time or part-time. I just never did let go of the interest and fascination of becoming a martial arts expert one day. Now that I had mastered a lot of martial arts skills, and my teachers had branded me an expert, the fascination had ceased to haunt me. Instead, it had become an integral part of me, standard stuff that I live with. I found myself bored and constantly seeking another fascination, which I, unfortunately, haven't found yet. But my adventurous spirit, the one that bothers my mom so much, remained intact and kept me going. I took whatever came my way but added to that now is my keen interest in taking safety as a first measure. I take more time planning out things more than I did before. I now try to make sure my life and those around me are not endangered. But then came along this job as a field agent for EdenCom. As a field agent, one had no control of what was in store for him or her while on assignment. You must entirely rely on your instincts and training while adhering to the assignment's rules and guidelines as much as possible. You see, the ability still becomes the key to safety for everything that we do in life, especially the outgoing, sometimes outrageous and daring adventurous life like mine.

"Couldn't do it," she said. "The school course load was too much, still is too much. This is my future, though, meaning linguistics. Perhaps I will rejoin the group after being done with school."

"Good idea, whatever works for you," I said. I settled back comfortably in the leather seat and closed my eyes, concentrating on all I could hear of the music. I probably dozed off, for when I opened my eyes, we were driving up a steep, winding slope, and around us were tops of numerous hills all covered by green vegetation. We could not see the bottom because of the dense morning fog that surrounded the entire physical structure except for the tops. It looked like a fluffy silver blanket sprawled around them. Salieya looked at me and smiled.

"You dozed off," she said. "We are in the rolling hills of the Garampoli highlands, which have a road built through and over them. It is beautiful up here. There is a place where you can experience what I am talking about, especially in the morning, at sun dawn."

"How long have I been sleeping?" I asked, feeling somewhat groggy. I now realized that I have been sleeping a lot since this assignment began less than a day ago.

"For about an hour or so," she replied. "You probably needed a Power nap. I hope you stay awake for the rest of the journey. There is a lot of countryside to see, if you are interested in that kind of thing."

"Yes, of course, and I think am fully awake now," I said.

"There is a spot my dad used to take me to up here every time we came this way," she said. "We used to leave the city very early in the morning so we could catch the sun dawning at the top of the hills. It is amazing, beautiful. I want you to see it."

We drove on in silence. The two-way, winding road had no tarmac surface, and potholes were common. At certain times we went around an entire hill upwards and then around another downwards, without ever leveling off. After completing a steep incline, we finally leveled off to the top of a big hill with big rocks between dense, green vegetation bordering both sides of the road. It was at one spot alongside this flat road phase that Salieya stopped the car and killed the engine. She pointed up at the top of a hilly escarpment to our left.

"Up there. That is where my dad used to take me very early in the morning to witness the sun's magic," she said, pointing her finger past me to her left. "Let's get out and do some climbing. It's not too far up, so you don't need to worry about stressing your leg muscles."

"Ready when you are," I said.

We got out of the car, and after she remotely locked it, we started making our way upwards and through the rocky vegetation. I was following right behind her as she climbed and made her way upwards over the big rocks, avoiding dense vegetation areas by going around them. Never once did she look back, just concentrating on leading the way. This all wasn't new to me since I had experienced hilly terrain navigation, both vehicular and hiking, during training with army rangers. We finally made it to the hilltop, which was flat and wide with low grass and smaller rock terrain. And she was right. It was beautiful up here, and the scenery was breathtaking.

But perhaps the most breathing taking sight was catching the sun coming up above the hills. We got there just in time to catch the golden waves of the sun's rays weave themselves through the thick blanket of cloudy fog like a golden ribbon wrapping itself around a big chunk of fluffy white cotton. The mix glowed so magnificently it made you want to jump on it and touch it or ride on top of it. As we looked on, the golden flow of rays finally joined together, creating a blanket that completely engulfed the fluffy silver ball of cotton. Great masses of vapor were now rising from all over the place as the dewed fog started evaporating due to the new heat from the sun's rays. It was like the place was full of golden steam trains. From where we stood, the smell of fresh, moisturized breeze was very over-powering.

"Amazing and beautiful, isn't it?" Salieya said, wrapping her arm around mine.

"Spectacular," I replied.

"That's what I wanted to show you," she said. "And now the show is all over. In a few more minutes, all the fog will disappear, and the hilltops with all the greenery will show. So we better get going back down. We still got some ways to go to reach our destination."

We started making our way down the bushy, rocky hillside. Going up seemed to be much more comfortable, and that is because of the downward pulling, or incline plane type force, which can quickly force you into a quick forward tumbling, rolling fall that would not stop till you hit the base of the hill. There were also a lot of small loose rocks, so every step was cautionary. This time, though, I was leading the way, and as we came closer to the road, I noticed that we were suddenly not alone. I stopped dead on my tracks. The sudden stop forced Salieya also to stop, almost losing her balance and grabbing at my arm to keep herself steady.

"What's the matter?" She asked.

"We have company," I said.

They were five tall, skinny men, armed with machetes and big sticks. One had an old rifle, which he now pointed at us. A quick review of my surroundings pinpointed their locations. They had already surrounded the car; two stood by the driver's door, one in front of the car, and the other two behind it. They looked shabby and scraggy in their dirty, old loose cloth and dirty, filthy looking hair. They also looked very ferocious.

"Miseges," Salieya said the word almost instantly. "Ruthless, hill thugs or mountain bandits knew not only to rob their victims but kill them too. These people are dangerous, Kiron. They kill travelers all the time with their big knives by chopping them into pieces. They rape their women victims, strip them naked, and take everything they can lay their hands on. Rumors have it now that they steal babies too and sell the children to people in Sudan. They are evil people, so I think we are in huge trouble right now. We have to get away from them as fast as we can, and the only way is to go back up."

The fifth man confronted us before we even got closer to the car. He stopped us halfway across from the other side. He said something very quickly, in a strong, heavy accent and a hoarse voice, very ferociously too. He had a machete in one hand and pointed at us with the other.

"What is he saying?" I asked Salieya.

"He is saying I am not supposed to talk," she replied. "Women are not supposed to talk around men. He also wants you to take all your clothes off and also hand over your shoes and watch."

"Really? Ok then, Salieya. Just do what I tell you to do, and we shall get through this with no problem," I said. "Step back behind me," I said. "Then try to make your way back up the hill. Do it now."

She immediately did as I asked her to do. She took a few steps back, and as I stepped up in front of her, she started scrambling back up the hill. Taking note of this, the man moved forward quickly, raising the machete up in a striking position. He, however, hesitated when I took a few steps towards him. Doubt crept into his eyes. The man with the rifle left his position from the other side of the car and came into full view, watching me very closely, and the gun still pointed at me. The gunman was now standing a few yards away, to my left.

Without saying a word, I quickly stripped off my dual-time Casio watch and offered it to him. The doubt in his eyes disappeared as he reached for it, the machete still raised. Now, I knew that if I hesitated and not act quickly, this man would chop me down. I could tell by his poise that he was an expert at using this kind of weapon. As his fingers touched the watch, I suddenly reached out and grabbed his hand. In one quick move, I twisted it around, forcing him to bend down, while I lashed out with my left foot and kicked hard at hand holding the machete. The big knife flew out of his hand, landing on the ground, not far away from us. Then I yanked him forward, using the same side I had grabbed. He was a light guy, and as he screamed in pain, I jerked him off his feet and tossed him aside like a scarecrow project.

Quickly spinning around, I jumped forward and grabbed the machete. Before the man with the gun could react, I fell to one knee, swung the knife upwards, and then threw it as hard as I can at him. At that close range, the big, sharp, double-edged knife buried itself deep into the area between his belly and rib cage. I saw the gunman's eyes widen in shock, and then he crumbled to his knees, dropping the rifle. In a flash, I was over his fallen body and picked up the rifle. Then I looked around at rest.

Even though I had knocked down two of their buddies in a matter of seconds, these guys were not about to give up that easily, and they knew exactly what to do next. One of the men dashed from behind the car and across the road, trying to get to Salieya. But I wasn't about to let that happen, because if he got his filthy hands on her, that meant game over for her and me. So, I went after him and quickly caught up with him before he got to her. **Salieya** was now quickly getting further and further away from the battlefield. Realizing that I had closed in on him, the man aborted his plans for Salieya and faced me.

I stared into those sunken, bloodshot eyes, and realized that I was dealing with ruthless, cruel, evil, cold-blooded killers. He was now like a cobra facing a mongoose. His eyes darting around in all directions; he raised his machete. I taunted him with the rifle, which I now held by the barrel, like I was holding a spade, overseeing him. He swung the big blade at me, and I stepped back, dancing around him, changing positions so I could keep an eye on the rest. The deadly blade swished past my stomach, and then instantly came back the same way. But I danced away again. He thrust at me again and again, but I kept dodging that big blade, and then in one move, I quickly went around him, and as he swung around to face me, I turned the gun butt-forward and jabbed it hard into his face. I then swung the rifle butt up again, bringing it down on him, hitting him again hard between his neck and shoulder. He screamed in pain and fell to his knees. I stepped in and kicked the machete out of his hand and then my foot came up and connected with his chin with brute but calculated force. His body flipped over backward into the air, landed onto the rocky, steep ground, and then rolled away down and into the middle of the road.

Three down.

Another man was now coming towards me with his stick. He lunged forward at me, but I was moving faster. I stepped in, blocked his flying wrist with my left, and then with my right, I brought the old gun down hard into his side. He buckled down to his side instantly. I then swung my foot up, and the steel-toed tip of my shoe connected carefully with his belly. At the same time, I was in time to duck as another man threw a machete at me with deadly accuracy. The thing cut through the air, spinning like a boomerang, but since I had seen it coming, I fell backward on to my back and rolled clear. The big knife flew past and above my body and landed harmlessly some yards away from me. Quickly getting up, I looked around, grabbed the rifle, and aimed at the thrower, pulling the trigger. Click!

The thing did not even have a single bullet in it. I threw the useless rifle of the ground and glared at the thrower. His eyes were now wide open like he was in shock, and then his whole body started shaking. It was as if he had just seen a ghost. He suddenly looked terrified as I took a step forward towards him. He mumbled something, and then turned around and took off in the opposite direction, away from me. In a moment, he was scrambling his way up the slope on the other side of the road as fast as he could. Breathing in heavily, I looked around at his fallen comrade at arms. The man with a blade in his belly was still curled up in a ball, his eyes wide open and his breathing uneven. A brown liquid was coming out of his nose and mouth. It didn't look like blood, so maybe it was the breakfast he had this morning. He didn't look too good, either. The other three guys were still trying to regain their sense of everything, while even down.

"Alright, Salieya, you can come down now," I shouted, looking up at her. She had gotten up that slope pretty fast. "It's safe now."

"It's safe? What do you mean it is safe? Those are bad men, and they are going to kill us…," she yelled back. She still sounded very frightened or scared. I could hear it in her voice.

"I took care of it. There are no more bad men, Salieya," I shouted back. "So, it is safe for you to come down. We have to get going, remember?"

Reluctantly, she made her way down the slope. When she finally got down and was standing next to me, she mentally took in the situation, and her face looked even more terrified. She stayed away from the fallen bandits and walked around them to get back into the car. She started the car, and once I was in, she drove off immediately. Her hands were shaking as she maneuvered the wheel, and her eyes were fixed on the road ahead, her head motionless.

"Want me to take over the wheel?" I asked after almost fifteen minutes of silence. "That will give you time to recover yourself out of that nightmare event behind us."

"No, I am ok. I almost got us killed, Kiron," she burst out. "And I know better not to make unnecessary stops in this area these days. I acted carelessly, and that's not a good thing." "But that was one of the best visions I have ever seen in my life," I said. "The morning sun, cloud combination was so perfect. It's awesome, and I think it was worth the risk."

"No, that's not true. I knew very well about the risks of stopping in a place like that. Lately, it has become hazardous out here," she continued,

"And by the way, what did you do to them? What happened?"

"Nothing much happened," I replied, looking away from her so she couldn't see the grin on my face. "I took protective measures. Acts of self-defense."

"Don't tell me that nothing happened, Kiron?" she said, "That man has a machete sticking out of his belly. He didn't do that to himself, did he? Seeing him on the ground like that wasn't very comforting. And the rest of his cronies were all laying around him like litter. The last one ran away from you like he's seen a ghost. And you telling me nothing happened?"

"Well, let's say I just happened to save the day," I replied carefully. "You see, I have some special skills that I can apply to situations like this, and as you can tell in this case, they came in handy."

"Like Karate? Judo?" she asked hesitantly, a questioning look on her face.

"Well, something like that," I replied.

She didn't say anything anymore after that. We drove through the rest of the hilly terrain quietly, a bumpy up and down ride that left a cloud of dust behind us. I must have again fallen asleep, because a hard tap suddenly aroused me on the head. I did not understand why I was falling asleep frequently, maybe it was a time zone issue.

"Aw, that hurt," I said, pulling myself up in the seat.

"Well, I tried to wake you up, but none of the usual wakes up methods were working," she said, smiling down at me, her big eyes twinkling. "You seemed to be so tired, so I just let you sleep on. And boy, can you snore! I thought you had rested enough last night."

"Where are we?" I asked, looking around me. We seemed to be in the middle of what appeared to be a dusty town area, with people walking around in all directions. The buildings on both sides of the street looked very old and dusty. A donkey stood at the sidewalk while someone loaded a big stack of stuff on to its back. Poor animal, I thought.

"This town is called Isibendo, "she replied. "It is a local big village or township still stuck in the old times. Nothing much has changed here since over five hundred years ago, I believe. Modern machinery, like cars and helicopters carrying politicians and tourists, maybe a tractor to pave a road, have shown up here occasionally, but not the ways of life for the people. And so perhaps that is why, if our mission's facts are true, it is not such a coincidence that this is happening here."

I yawned as I straightened up in the car seat, while rubbing my eyes, then asked, "So what do we expect to find here?"

"According to my cousin, a cadet priest of the religious sect known as followers of the God of Abraham, which is very rooted in the lives of the people of this and other surrounding towns, the item in question for our mission is here. When EdenCom first tapped me to investigate these events, I contacted my cousin through an aunt of mine who lives here. It was then that I found out that he belonged to the same religious group that involved the boy with the stick. He promised to take me to the house where the boy is kept and guarded. The house is in this township or village. He also promised to get us in so we can talk to the boy, interview him."

"Great, we are getting close," I said, instantly feeling the enthusiasm building up inside me. "I can't wait to get to the bottom of all this; so now what next?"

"For now, we are going to visit his mother, who is also my aunt Mumia," she said, "she partially raised me when my father was dealing with post-grad studies and separation issues with my mother. She and her husband have big farmland here and some residential rental property near the capital city, Addis Ababa. They are doing well. My cousin is one of the twin children they have. God only blessed them with two. His sister is somewhere in Europe finishing up with medical doctor studies. We will spend the night with aunt Mumia and then embarks on the assignment again tomorrow. We are sort of early in town; my aunt is expecting us in one hour from now. So, with this extra time, I will show you around. It's a unique environment, one that you definitely are not accustomed to."

We were parked in one corner of what appeared to be the main street in the town. Like I noted earlier, it was filled with a lot of people moving in different directions, and a lot of sidewalk activity was going on, notably small time vendors with all sorts of shiny ornaments, cloth, utensils, and even food was being cooked live on the streets. Someone was roasting some fowl on an open fire on one side while what appeared to be like a whole pig was being roasted on the other. I could see people dishing out some sort of money and the vendor cutting off slices of meat. The smell of burning food, mingle in the dusty air plus fumes from exhaust pipes of some ancient cars driving by overloaded with bags of stuff created a sort of misty colored environment which nobody, except perhaps me, seemed to care about. A group of musicians with drums and a forefront female dancer doing a belly roll was attracting a large crowd in another corner of the street a few yards away. Other people were coming in and outdoors, which appeared to be entrances and or exits to indoor shops, restaurants, maybe back alleys. I hope you get the picture. We then had to slowly make our way through this active zone, with Salieya trying to explain a few things about what was going on and trying to make sure I can hear her with all the noise around us.

At a certain point, we crossed the street to the opposite side. Salieya wanted to show me something up close, an item made locally. But just as we approached this one vendor, we were suddenly swamped by a multitude of local vendors trying to entice us to buy something, having spotted an opportunity. It was then that I felt a sudden grip on my right ankle. It was so tight I could not move my leg forward. I instantly looked downwards and found myself staring into big round eyes that almost appeared too white for my liking, inset in a roughly bearded face, dirty dreadlocked hair falling all over a broadened shoulder base, a big nose that was front blocked by a thickened moustache and with prominent cheekbones, all these complimented by a dark coffee brown skin with some darker areas. I also came to realize that my anchor is a disabled individual who was sitting on a pair of crumpled legs, basically a crawler, but with what appears to be a well-developed upper body. Years of using the upper body for constant mobility purposes probably led to the upper body development and strength, which perhaps explains the firm iron grip on my ankle.

"Hey, let go of my leg now! "I shouted at him, as I tried to free myself with vigorous forward attempts.

He didn't let go. Instead, he burst out laughing, giving me a glimpse of surprisingly very white teeth and pink tongue. His laugh was a congested type guffaw that made me wonder if I was dealing with a deranged, possibly frustrated individual who was capable of inflicting physical harm to others without a second thought. I started to quickly think about other means of freeing myself, which would include a kick at his gripping hand with my free foot or clubbing him with a fist in the face, which would divert his attention from holding on to my leg. As if he was reading my mind, he abruptly let go.

"Give me some money, I want to buy food," he said in what came out now as a deep, rich gruff voice, and in broken, but surprisingly, understandable English.

"Yeah? But that wasn't exactly the best way to ask for it, grabbing at people's ankles!" Salieya yelled back. "That was rude, and it's unacceptable. Come on, Kiron; let us get away from this maniac before he does something bad to us."

Ignoring her reaction, the man took hold of my leg again, but this time gently. "Please, help me. I haven't had food in the last three days, and I am starving. I am sorry for appearing to be very aggressive, but it was the only way I could catch your attention. Look at me now, man. I am way down here, and nobody can see me. Every normal human being looks upwards. Please help me with some money so I can buy something to eat."

I looked down into those big grey eyes that almost seemed so white except for the enormous brown pupil in the middle. There was something in those eyes, something in that face that gave me second thoughts about this guy. It was like staring into the eyes of an innocent, distressed child that has suddenly found hope in you, the only hope, and expressing those feelings without saying anything.

"Salieya, give me some of that native money," I said, looking up at her and stretching my hand out. At the same time, I felt the man letting go of my ankle. Salieya hesitated briefly, looking at me in a questioning way. I nodded my head at her once and then winked, a wry smile coming on my face. She reached into her shoulder carry bag and pulled three thick bundles of Ethiopian Birr notes, the crisp notes held together by a rubber band. She handed me one package.

"Will that be enough?" she asked, mimicking my wry smile by applying the same look on her face.

"That will do, thank you," I said, and with all the local vendors looking on in disbelief, I handed the bundle to the man at my feet and added, "There, I hope this can keep you afloat for a few days and perhaps rent you a nice bed to sleep in so you can rest. Now go, my friend, and be happy."

The man's face instantly lit up as he took hold of the money, with a look of disbelief, and once again reminding me of a happy child who had just gotten what he or she had been longing for.

"God bless you again and again, and again, my child," he said repeatedly. "May he grant you tenfold or more for the good deed you have done towards me today. May the good lord grant you success in all that you do."

But just at that same time, the local vendors all suddenly jumped on to Salieya, engulfing her like a noisy swarm of bees entering a hive. I went to her rescue, instantly forgetting about the crawling beggar man. The crowd that suddenly engulfed her was so overwhelming she lost her balance and fell backward to her bottom. She started screaming, in the native language, obviously asking them to back off, but this was to no avail. Reaching over, I grabbed at two lightly clothed bony shoulders and pulled them backward. The shoulders and their attached bodies instantly fell back, losing balance too. I bumped someone out of the way with my left shoulder and heard a grunt of pain before grabbing two other arms and pulled sideways, finally getting to Salieya. Someone in front of me placed his dirty palm suddenly in my face and pushed me back roughly. But I maintained steadiness on my feet.

"Alright enough, stand back!" I shouted and in English. To my relief, my call was compelling, for everyone pulled away from Salieya and left me standing over her. I stared angrily around me, at them, and suddenly they all faded as fast as they had appeared, some muttering or swearing loudly to themselves. I offered my hand to Salieya, and once she grasped it, I yanked her back to her feet.

"Thanks," she mumbled as she patted the dust off her cloth. "See what happens when all your attention is taken away from me. Other people try to take advantage."

"I can see you are tightly holding on to that shoulder bag," I said, grinning. "Sorry, I guess I caused this whole thing to happen. May be I should not have asked you for the money openly. I just wanted to help this guy out immediately." I said, pointing at ... nothing.

The crawling beggar-man had vanished.

"I can see he took your money and simply vanished," Salieya said.

"So much for getting what he wanted and after that, simply vanishes without a word."

"Well, actually, he said thank you, and even splashed some blessings on me repeatedly," I said, grinning.

"Well I hope those blessings enable us to get through this assignment quickly, be done with it. I am already getting exhausted," She said.

"Yeah, I guess we could use some blessings in a place like this. It's so ancient," I said.

After the brief mix up with the locals, Salieya appeared to have had enough of the busy environment already and suggested we go ahead and go to her aunt's place. So, we made our way back through the muddling crowd again, to the car. We found it much easier driving the big car in the crowded street, honking our way through, than when walking.

It wasn't long, maybe about ten minutes before we left all that behind and started driving through what looked like real farmland, with neat rows of crops on both sides of the bumpy, narrow, and dusty roadway. I also noted lots of animals grazing on the grass around the area. This is, reasonably to say, what one could call the pure countryside.

Aunt Mumia and her husband, Enoch, lived on a huge solitary piece of land, with her house, in a one-level sprawling house right in the middle of it. The land appeared to be very carefully cultivated with neat rows of cocoa and other crops. She had several workers helping her out.

Aunt Mumia came rushing out of the house to greet her niece with open arms. She was a relatively big, tall woman, in contrast to her husband, who was as tall but rather skinny. Everybody, including the whole worker group, seemed to be so happy to see Salieya. Salieya later told me that she had spent a good part of her early life here with her dad's sister and that aunt Mumia practically raised her. Most of the workers had seen her grow from infancy until she became a teenager, then to a young adult who soon departed for the city. Uncle Enoch quietly hugged his niece, with less enthusiasm, but I could tell by the look in his eyes that he was glad to see her.

"Aunt Mumia, this is Mr. Kiron Day, and he is working with me on my current journalist field assignment," Salieya introduced me to the couple. I briefly shook hands with uncle Enoch, but aunt Mumia gave me a big bear hug.

Enoch showed me around his farm briefly, and then after asking me a few questions about where I came from, sharing dinner with us, this soft-spoken man with a deep voice excused himself and retired to his resting chambers for the day. I found him to be less outspoken, unlike his wife; aunt Mumia was just the opposite, cheerful and talkative. Salieya appeared to be where she belongs, for she was fully engaged in the verbal exchange. It seemed that the two women had a lot to catch up with. I was shown more of the house, and the surrounding farmland rode on a tractor with the farm mechanic, played with a bunch of local kids, and watched cows and goats being milked. I even participated, but mostly observed, in slaughtering some chicken, by hand. Then we helped take some stuff back to the town center in our car, by hitching a big-wheeled wagon full of farm vegetables to the market place in the middle of the town. We then had lunch outside on a dining table made out of open wood plunks. I sat amongst the workers, and the food was served from a big pan of a free wood log fire. This, to me, was lots of fun, and time went by fast for the rest of the day.

After the meal, I was shown to where we were to stay for the night, in the guest wing on one side of the big house. Salieya, later on, mentioned that aunt Mumia actually, and quite frequently, rented out this wing to tourists or other visitors to the area. To that effect, our stay was business for aunt Mumia, thanks to her niece. We were effectively renting, and EdenCom was paying.

While the two women talked, I went to my room, which contained a twin bed with a desk and chair, and wall to wall light carpeting. A single glass window with metal bars gave you a view over the overlying fields, but that was now closed since it had gotten dark. A generator was now running and provided lighting to the house at night. I could hear its noisy drone from the outside.

I started to assemble the necessary equipment that I knew was vital to our assignment. One of the workers helped me to carry the bags from the car to the bedroom. Setting this stuff up was a piece of cake for me because I had done it several times, and it was all small gadgets, nothing big. The most important item was the laptop, which also doubled in as a base - satellite relay transmitter.

But the coolest gadget in the package was this pair of sunglasses that had special, shatter, and waterproof lenses that could focus even in the dark, with thin ear holders lined with tiny sensors that served as aerials. These shades came in a package with a pair of special buttons that are high density, unidirectional microphones, and unusual eyes that instantly come alive when the shadows started focusing on anything. The eyes could be thrown or attached to something in an area and still focus and transmit independently. Together they transmitted live sound and picture back to the computer that instantly relayed it to satellite in space which then sent it to a super computer at EdenCom headquarters.

The operators at EdenCom then would receive and record live whatever we focus on from wherever we are. Cool, isn't it? We each had a pair of these gadgets. I was responsible for making sure Salieya got wired well. After I set up the laptop with its pre-installed super extended battery and tested its satellite transmission capability and function, I was able to confirm that the small audiovisual transmitters were operational. I was even able to get a confirmation Text live from the IT team at EdenCom that everything was a go.

After that, I decided to step out of the building and get some cool breeze around me. I bypassed the living room area near the guest's wing entrance, and I could hear the two women still talking and laughing. I opened the front door and stepped out into the dark outside. The breeze was light, and indeed the air very fresh. It felt so good I stripped off my shirt and was able to feel the air directly rub against my body. I could make out the big car's silhouette in the darkness. An idea hit my head. To maximize the cooling effect of the breeze, I could climb to the top of the car and sit up there for a while, watch the star-filled sky above me. That is if I could handle the mosquitoes. The tiny monsters were buzzing all around me, probably attracted by the warm heat from my body. I made my way towards the car.

As I got closer to the car, I noticed something in the shadows to my far left. But I wasn't so sure if I saw something or it was an imagination thing, especially that I was making some noise from spinning my shirt around my body with my hand, trying to ward off the flying bugs. I moved more towards the left because the back of the car was to that side.

Suddenly, something leaped out of the shadows, coming straight at me. It was a human form and was moving quickly.

I stopped moving, but I had to instantly jump aside as the person lunged at me with the object in his hands. My body slammed against the car, making me aware that I had no more room behind me. So I turned around and faced my assailant again. He was coming in from the left to the center. Even in the dark, I could still make out his silhouette. He had something in his hands, like a wooden log or big stick, and was raising it and swinging at me again, another attack. I jumped clear to the right as he struck out to my left and then saw him stumble. As he regained his balance, I quickly stepped in and, in a flash second, lashed out with a mid-level kick at his wrists. That knocked the object out of his hands. In an instant I spun around and slammed my shoulder heavily into his body, sending him sprawling to the ground. I heard him grant heavily. I scooped up the object, a thick wooden log, swooped up, and came down at his leg. I heard him holler out in pain, and I was about to do it again when he raised his hands frantically in a gesture of surrender. I decided not to hit him back, but I still had my hands up with the log.

"Who are you, and why are you attacking me with this piece of wood?"

I demanded instantly. "Speak up, or I will smash your leg again."

"Please, please, don't hit me again," he said, still waving his hands at me. "It's me, Enoch, Mumia's husband. I think you broke one of my legs. Please don't break the other one."

"Mr. Enoch? But…what are you doing out here, and why were you trying to hit me with this wooden log?" I asked, completely surprised. I dropped the stick and slowly squatted down beside him, staring at him blankly. Yap, it was aunt Mumia's man right there before me.

"The night watchman… I gave him an off tonight and then decided to come out here and make sure everything is alright," he said. "We have people who come around at night and steal things. I thought you were one of them, and that is why I came after you."

Ok, this wasn't good, not at all, I thought. Here I was being attacked by a protective host, and I just broke his leg. Maybe I should have stayed inside the house after all, instead of meddling around with the outside. What was Salieya, or her aunt, or both, going to say about this? I had no immediate answers, but perhaps it was best I apologized immediately and then wait for the reactions from both women.

"I am very sorry, sir. I didn't mean to harm you in any way," I said to him. "I came out here to enjoy the fresh breeze and didn't know you were out here too. I reacted in self-defense when you came at me with the log. Let me help you back to the house, and then we will look at your leg. I have a first aid kit in the car, and I am trained to administer urgent care."

"No, it's ok. I will be fine," he said quickly. "It's my fault, all this. I should have asked first who you are before attacking you. And boy, you are fast, too fast. I must be growing very old; I can't even keep up with the simple momentum of a one on one fight. Just don't tell my wife about this incident, ok young man? I don't want her to panic or start farcing about things. My old girl always takes things way out of context."

"Ok then, I won't say a word, sir," I replied quickly, feeling more relieved that he didn't want me to go tell. Perhaps, I thought, he has his way of explaining this to the women what happened to his leg. "And I am canceling my outing tonight. You sure you don't want me to help you back to the house? You can do it yourself?"

"I will be fine, just go back in," He said, sounding a little impatient.

Without another word, I stood up and walked away from him and back into the house. I didn't look back, but I am sure he was staring at me. It isn't your age that is slowing you down, Enoch, it's my special military ops training, and my fighting skills enabled me to act faster than the average man or woman, I thought quietly.

I found aunt Mumia standing right in the doorway when I got back to the house. She was peering out into the darkness. Salieya was right beside her.

"We heard some disturbing noise out there," she said, "sounded like someone hurt. Are you ok, Mr. Day?"

"I am fine, thank you," I said. "I heard the noise, too; I just don't know what it was."

After I said that, I walked past the two women, still staring at the dark outside, and headed for my room. I got inside and closed the door without locking it. I flopped down on the twin bed, and after thinking about the evening events for a while, I decided to take a bath. Salieya had shown me a bathing room inside the house and a few yards away from my room. I gathered my fresh cloth and soap and headed for it.

It wasn't exactly my usual shower place, with no bathtub, but a raised cemented platform with a faucet attached to a water pipe to feel up the basin. There was a clean, plastic basin that I filled with lukewarm tap water and towels hanging on a rack, all fresh and clean. There was no hot water, and aunt Mumia had mentioned that if I wanted hot water, the workers could boil me some and bring it. But who needed hot water in this tropical setting, anyway? The lukewarm water was very refreshing. I washed up quickly and in ten minutes or, so I was back in my room. I turned off the light and tucked myself into the fresh, ironed bed linen. The bed had a mosquito net around it, although I had not seen any of the flying bloodsuckers in the room yet. I must have unknowingly fallen asleep, but only to be awakened by a gentle tap on the door. Not again, I thought. I didn't want to engage in another active encounter similar to the Enoch incident.

"Who is it?" I asked after a few moments' silence. I sat up in bed and listened intensely.

"It's me, Salieya. Please open the door and let me in." It was her alright, so I got up from the bed. I didn't have to change anything, for I had a pair of fresh jeans on and a light undershirt. Unlike in my own house, I stayed partially dressed and sort of ready for any surprises that might come up, a side effect of cobra mission training.

I opened the door and did not hide the surprised look on my face. There she was, in plain white pajamas, her feet sheathed in a pair of sandals.

"Is everything ok, Salieya? I thought you went to your room to sleep or you were simply still talking to your aunt." I asked.

She stepped into the room, and I closed the door behind her.

"I don't know. I don't want to stay in that little room by myself anymore," she said. "I must admit, and you may laugh at me if you want to, that I get scared of the dark sometimes. And so being in such a place by myself now, especially in a place where we just heard someone cry out loudly like he was hurt, makes me more afraid. We sent out some of our male on-site workers to look around, but no one was found." She sat down on the bed, hands in front of her, looking up at me. She looked so innocent, like some little girl trying to tell her daddy a secret. "Can I please stay in here with you tonight? I will sit up in that chair till morning. I have no problem with doing that because I did so much of it during my earlier school days."

"Sure, that's ok," I replied. I got off the bed and pointed at it. "There, you can use the bed, I will take the chair. So, how about your uncle Enoch, did he hear anything?"

"Uncle Enoch is still out there, doing his thing with other guys, his neighborhood friends," she replied. "Aunt Mumia told me that she is worried about his drinking habits these days. He goes out every evening and comes in late, very drunk."

The man was probably drunk when he attacked me, I thought. He perhaps mistook me for a thief on his property, trying to get something out of the car.

"Well, the man is going to do what he wants to do," I said. "Maybe we will find out the real deal behind the screaming in the morning, so, for now, its sleep time." I yawned widely, stretching out my arms above my head. Talk about contagious action; she too yawned, stretching out her brown arms sideways, and then giggled lightly.

"How about this: we share the bed. It's a twin made from solid wood, and I think it can handle two adults. That way, we both get comfortable rest. It could be a long day tomorrow, you know. That is if you don't mind sharing a bed with a girl, "She said.

What was this, an invitation to a treat? I certainly didn't mind sharing a bed with a girl, more especially a pretty bombshell one like Salieya.

"Sure, good idea, if you don't mind me snoring my head off," I said. "Jump right in, make yourself comfortable. I will follow."

"I am sure I can handle that; I am a heavy sleeper when tired, like now, so I won't hear you snoring. You get in; first, it's your bed," she said.

"No, you first. I tend to give my guests the priority first, especially the first timers. So, you first and hurry up before I change my mind and kick you out of my domain," I insisted.

She giggled again, and got into the bed, moving over to the far-left side. I turned off the light and got in beside her, and we both pulled the cover on top of us, at the same time, then laughed about it. A fresh scent like baby passion fruit aroma tinged by a faint jasmine whiff blossomed in the entire environment, originating from her body, and the bed was suddenly hot and cozy.

"Now, I feel safe. Good night Kiron", she said softly and then turned her body gently around, turning her back to me. I echoed back the good night, and then turned my back to hers too. I could feel her warm, soft buttocks against mine, her long legs lightly touching mine.

And that was it. It was all civil if you understand what I mean, and later on, in the morning of the next day, I had to acknowledge that this was one of those nights that I truly and fully slept well.

Chapter Three

S HE WOKE UP first. "Did you sleep well?" she asked.

I nodded in affirmative, yawning, and stretching. Sun rays were streaming through the glass windowpane, dulled by the silky white curtaining.

"Good. I thought I had ruined it all for you," she said, sitting up in the bed. "Thank you for letting me stay in your room and sleep in your bed too."

"You are welcome," I said, sitting up on the side of the bed. Salieya rolled over to the edge of the bed beside me and sat up. She then gently parted me on the back.

"Now let me get back to my room and freshen up," she said. "I will be back here in a few minutes so we can go over our plans for today."

"I will be waiting," I said. "Hurry back."

By the time she came back, I was myself ready, having stepped out to the little bathroom to wash up and brush my teeth, and then fully dress up in fresh cloth, which consisted of black Khaki cargo pants, blue short-sleeved T-shirt covered by a black, leather all-weather jacket that looked like a pro fisherman's deal. I topped it off with a black beret over my clean shaved head, and my feet were back in the steel-toed boots. She was dressed in a pair of blue jeans and a black, long-sleeved Tuttle neck top overlapped by a sleeveless denim jacket flat, thick-soled leather sneaker shoes completed the attire. Her hair tied back, she looked tall and elegant.

I then introduced her to the field gadgets again, but this time in detail, about what they were for and how to use them. Quick learner: She demonstrated back to me on what I had just taught her perfectly well. I attached everything in place and then gave her the sunshades equipment we were to start using at my signal. That took about fifteen minutes. Then using the satellite phone, I called Jim Holmbeck to let him know that we were now hooked up and anytime the storyline would go live to him via the equipment. He told me that he had been expecting my call and was at work at this moment. He was going to go ahead and give a head start briefing to the communications team at EdenCom and needed about fifteen minutes to do this. He also wanted us to be careful. He spoke to Salieya briefly before we hang up. After that, we packed whatever stuff we had to pack. The laptop was to stay behind, running to keep the satellite connection going. So we retained the room for use pending our return from the field and locked it up. Aunt Mumia was still making money.

We had breakfast with aunt Mumia. There was no sign of Uncle Enoch anywhere, and I didn't bother to ask. We briefly discussed our next move over the breakfast when and while aunt Mumia stepped out to direct her workers on what to do today. We were to meet with Salieya's cousin, the cadet priest, and after that, he was to take us to the monastery and help us to gain access to the boy. Ten minutes later, we said bye to aunt Mumia and left the farm.

We drove back to the old town and went to a small coffee and tea shop. Her cousin was waiting for us there. His name was Haile Gere Mariam, a tall brown fella with a light mustache and dressed in a priestly black combination of black pants and a shirt with a white-collar all around. He stood up to greet us, shaking my hand, and lightly hugging his cousin. Like his cousin, he spoke fluent English, with a very faint accent.

Haile Gere Mariam explained that the issues at his monastery had generated a lot of interest locally and nationally, if not, by this time, worldwide. This had prompted the Ethiopian government to intervene, and at the request of the head priest. He wanted full protection from what he saw as a danger to his church and subsequently to the surrounding local area. As a result, the monastery was now guarded by armed Ethiopian police personnel, and there was a checkpoint a couple of miles down the road that led to the monastery's main gates. Vehicles are being thoroughly searched, he said, and a lot of questions are asked. Visitors also had to have a special pass provided by and signed by a monastery official to enter the compound, except the priests who worked there. That is why he was here to take us through these hurdles and make it easier for us to gain access. I later learned that these services did not come free. Salieya had bankrolled him to the project as part of her expenses, and Jim had no problem with it. He now wanted to know if we had excessive baggage because this could cause a delay. We didn't, as we had left most of our gear at aunt Mumia's. Good, he said, we then were ready to roll.

After about thirty minutes of driving through tiny village townships, we drove up a dirt road and encountered the police roadblock. We were asked to get out, although the priest was told to stay in the car. They then opened the car's liftgate and looked around inside the vehicle. They didn't ask for our credentials, and after finding nothing that caught their attention inside the car, they let us move on. A few minutes later, we arrived at the main gates of the fenced-in compound. There were more guards here, and once again, we were ordered out, this time the priest inclusive. All of us were carefully strip-searched, and our credentials were now thoroughly examined. Haile Gere Mariam did his best to explain that we were student journalists on research work at the monastery and that he had been assigned to assist us. The car was also carefully searched again before being finally let through. As this went on, I counted the number of guards on duty. Twenty-four guards altogether, at the main gates, and eighteen of these were armed with automatic. rifles. The armed personnel had remained on full watch while four searched the car and our bodies, and the other two examined our credentials. After what seemed like eternity, we were finally allowed to proceed.

With Salieya driving, Haile Gere Mariam directed us from the gates through a narrow, neatly paved, winding driveway that led us to the back of an old sprawling, red brick house with asbestos roofing. Around us was all green grass lawn, neatly cut and clean, with flower beds in between. Everything about this compound, surrounding the entire building, was all neat and clean and appeared well maintained. The red brick house was the center of other smaller, detached houses or units that surrounded it. There was a parking area for cars in the back, with two mini vans packed in it. There was also an old lorry from which two men were unloading bags of stuff. We parked our vehicle further away from the lorry but closer to a door to the building. Haile Gere Mariam got out first and beckoned to us to follow him.

"Normally, all visitors have to go to the main priest first and meet with him, and then from there move on with their visitation purpose," he said. "We get a lot of tourists, because this monastery has been around since the late eighteen hundred. And we also get a lot of theology students and clergymen who take this as an exhibit of Christian faith. But today the main priest is out of town, gone to meet with the highest priest in the hierarchy of our faith. He won't be back until next week. So, I will now take you straight to where the boy is, and leave you there, but only for a few minutes."

"Here, keep these, "Salieya said, handing the car keys to me. "I have a bad habit of misplacing stuff sometimes, especially at a time when I need them. It's a curse, sort of." She giggled when she said that, the usual girly giggle. I was getting used to it.

The inside was all marbled and beautiful, but also eerily quiet. Not very many people inside, and the few that we came to meet on our way seemed strangely quiet and only nodded at us, not a single word said.

"We must maintain silence in most parts of the inside of the building," Haile Gere Mariam said. "That allows us to continuously meditate and stay in touch with the lord, the only way we can feel his presence."

We entered a corridor and followed it shortly into another that led to a big open room that looked like a classroom, clearly illuminated by numerous candles, lined up on unique shelves all along the four walls of this big room. The floor was neatly had neatly arranged marble tiling, and all walls had well-arranged brown wood paneling on which hung old paintings of ancient-looking men with big dark beards, all dressed in dark monk style robes, staring at you with empty big brown eyes. Their eyes seemed to follow you in whichever direction you took, which made it even more eerily around here. It had a few desks and chairs all neatly ranged in rows and a pulpit in front of the arrangement. On all sides of this classroom were doors, about four on each opposite side.

Haile Gere Mariam pointed to one of the doors on our left. The door was painted bright white and had a long gold ribbon pinned to the top and hanging to its bottom

"That is the door that takes you to the boy. Just follow the short corridor, and there will be one more door before you come to a room with a lot of dimmed lighting inside. This is where he is. Please knock before you enter," he said.

I nodded and said thanks to him and then opened the door to reveal a dimly lit corridor that led to a single door at the end. The door was painted white too, had a gold ribbon as the other one, and had a single lit candle right above that illuminated it. I stepped into the corridor and made my way towards the door, with Salieya right behind me. Once outside the door, I gently knocked and waited. After about a minute of uninterrupted silence, I knocked again, this time louder.

The door opened, and a woman with loose black hair, dressed in a white robe held in place by a thin white sash around the waist, her cleavage clearly exposed, and bare feet, stood staring at us with blank eyes and said nothing.

Salieya gently pushed me aside and confronted the woman. She started speaking in rapid local lingo, which, of course, I could not comprehend. The strange woman answered back in slower, gentler tones, but her face looked rigid and suspicious. It was when Salieya stood aside and pointed at me that the woman's face suddenly changed to an astounding look and her hand went to her mouth. Suddenly, she stepped back into the room and tried to close the door, but I had already anticipated her action and moved quickly to block the door with my foot. I gently pushed back the door until it was wide open and stepped into a dimly lit room fogged up by light scented, fresh rose flower, incense smoke. Not taking her eyes off us, the woman slowly walked back towards another door, but just as her back met it, it opened inwards, and a figure emerged.

He was probably about twelve or fifteen years old, skinny, and quite tall. But he looked healthy, his golden-brown skin tone distinct, and his long dark hair was straight combed to the back into a silky, shiny, flow, held in place by a long, white cloth band. His big brown eyes stared at us without blinking. He suddenly spoke, with a lot of ease, like someone who has never been bothered by any problem. He paused for a moment in his speech, and then uttered a single word before slowly turning around and walking back into the room.

"He says that you are finally here, and was wondering what had taken you so long," Salieya interpreted. "He wants you to come in and sit with him. And only wants you, not the women."

"Tell him I need you in there to interpret what he is saying," I said. Still, the boy had already disappeared behind the numerous white drapes and veils that shielded the more profound insides of his mysterious chamber, the mysterious woman close to his heels. I didn't wait for the answer to that from Salieya either, as I found myself following him without looking back. I was now excited that we had meet the core of our assignment. I touched a tiny switch on the right side of my communication eyewear lens frame, and a little red blip flashed twice before turning into a constant green light. The satellite transmission was now on. We were finally live on location.

Suddenly the whole hanging veil, or drapes, ordeal came to an end, and I entered the center of the room, which revealed a big glass window draped by transparent white curtains that a light breeze from outside was gently blowing inwards. In the center of the room, in front of me, was a neatly made queen-sized bed with plush linen, again all white. The floor was carpeted, and clean, and personal items were neatly arranged on one side of the room. On another side were a single chair and desk with neatly arranged writing pads and a couple of fountain pens. At the foot of the plush bed was a video game console hooked to a television set. The still picture on the screen made it evident that the boy had been playing a game on the machine at the time we made our debut. That was probably why he didn't look pleased when he came out of his sanctuary and saw us. We had interfered with his game.

The boy jumped onto the top of the bed, sat down, and faced me. He pointed at the chair and then spoke.

"Bring that chair over here, Mr.," he said in clean, clear, and crisp English, a word by word pronunciation, but a surprise. I now realized I didn't need an interpreter, after all. There was more to this individual than I had thought, I told myself. His voice was light, that of an up and coming teenager, of course.

"Thanks," I said, and pulling the chair around so I can face him, I sat down. "You don't appear surprised to be sitting in here with a total stranger, and I find that quite intriguing."

"It's because I was expecting you to show up anytime from now," he said. "I have seen you very often in my dreams as a shadowy figure that told me it's the deliverer from God. Only in yesterday's dream was the figure much brighter than usual. I couldn't see the face, for a thick white veil always obscures it, but the rest of the body was transparent and shone brightly. I could see its heart as a shiny object beating in the center. The figure spoke to me for the first time yesterday since it first appeared in my dreams several days ago. I was able to instruct my aides to look out for a man coming to see me, who fit the description of the person in my dream. So, when my aide told me you were here, I had to come to look at you myself to make sure it was exactly that. Then, I have this headache had since the shadowy figure started its daily control of my dreams. It just stopped a few minutes ago, and I feel very different now. No more headache, but I can feel my heartbeat going faster, and I don't know why it's suddenly."

"And what did the shadowy figure say to you?" I asked.

The boy stood up and started slowly pacing the room, hands behind his back. He was dressed in white, wide pajama pants and a white robe, but no shirt.

"He said that my task was about to be over, that my freedom will start as soon as the stranger showed up," He replied.

"How do you know I am that stranger?" I asked. "I am sure there are more people out there like me who are interested in talking to you."

"I know because you identified yourself that way, as a stranger that I am not afraid to be with in the same room," he replied. "It's the first thing you said in your opening words to me, remember? The dream figure said I won't be afraid of you, I will feel at ease when you come, even though it will be somebody I had never, ever met before and that you will come in the form of two. That explains the woman you came with."

"I don't understand how you are meeting a stranger in the form of two," I said. "Basically, its two people who want to talk to you about…"

"You are both here in the capacity of one, after one thing and with one task," the boy cut through, sounding impatient, "You take over from me now. The instrument must be delivered and given back to its rightful owner through the right hands. And that is why you are here."

"And what is going to happen to you, now that I am taking over?" I asked. "You are going back to school?"

"I don't know yet," the boy replied. "But I am glad it's all done, am glad it's over with me. I am finally free."

Suddenly the boy clutched at his face and winced in pain.

"Go, go now and do what you must do," he said, almost crying out. "The terrible headache is back; I can hardly see it; it's so painful. But it would help if you were fast or terrible destruction will start. I have given you enough warnings…"

I couldn't see his face, for now, his back was turned to me, and his body bent down as he buried his face in his hands.

"You mean the stick? Where is it now? "I asked quickly. "I have to see it. Show it to me now…"

He suddenly turned around and looked up, facing me, and it wasn't a beautiful sight. I jumped up from the chair and stepped away from him. There was nothing in those eyes anymore except plain white eyeball tissue, and the golden skin tone was gone from the face, replaced by an all-red blemish. The carefully combed back, silky hair was all now a tangled mess with no cloth band holding it back, all spread out in straight, stiff lines. It was like he had been hit by a hot, live, electric current. And when he spoke, it was more of a harsh, very menacing whisper, sounding more feminine than masculine, but that of a furious human female. "You will be shown the way to where the stick is. It's been taken away from me already. You must hasten!

There is no time; he will destroy everything in order to get back what is his, to get what he wants. He will not spare you! And now that time of destruction is near. My part is done, so goooo, go now! Do not waste any more time with me …."

As he said the last part, he raised his hand and pointed at the ceiling. I instantly looked up to see what he was pointing at, but of course, there was nothing there except clean, white, cardboard ceiling material. I looked back down at him. He was now on his knees, and his whole body was shivering uncontrollably. I quickly pulled the top cover off the bed and threw it at him, to cover him up and maybe retain some warmth. But the cloth did not fall on him, but remained suspended in the space above his body, spread or stretched out in its entire length! Now that's crazy, I told myself.

I looked at his female aide, only to find that she was lying on the floor, undergoing a massive seizure activity. I will be damned, I told myself, if I don't get the hell out of there fast! I turned around to realize that the numerous drapes, curtains, and veils were all parted apart, held back by a mysterious blowing wind as if to make way for me to go through. What the hell …

At the same time, and suddenly, there was a loud explosion and the unmistakable sound of gunfire coming from outside. The noise was very clear from the open window. More explosions followed with the rapid shooting. I dashed through the patted veils, but then halfway stopped and turned around to look at the boy. The bed cover was still spread out above his head but had self-shredded itself, the pieces remaining suspended in the air in equal sequence. It was as if someone was cutting it into bits with a pair of scissors, only that there was no person and no scissors. The boy was now on the floor, his body looking lifeless and stretched out straight, his face turned upwards, his hands stretched outwards, like he was staring at, and at the same time reaching out for something above him. There is nothing I could do anymore to help him; I decided. I stepped into the next room and found Salieya kneeling over the limp form of the woman who had opened the door, the same woman who had been in the room with me and the boy and who, just a few minutes or so ago, I saw laying down on the floor, experiencing a massive seizure. How she now came to be out here, I did not have the slightest idea. Suddenly, the woman's eyes opened, and she sat up straight. Salieya jumped back, looking frightened. The woman, not blinking, raised her arm and pointed at the door, then shouted out at us, but in the local dialect, her voice sounding like that of a crazed, maniacal child.

"She says we must leave now, and should not look back, or she will kill us both," Salieya interpreted quickly. "What happened in there, Kiron?"

"No time to explain," I said, grabbing her hand and pulling her after me as I made for the door. "We must leave at once. Let's find your cousin and get the hell out of here."

"She suddenly appeared from nowhere, then collapsed, fainted …" Salieya replied, sounding shocked and looking very confused. "Did you see the stick? Where is the boy?"

"I don't know what's going on right now, and the boy is in there doing his thing," I replied. "The stick is not here; he doesn't have it. But he told me that we have to find it and deliver it. He said we should be led to where it is. With the gunfire and explosions out there, I don't know what's going on. We need to be out of here first, because it's not good anymore."

We dashed through the corridor and got back into the big room that looked like a classroom, with all the pictures of the older men with blank stares. The only difference with this room was that it now had more than one person in it. Salieya's cousin, Haile Gere Mariam, was standing in the middle of the room with someone pointing a gun at his head. In random areas of the big room, three more men stood apart, and all were armed with submachine gun pistols. I recognized them immediately. It was the Hebrew speaking guys we had encountered in the bar at the hotel inside the lobby. The man with whom we had a scuffle over Salieya held the gun that was pointed at the priest's head. The man who had earlier intervened in that scuffle stepped forward again, with a big smile on his face, and clapping his hands randomly.

"My friends, we meet once again. I am beginning to wonder if our destinies are interlinked somewhere," he said."

"I am beginning to think so too," I said, still holding Salieya's hand.

"I am also trying to figure out why every time we meet, your side is harassing us. Yet we have done nothing bad to you guys; we don't even know who you guys are. For example, why are you pointing a gun at the priest's head? Has he done anything wrong to you to deserve that? I am sure something is missing in this whole puzzle, and maybe you can help fill us in on what it is."

"You are indeed very right, my friend," the man said, now standing much closer to me. "We want the same thing that you two are looking for."

"And what is that exactly, and how do you know that it's the same thing?" I asked.

"Ooh, well . . . even classified information gets to leak out over time," the man said. "But let me cut the bullshit out of this business now. We want to know about the stick; we want to know what the boy in there told you about it, and maybe you can lead us to it. In short, we want to find the stick and retain it."

"Retain it? Nonsense!" Salieya intervened, breaking her silence. "How can you retain what is not yours? It doesn't belong to us either. We are here as journalists working for a private company, trying to learn as much as we can about this stick so we can write some details for our clients. We are not here to take over or retain, as you guys say, the stick. It does not belong to us, period. Neither does it belong to you, I am sure."

"You are very right, Madam," the man said. "It does not belong to you or us. But while your organization wants you to write a story about the object, our organization wants us to find it, retain it, and take it back with us. That's our job period. Now tell us what you already know about the object and maybe even where to find it."

"And if I don't?" I asked, trying to bet our chances.

The man laughed lightly and pointed the finger at me.

"You don't get it, my friend, do you?" he said. "You are not in a position to negotiate anything. We will get what we want, even if it means executing both of your two friends here."

"Why don't you go in there and ask the boy himself?" I said, pointing at the doorway behind us. "He didn't tell me much, except that the stick was taken away from him and that I have to quickly find it, or else God will destroy stuff and people. I left him in there, and I am sure he would be glad to talk to you about it."

"And you will get to chat with his beautiful female aide too," Salieya added.

The man turned around and signaled with his hand to one of his armed men. His man nodded, quickly walked to the doorway to the boy's chambers, and disappeared inside. Then he turned back to me.

"Now you better be right, son. The fate of your friends, and ultimately yours, depends on what we find out from here."

The man that had entered the boy's chambers returned in no time. He spoke in another language, the same that Salieya had defined to me as Hebrew.

"He says that he found two people in there, a boy and a woman, and they both look dead," Salieya interpreted.

His commander now turned to me, his face looking very grim and tight. "Did you two kill those folks, huh? You probably did. But that doesn't save you from anything. You either tell us what you know, or he dies." he said, pointing at Salieya's cousin.

Salieya stepped forward quickly. Her sudden movement prompted the lead man to take a step back and raise his gun at us instantly. The other men also moved forward a step or two, their weapons raised, poised to shoot. I immediately stepped in front of her, shielding her body with mine. But she instantly shoved me aside, a move that surprised me.

"Gosh, you people seem to be so eager to kill, that slight movement from a harmless girl appears to make you very nervous," she said. "And all I am doing is to ask you to let the priest go. He has nothing to do with this. The reason why he is with us is that he was our guide to this monastery, and to the boy. I will take his place. You can have me as your captive."

The lead man hesitated for a few seconds and then nodded in affirmative to the man holding the priest with a gun pointed at his head. It was Mukash, of course. Mukash lowered his gun and roughly shoved the priest to one side. At the same time, Salieya walked over to where he was, and in a moment, the gun was pointed at her head. As for the priest, he didn't perhaps appreciate that shoving from Mukash, for he turned around and glared at the operative with a mean look, slowly shaking his head.

"Don't worry, sister, everything will be ok," the priest said to Salieya, not taking his eyes off Mukash. "These bad men will learn their lesson later." He then turned around and faced us, particularly me, and the lead man.

"The stick is with the high priest, the head of this establishment. Some people came with him the other night, and with the blessing of his eminence, they took the stick from the boy. I spoke to the boy myself, and he told me that he was forced to hand it over and that we must get it back quickly, or a lot of bad things would happen to us."

"The men with the high priest, did you see them?" the lead man asked. "Do you know who they are?"

"I think one of them is BJ Junior, the oldest son of the wealthiest man in this country," the priest answered." I have seen him here a few times recently. But I didn't recognize the other people," the priest replied.

"I know where BJ's house is," Salieya said quickly. "I was there twice on a journalism assignment. I can take you there."

I instantly reacted." Salieya, you just can't do that. These people will probably kill you after they get what they want, or if you happen to be wrong. You can't just give yourself away like that."

I turned to the lead man and faced him. "If anything happens to my partner, I will look for you and I will kill you myself," I almost shouted in his face.

"And how are you going to do that, huh?" the lead man asked. "My dear boy, you still don't get it, do you? You end here; you are outgunned and useless now. And it's all quite simple to me. She better be right on. She will now take us to this man's place, the right place, or she will die too."

"Kiron, how dare you to talk like that in front of me?" Salieya said, staring at me with horrified eyes. "Don't tell me you are like these animals. No one kills anyone today; do you all get that straight? No one here needs to die, or be killed, for that matter; Because no one, except God, has the right to take away any person's life. Now, can we go so that this whole ordeal can be over with?"

"I won't let you do this," I said menacingly, taking another step towards the lead man. But his revolver was up and pointed at my face.

"You are such a loudmouth, boy!" the lead man snapped at me, his face grim again. "What makes you sure I can't put a bullet through your head right now, huh? Your friend is right, no one must die, but it appears you want it to be that way for you. Maybe you think I can't do it, right? Well, now, try me out. I dare you to make one more step forward and let's see who will be standing upright in the next second. Could you go on, do it, take that step forward? Only one step forward, my friend, and your brains will be all over that wall. That means, my friend, that you will be one dead, crazy bastard!"

The priest, who had made his way to the exit door, quickly intervened. "Don't do it, Kiron. Don't even move an inch, for he means it. I can see it in his eyes, feel it in his voice. He will kill you if you do so. We don't want you to die now because the lord needs you to do his work."

"Well, maybe the lord should protect me now against this mad man's bullet, that is if he needs me," I said, not taking my eyes off the lead man. The man had a faint smile on his face now, and I knew what it was, what that look means. He wasn't bluffing. The left side of his mouth was twitching. He was ready to kill me if I challenged him again by making that step. I looked briefly over at Salieya. She was breathing heavily now and looking at me with terrified eyes. I decided to stay put.

"Yes, he will, he does. But God also doesn't want you to tempt him," the priest said." You are his creation, not his creator. You do not tell

The most high what to do, Kiron. He alone decides what you can do, he decides what communities and nations can do. The fate of our lives, of the whole world, is in his hands. This human being is ready to end your life, but that is if you let him. It is ultimately your decision at this time, not God's."

Seeing that I wasn't taking that step, the lead man shook his head and said. "I didn't think so. You are not man enough to do it. Like I thought, you are just another loudmouth, scared of dying. Let's get going, people. I am getting impatient with all this. And you, my priest friend, get out of my sight before I change my mind and take you captive again. You just saved his life, just like your sister saved yours. But remember that since we don't need you anymore, I can dispose you off the same way."

The priest nodded his head quietly, and left the room, but not without smiling broadly at me. As the group got ready to leave the room, Mukash, still holding a gun to Salieya's head, cleared his throat.

"Hey boss, we don't need him either. Why don't you let me finish him off? After all, he and I have a previous score to settle."

The lead man hesitated, and then shrugged his shoulders. "Yeah, sure, why not, "he said, "We don't need his loudmouth anymore. Just make sure you shut his loudmouth permanently, Mukash. Join us when you are done. We shall wait for you in the small-town café. Radio me when you are done. The woman will take us to where the stick is. Goodbye, my friend. Let's go, now."

The goodbye was meant for me, of course.

"With pleasure, boss," Mukash said, grinning profoundly. Big, tall fellow too, with bulging biceps and broad shoulders, I reassessed closely. The beret on his head sat at a jaunty angle, revealing half of his clean shaved head. On that side, half of his ear was gone. I wonder what had happened, and whether the causer had gotten away with it. His bloodshot eyes told me he enjoyed being a member of the human killer club. As the group left the room, a now visibly shaken, hard breathing Salieya would not stop looking my way with a terrified look on her face, but another man, with his gun pointed at her, started dragging her out of the room. They closed the door behind them, leaving Mukash and me in the room by ourselves.

Mukash raised his submachine gun, in his right hand, and pointed it at me. "Alright boy, turn around and face the wall, now!"

"I thought we had a score to settle," I said, looking directly at him now. "Why don't we start where we stopped? Or you are not man enough to kill a man with your bare hands, huh Mukash?"

Mukash grinned, and shrugging his broad shoulders, he uncorked the gun and laid it down on the floor. He moved the gun further away from him, to his left, by kicking the machine with his booted foot. He still had something stuck to his leg, I noted. It was probably a knife.

"Suits me fine, boy, because either way, I am going to kill you anyway. So come on, let's get over with it," he said, slowly advancing towards me, his clenched, gloved fists raised. "I am going to tear you apart bit by bit; you are going to scream like a little kid, maybe call your papa or mama, I don't care which one it is. But I am going to enjoy every bit of it."

He was dancing around now, showing off some fancy footwork and rolling his neck. I watched him closely, at the same time slowly moving sideways, my arms still down. He had this maniacal look, a sort of stupid, half open mouth grin on his face. He meant what he said, he was out to mess me up in the most excruciating way possible and probably kill me afterward. He looked very confident in his determined, and ego-fueled, stunt. Why not anyway: he was more prominent, taller, leaner, more muscled, and most likely a well-trained, seasoned, fighter, or killer operative. In his eyes, I was just a little nothing, a pawn to prey on.

What he didn't know at the moment, however, was that I wasn't about to make it very easy for him. He was judging the book by its cover. All my survival fighting instincts were fully tuned up and turned on now. I just wasn't visibly showing that off yet. Instead, I let him overflow himself with that confidence. He danced, I walked, his fists were up, my arms were still down, he grinned, I looked grim and kind of terrified, he was talking, I stayed quiet.

I made a move towards the door. He instantly jumped, blocking the way.

"Oh no, little man, don't try to escape. I will not let you do that, "He said briskly. "Why, aren't you going to try and make this a little more enjoyable for me, huh? Common on, put some bone in my meat, I like crunchy stuff. Please show me some of that action you showed off at that hotel. You had all my buddies laughing at me later. They told me a smaller guy shunned me and I couldn't do a thing about it. Well, now it is time for you to prove it."

"So that's what all this is about, Mukash?" I said, moving away from the door. "To prove to yourself that you are the better man? Your audience is not even here to applaud. So, when you are done, are you going to cut my head off and take it back to them as evidence that you took me out? Grow up, Mukash. I acted the way I did, at the hotel, because you were threatening my colleague. You were acting like a bully. I did nothing wrong to you but wanted you to back off and let her be. You would have done the same if it were, say, your sister or her best friend, or even your former classmate. And for that, you want to kill me, right? What kind of human being are you, Mukash? What happened at the hotel was just a brief boys' scuffle, and it ended with no one getting hurt. So why don't you just move on and follow up with the rest of your cronies to get that stick? Killing me wasn't part of your mission."

"Well, I have my orders, and that is to get rid of you permanently," he replied. "And I am going to make sure that it is done well."

Suddenly he lashed out, a left medium jab meant to lure me to the opposite side so I could collide with a much harder, on coming right hand hit. I knew that, though, and instead, I jumped backward. In came that flying right, swooshing through empty air. So hard tuned was it he stumbled. But now that made him sort of angry. He jumped forward again, his jabs now more rapid, but I kept ducking and dodging. Left-right, upper then quick lower jabs aimed at breaking my ribs, but I wasn't there. Then in one surprising mad rush, he grabbed at me and rushed me backward until he rammed my back hard into a wall. That drove the air out of me, and grinding pain hit my shoulders. That pain loosened up my guard, and I knew I was enduring hard, heavy fists pounding into my sides before being yanked away from the wall and tossed across the room like a rag doll. I automatically spread out, having been taught how to fall by my martial arts trainer, and hit the floor in such a way that as much as it was supposed to be a hard floor fall, it became more of a smooth rollover. I faked a loud groan and slowly got myself up.

"How did you like that, eh, boy?" he asked, obviously happy with himself.

"What do you want from me?" I asked, stumbling to one side. "Why don't you go after your prize instead? Go get that stick, Mukash. That's what your government paid you to do, right? Killing me isn't part of those orders."

"We have orders to eliminate any opposition to those orders," he replied, approaching me like some starving wolf approaching a harmless rabbit.

"Orders to kill anyone who stands in our way. And for your information, the rod doesn't even belong to the Israeli government. It belongs to the Malachi tribe, my tribe."

"Well, it looks like you are about to let the government have it. They probably know it doesn't belong to them, but they want it anyway," I said, wanting to stall his brain. "Someone in the government wants it for themselves. That is why your buddies left you here to do the dirty job of disposing of me, while they go get the stick and take it back. A good way to get it without having you in the way."

I said all this is hoping that these words could make him change his mind about trying to kill me instead of going after the stick. I was very anxious about Salieya being out there alone with those other men. I feared they would most likely kill her after they got what they wanted.

But that wasn't working out either.

He swung at me, a jabbing right that I blocked quickly, but he was ready for that. He stepped in quickly and lashed out at my legs. My knees buckled, and as I went down, he rolled in and, in one quick move, grabbed at my blocking arm, spun around and forced my upper body to lean further downwards, to his advantage. I knew this hard sled hammer elbow slamming down hard between my shoulder blades, before being flung again into space, ending up smashing into two wooden tables and chairs. This time the fall was hard, and the pain was excruciating.

I slowly got up, breathing in hard, but he was on me, his hands around my neck. A hard knee went into my stomach, likely meant for my groin, but I quickly spread out backward, hence avoiding that.

Another two more knees came up again, rattling my ribs before I was spun around and tossed. Down came another set of tables with this crush, and more pain. I felt I was losing my strength. I now had a superficial cut on my forehead. I wiped the area with the palm of my hand and looked at the residual.

Blood. I was bleeding, and at the same time feeling somewhat dizzy. A few more of these crushes, I thought, and that would be it for me. I slowly got up, staring at him. His face was now grim, his eyes not blinking. He was now ready to kill. He was prepared to murder a human being in cold blood.

He started advancing on me again, kicking stuff out of the way, left and right, with his feet. A hard kick slammed into my left thigh, meant for my ribs, perhaps, but I slightly moved, and then he spun around, and the same kick came my way. I blocked it with both my arms, but its concrete fury sent me staggering backward. I found the energy to jump clear as another foot blow came my way, and on my way, grabbed hold of a wooden chair and threw it at him. That chair received the wrath of that kick and was completely shattered to pieces.

We rotated positions, glaring at each other, his look now a maniacal, grinning glare, mine a serious, wounded animal, give me a- break- man, outlook.

"You are wasting precious time on me, Mukash," I said, trying to catch my breath. "Go after your prized artifact. Killing me won't get you any closer to it."

"Well then, the sooner we get this over with, the better, so I can get back on track," he said. "As my commander said, you talk too much, little man. And wait a minute; just think of what I am going to do to your little woman after I put you down. All kinds of things will happen to her before I kill her, just like you. And it will be much easier, and much sweeter. I just can't wait for that time to come."

Now, those words touched a nerve point somewhere deep inside me, forcing me to summon my innermost strength, the will to do whatever it takes to survive, to push through at whatever cost! I felt the warm blood rush through my veins. The thought of this man bearing down on Salieya with all that murderous lust was viciously unbearable. It wouldn't be fair; I decided! It wasn't going to happen either, I concluded!

"I warned you, Mukash, not to mess with my friend, and so I won't let you do that to her," I said, and I meant it this time. I was tired of this guy talking about Salieya like she is some dirtball. "You are right. Let's get this over with."

I now took a stand, swinging my hands around my side, loosening up my muscles. Suddenly, I no longer felt the pain.

Swish … he threw out a leg at me, a high-flying leg, and then did a quick spin, sending another kick at me. I ducked both, for I knew that those are hard bangs meant to weaken me more. My fists were now clenched, arms ready for an opportunity to strike, and it came sooner than I expected.

"Are you going to dance around and avoid being hit, huh? Stop wasting my time, boy," he said, he rushed at me, the same rush he did for his wall crush. But I rushed at him too, and I was a shade faster than he was. Since he was the bulldozer approach, his upper guard was down, face lower. I stepped in and implemented two rapid hard punches into his face, with a snap yell from my mouth to enforce them. Known as Jong hammers after its Korean master creators, these blows are meant to be the equivalent of driving two hard nails into a hardened log of wood with a carpenter's hammer, only that our training required us to do it every day with protected bear hands until the nails were firmly rooted into the wood. By the time the nails were firmly rammed in all the way, the brain had registered what kind of force to apply to finish the job. To a human head, the blows are bound to pack in some nasty, instant bang, and or dizziness. And that stopped him alright, in his tracks. I saw him stumble backward, and his hands went to his head like he had lost some vision. I decided not to jump in instantly, let him feel it.

"Maybe it's you who talks too much, "I said, watching him carefully. When he looked up again, blood was dripping from his nose, and his left eye was barely open.

"I am going to kill you for this!" he growled and came in at me again, fists raised. But I wasn't there. I was down on the floor, and in a quick workup, I tripped him with my legs, and he went sprawling down onto the floor with a thud! I was up on my feet again in a matter of seconds.

"Goddammit!" he bellowed and tried to get up. But I stepped in and sent a flying power-packed kick into the side of his head that sent him sprawling again. He hit the floor again and rolled over onto his back. Now looking very dazed, he balanced his upper body with his elbows and shook his head vigorously, probably to try to shake off the dizziness.

"Get up, Mukash, get up and fight like a man," I yelled at him. My arms were up now, fists clenched. I saw him get up, the look on his face of that of a man not knowing what had suddenly hit him. He looked at me viciously. It was the look of a wounded animal, may be ready to kill in self-defense, his head slightly lowered, and his body swaying slightly forward.

"Ok, I am now ready," he growled. He came at me again, but this time it wasn't a mad rush. He had just learned, perhaps the hard way that the mad rush wasn't going to do it anymore. He swung a right at me, but I blocked it mid-way with my left and then quickly stepping in closer, I slammed three rapid fist blows into his mid-body, which felt like hitting stone, and then slammed a forth one upwards into his chin, just above that Adam's apple thing. Being a heavy guy, he stumbled backward, but remained on his feet, his arms flung outwards on his sides, body slightly bent forward. I then leaped up high, off my feet, spinning around in midair, and my foot connected with his face in a smashing hard foot crush that this time sent him down to the hard floor again. As I landed back on my feet, I noticed he was already trying to get up and get to his pistol, which was a few feet away from where he was. I instantly went after him again, knowing what was going to happen if he got hold of the gun. I was getting to him when he turned around suddenly and swinging upwards, landed a hard elbow into my face! It was my time to fall back to the floor. The hot gush of blood that rushed through my head was also followed by this intense crush of pain that gnawed through my entire system, and I thought the ceiling was spinning. That elbow had some hardcore power molded in it. I tried to get up, but my head was reeling, and I fell again on my stomach.

Through all this, I was able to see Mukash slowly spin around on his heels and fully rise, like some bloodied monster coming out of a grave. But instead of reaching for that gun again, he came after me, bellowing with recharged power. He was now a wounded bull with no boundaries, ready to knock me out of the way for good.

Big mistake: he should have gone for the gun. He was almost right on top of me when I rolled over to my back and lashed outwards with my right leg, snap kicking him hard in the face, stopping him in his tracks. He was still reeling from that when I rolled around again on the floor and flip twisted his ankles with both my legs and threw him off his feet and on to the floor, which he hit with a thud. I rolled away again, got up to a squat posture and then flipped my body over his, and in a flash, I had his pistol in my hand. He looked up to see the barrel of his own gun a few inches away from his bloody face.

"Go ahead, shoot. You don't have the guts to pull the trigger," he taunted. "You don't have the guts to kill anyone."

But he shuddered and pulled back when I flipped the safety catch off and touched the side of his head with the mouth of the gun barrel.

"Ok, maybe, but don't push me into making you my first experience because right now, I have every reason to do it, "I said. "Don't be so sure of me not doing it, especially when both of us know that you intended to do the same to me, Mukash. Now you listen to me carefully. I will spare your life right now if you promise me you will leave us alone. We are just plain journalists on a mission to find out the truth about this stick mystery. We don't want the stick; we want the facts about it. So, you guys can go ahead and have it. Do your job and let us do ours. I just now want my partner back and will stop at nothing to get her back. I will kill someone if that's what it takes to get her back. Do I have your word on that, or do we end it here and now?"

Mukash looked at me, and for the first time, I noticed that the damage I had done to his face was quite noticeable. Both his eyes and lips were puffy, swollen; his nose was covered with dried blood and looked like a chunk of it had been torn off. His chin had a cut on it, and his right jaw looked swollen near the ear. There was blood all over his neck like he had sweated it out.

I also saw him, for the first time at this time, smile, and then he started laughing. He looked like the devil himself.

"Are you serious, man?" he asked, staring at me like I was something out of nowhere.

"Yep, I am dead serious," I said. "All I want is you to leave my colleague and me alone. If you give me your word on that, I will not kill you."

"Ok, you have my word," he said, shaking his head slowly like he couldn't believe what he was hearing. "Good. Now here, take your gun back. I don't need it anymore," I said, and knocking the safety catch back in place, I placed the heavy caliber pistol in front of him. I stood up and walked away from him slowly, turning my back to him. I watched him, from the corner of my eye, scoop up the gun quickly and then slowly rise, pointing it at me, a big smile on his face.

"Now I am going to kill you, foolish man," he said, and I heard the click as he took the safety catch coming off.

I turned around and looked at him, shaking my head. "Come on, man, you don't have the guts to kill someone who just gave you a second chance at life, do you?" I said. "Why, instead, don't you just come with me so we both can go find, and take possession of, what is currently very important to us, huh? You find your stick and take it, I find my girl, get her back, and then we both go our ways, peacefully."

With that, I walked out of the room without looking back, through the single entrance to it, and into another corridor. At one end, I could see the light coming from the outside. I headed for that opening. But there was no sound of anyone coming behind me as I made my way for the exit. He was probably thinking it over, cursing himself for failing to kill me, even when he had a clean shot with a gun. I shuddered at the thought that he still had the time to come out of there and shoot at me. I moved faster towards that light and breathed a sigh of relief when I finally stepped outside.

But outside was another mess too. There was smoke everywhere, and the smell of burning stuff. I spotted the range rover immediately further to my left, where we had packed it. The lorry was still parked nearby, but half of it was all messed up, like someone had hit it with a grenade. One of the vans was gone, probably taken by the Israelis.

I immediately headed for the big car, instantly reaching into my buttoned cargo pants pockets to retrieve the keys. It was then that I realized the strange, odd fact that Salieya had handed me the keys to keep, just like that and out of the blue. I doubt that she knew all this would happen, and I would need them when she was gone.

I was inserting the key into the door lock of the driver's door to open it when a uniformed man suddenly came out of nowhere and pointed a gun at me. It was an Ethiopian policeman with an AK 47. He shouted at me, ordering me to get down to my knees with my hands up. He looked frantic, and frantic people can mess you up because, well, they are frantic. So, I exactly did as he asked. I dropped the keys to the ground, raised my arms up, and went down on my knees immediately. I didn't look at him anymore, just stared down at the ground …

Bang, bang, bang! I closed my eyes hard when that loud, repeating sound of gunfire suddenly erupted around me, which was then followed by a heavy thud on the ground next to me. In the next few seconds, I opened my eyes to see the Ethiopian policeman on the ground, a hall in his head dead. I instantly looked up to see Mukash lower his pistol.

"Get up, man. Let's get out of this hell hole," he said.

I scrambled to my feet, my heart beating rather fast. The sight of a dead man, who was alive just less than a minute ago, proved to be a little unnerving. It can happen to anybody, you know. On the other hand, maybe it could have been me. Perhaps the Ethiopian policeman was going to blow my head off; he just wasn't ready yet. His get down to your knees, with hands up routine, perhaps a by-the-book original most likely cost him his life. I wasn't sure why, but I sure was up and running again.

As Mukash walked past the dead man, he grabbed the AK 47 from the dead man's hands and proceeded to go around to the other side of, and jumped into, the big car. Once behind the wheel, I started the car and reversed. Driving forward, I stepped on the accelerator and felt the massive machine jump ahead. I twisted the wheel around, so we made a sort of u-turn, then forward and made it around the corner of the building. Up there, several yards away, were the gates to the compound, all visible. If I made it to that, we could be well on our way to our next destination, which I wasn't very knowledgeable about.

But that appeared to be an illusion, at least at this moment. We could see a green military truck pulling up and armed men in uniform, jumping off at the gates even before it stopped. Then another one pulled up next to the first one, and it was full of uniformed men with guns. As they got off the vehicles, they quickly started spreading out, at the same time advancing towards the main building, towards us, guns aimed. I stopped the car and shook my head slowly.

"Now, there is a big problem," I said. "We have to find another way to get out of this place other than that because if those guys get to us, they sure will kill us. After all, we just killed one of their own."

"No, just keep going forward," Mukash said, putting the heavy pistol down near the gearbox and raising the AK 47. The gun had two extra magazines full of rounds attached to it with rubber straps. He unstrapped the extra magazines off the gun and laid them next to the pistol and then expertly worked on the gun. Meanwhile, I saw another truck pulling up. More armed police had just arrived on the scene.

"Man, are you crazy? "I asked, staring at him just like I envisioned him to be, crazy. "We are going to get killed quickly if we go that way.

Look at those guys out there; they are like ants; Armed ants, Mukash.

We are outnumbered and outgunned. I see no way we are going to make it through that front line alive."

"I said keep driving, forward, towards the gates," he repeated, glaring at me with bloodshot, swollen eyes. "If you can't do it, I will kill you and then drive the car myself. And this time, man, I won't spare you like I did before, understand? Now drive the damn car forward, towards the gates!"

The growl and menace in that voice put me back into active mode. Without another word, I stepped on the accelerator, and the car moved forward, towards the gates. It didn't take long for the other guys to spot us as we walked towards them. I saw someone point at us, and almost instantly, a group of men started heading in our direction. By this time, Mukash had also rolled down the car window and was staring at the advancing group of uniformed men, the gun on his lap.

Suddenly, and without warning, he whipped the gun up, thrust the gun barrel through the open window, and opened fire on the soldiers. The loud automatic rifle firepower was deafening, and hot shells rolled out to the floor as he moved the gun skillfully from side to side, and I started seeing the uniformed figures quickly go down. I was now close enough to hear the men screaming and shouting. I kept driving towards the gates, increasing the speed.

Then, of course, the remainder of their guns turned towards us. Instantly taking cover and aiming, these guys opened fire back at us. But the damage had been done; Mukash had wasted a lot of men in that initial gun down mode a minute or so ago.

Nonetheless, they were a lot of uniformed armed guys out there still standing upright, and thanks to Mukash's nasty welcome call, we had now caught everyone 's attention. Everyone was now going to be shooting at us, for this was now war. It was either them or us.

The spread outline on my left was circling towards us, their guns blazing. Bullets hit the car hard on, sounding like rocks pelting the metallic surface. I heard the shattering of the glass in the back and all around us, but that didn't stop me from driving, and certainly did not stop Mukash from ejecting an empty magazine and quickly reloading a new one and opening fire again. On my left, I saw this line of men advancing quickly in a half-broken pattern, their guns blazing. I quickly figured out that with Mukash busy wiping out the frontal and right-side confrontation, it would be impossible for him at the same time to take care of the left. I stopped the car and whipped up his pistol. Aiming the piece with both hands for stability, I aimed out of my window side and started shooting at the advancing line. The army rangers had trained us well on how to shoot at both still and moving targets at numerous gun ranges, and my aim was good and steady, so I dropped those guys down quickly. I kept firing until I couldn't see anyone standing upright on my side anymore. I then put the gun down again and resumed driving.

"Now that's what I am talking about, " Mukash bellowed, looking insanely excited with a big, wide grin on his swollen face. A gruff guffaw instantly complimented this reaction! As we got close to the gates, another pick-up vehicle was pulling up, loaded with soldiers. Someone in their military apparatus had pressed a panic button on this because sending these many armed military personnel was indeed like engaging in a mini war.

We got to the gates…

I stopped the car again, picked up the pistol, and went bang, bang again. And each bang brought somebody down until I heard a click which told me I was out of bullets. I looked out and this guy was running towards us, firing from the hip. Mukash saw him and aimed at him, sticking half of his body out of the car and twisting his body slightly towards the advancing figure. The man went down, but then Mukash's rifle went silent. We were both out of ammo!

His door instantly flew open, and in an instant, he was out, hitting the ground and rolling. When he came upright again in the next five seconds or so, he had another gun in his hand, another ak47, and shooting. He had probably spotted it on one of the fallen soldiers all over the place. This guy was good at this, I am telling you. In no time he had shot down almost all of the upright uniformed men around us. Then he jumped back into the car, slamming the door shut quickly.

"Drive, drive, drive ..." he shouted. But the car was already moving by the time those words finished coming out of his mouth. Pushing himself up until his body was halfway past the window level, he continued firing at anybody, anything in his way. In one final mad rush, we drove through the gate, pretty much leaving everything shattered and no one still standing. I almost crashed into one of the vehicles, missing it narrowly. Mukash continued firing the automatic rifle, flattening the tires on the police trucks as we drove by until we were way clear of the gates and got into the main road. He then pulled himself back in the car, panting heavily. He stared at big his hands, all blistered heavily from gripping the guns so tight. He looked at me again, sweat running down his face, and grinned.

"Bloody hell that was alright," he exclaimed.

"Yea, like the bloody hell, we made it out ok," I said, grinning too.

"I must say you are damn good with the guns, man. Astounding! You've got to be one of those well-seasoned, battle-tested, warrior commandos."

"You bet, and thanks!" came the abrupt answer.

And that was how we got out of Mukash's bloody hell hall.

Chapter Four

I REMEMBERED THAT I had taken off the "tele- shades" once we left the boy with the divine predictions and had placed them in my pocket. I reached in there and felt inside. They were in there and felt complete and intact. So, I focused on the road now, even if I had no clue where I was going. Driving down the winding, dusty road with jolting potholes, two Lorries loaded with armed, uniformed personnel sped past us going in the opposite direction. They were probably headed for the monastery.

"Helicopter," Mukash said, pointing at the sky in front of us. "Looks military too, probably responding to our little war. Too bad, they will find only dead bodies and no war waiting for them, and by the time they figure out what happened, we will be long gone."

"They are bound to set up roadblocks and security points all along this trail," I said. "We better get back to that old town and out of it before they surround the area. But I have no idea how to get back to the town. Do you?"

Mukash looked at me, shook his head slowly, and then lifted up his left-right arm, he revealed a thick watch-like object strapped to his wrist. The big ornamental, oval pan surface was a casing that enclosed a special military compass, at the same time, served as a watch. Mukash stretched his arm out, stared at it for a moment, and then pointed ahead.

"You have no clue of anything in this world, I can well see that," he said. "Just carry on straight, civilian. That's going west. I memorized it when coming down to the monastery. And drive faster, man, or I will take over the wheel. But I will shoot you first, though, because I won't be needing you anymore. You have no sense of direction, and you can't drive. I am curious, though, where did you learn how to fight?"

"Oh, not anywhere or anything serious. Just back street survival stuff," I lied. I thought that telling him that I am nothing in the combat business would make him feel at ease and make him believe he is in total control, even if a few hours ago, I had proven different. This guy was one edgy, trigger happy, quickly excited monster, who could do anything if he feels threatened by even the tiniest, minute issue from his surroundings. He wouldn't hesitate to shoot me in the back if he thought at any moment that I was trying to run away or do something behind his back, more especially if he gained knowledge that I was ex-military, not a simple-minded civilian.

And it worked. He didn't ask any more questions but settled back in the car seat and dozed off, the pistol, now fully reloaded with a full magazine, in his hands, a finger inside the trigger ring.

About thirty minutes later, we drove into the outskirts of the old town. As I recalled, when leaving the town for the monastery, it was straight out of the town center. So, once we closed in on the town, I drove on straight, because this same, narrow two-way road would lead us back there. In less than ten minutes, we drove right into the smoky, dusty, crowded, and noisy town center. It was then that Mukash woke up, suddenly sitting up like he was coming out of some terrible nightmare. His hand tightly gripping the gun, he frantically looked around him, behind us, and then stared at me with some weird, suspicious, frowning look. I stared back at him and grinned.

"Welcome back to the real world, Mukash, "I said. "I am sure that was one nice, refreshing nap. We are back in town."

"We must find the other guys quickly," he growled, rubbing his eyes vigorously. "We also need to secure that rod as soon as possible, so we need to find it too. But first, we have to find them, or let them know we are in town."

"We? I don't think so, Mukash," I said. "You are supposed to kill me, remember? Imagine seeing you with me; they would probably think that I have teamed up with you or that some conspiracy is going on. They wouldn't trust you anymore and would probably shoot at you. I suggest we split up from here. I look for my girl, you look for your buddies, and I hope that we won't be shooting at each other when we meet again."

"No, we stick together. No splitting up, you hear me? As for those guys seeing you and me together, they will get over it. But if they try to kill me, I will be ready for them. I will kill them first," he said. "Now I need to hear your plan, little man. Tell me what's next from here."

"Hey, quit calling me little man, "I said, now beginning to feel that the term was rather annoying. "From now on, we are partners. We are working together, helping each other. You find the stick, grab it, I find my girl, take her back with me. We already agreed to that."

Mukash grinned widely, the same grin I noted when I handed him back his gun, back at the monastery. He looked at me, shook his head slowly, and said, somewhat reluctantly, "Alright, partner, you got the deal, so now what next?"

"Remember the priest that was with us?" I asked.

"Yea, I remember that fool. What about him?"

"He mentioned that the head priest was going for a private meeting with some people back in the city," I said. "And that was pretty much the same thing that the strange boy told me, except that he said it differently, and also he wanted me to stop the head priest from whatever he was going to do. The priest also mentioned that a man known as B.G Fawas Jr. had come down to the monastery a few days ago and met with the head priest, just before the head priest left for the city. I bet you my bottom dollar that's where he is, and that's where the stick is right now. We need to find this B.G guy's place. And I think that's what your friends are looking for, that's where they are headed to."

"Ok. So how do we get there? How do we find this guy?" Mukash asked.

"That's the problem, how and where," I said, rubbing my chin vigorously, "because just like you, I am foreign to this country, and your friends have kidnapped my guide. Maybe I should ask around and see if someone knows and can take us there."

At that very moment, something started banging on the side of the car, on my side, repeatedly. I saw Mukash's grip on the pistol in his hand tighten, and they heard the safety catch slowly click. I peered through the glass pane, but I didn't see anyone or anything. So, I rolled down the window glass pane and carefully stuck my head out, looking up, around and then down below. I found it down below, whatever it was repeatedly banging on the car side, and it wasn't a thing, but a human being. It was the crippled man I had encountered the day before, the one that had grabbed at my leg and wouldn't let go until I gave him some money. He was the one banging on the side of the car with one of his big, clenched fists. I looked down at him, frowned, and slowly shook my head.

"You again? Now, what do you want? I thought I gave you enough money to keep you going for at least a week," I said.

"Need some help?" he asked. His big, round, sunken eyes stared at me without blinking. "Maybe I can help you, Mr.; you helped me once, so now maybe I can help you too."

For some reason, I didn't immediately back off. I stared back at the man, corked my head to one side, and asked the man how he can help me.

"Depends on what you want to do," he replied.

I was trying to figure out how a crippled man like him would help me with what I was looking for. But once again, for some reason, I didn't hesitate to blurt it out. "I am trying to find someone who can take me to B.G Fawas Jr.'s place. Have you ever heard of that name? I need to get there as quickly as possible, and I will pay well for anyone who can take me to his place. Do you know of anyone who knows this man and can also take me to his place?"

"Oh, everyone knows that idiot," the crippled man lamented loudly, raising his arms above his head. "His father is the richest man in Ethiopia, a businessman who owns a lot of lands. He is also one of the most powerful men in the land, if not perhaps the most powerful, and most of the politicians listen to him. But while the father is away on his overseas business, he will let his oldest son, Jr., take care of business, and that's where the problem is. B.G Fawas Jr. is a flamboyant, wasteful man and very arrogant."

"How come?" I asked, trying to boost up some more data on the Jr guy.

"He doesn't care about the poor people and treats them like trash. He is also a very dangerous fella, rumored to be behind several people; some found dead later. Some say he is a drug and gun dealer too. Nobody likes him; people are afraid of him," he replied.

"Hmm…, thanks for letting me know about him," I said, shaking my head in wonder. "But I still need to go to his place, and I don't have much time. Do you know of anyone who can take me there?"

"I know where he lives, and I can take you there," he replied. "Just help me get into the car, and I will lead you to his place. He lives on the other side of the city, Addis Ababa."

I sunk back into my seat and looked at Mukash, still holding the pistol tight in his hand. "I have found someone who can take us there."

"Where is he? I can't see him. Who were you talking to?" he asked, leaning forward and trying to look beyond my side of the car.

"He's a crippled guy I helped once, yesterday," I said. "His legs are completely shrunk, twisted, so he can't stand and crawls around. He is down below, near the car."

"I don't get it, man," Mukash said. "How is a crippled man going to take us there when he can't stand or walk?"

"Mukash, we have to help him to get into the car," I replied, shaking my head, wondering if he ever thought of anything positive, away from his guns and killing people. "We can grab him, and toss him in the back seat, and then get going."

"And who will bring him back, huh? Because, and obviously, he can't walk back, and neither can he drive. When my mission is done, I am not coming back to this filthy, God-forsaken place," he said.

"Well, I guess it all falls on me," I replied. "But for now, let us focus on the problem at hand, to get to this guy Jr.'s place. We also need to get out of here quickly before the Ethiopian police or army comes rushing in, searching for the culprits who killed their own. You don't want to engage in another mini war, do you? That will only serve to delay us."

Having said that, I opened the door and got out of the car. I had a click behind me and slowly turned around. Mukash had the pistol pointed at me.

"Where do you think you are going, Partner?" he asked, that stupid grin on his face.

I shook my head vigorously, now definitely annoyed. "Man, you must have your wires crossed! "I said. "Something is wrong with you. Do you think I am going to take off? Just Poof! Vanish? Stop acting like an idiot, Mukash. I am not going anywhere until I get my friend back; you get it? But I don't think I can do that alone, because I can't confront your friends by myself. I will most likely be outmanned and be outgunned. I will need your help, much as you need mine right now to get to that stick. So, stop playing with that gun, get out of the car, and help me get this man inside. If not, go on and shoot me, but I will have to get going if I am to help free my colleague. With or without your help."

And with those words, I turned back around and took a few steps away from the car. I didn't think he would shoot me in the back, but I was not sure if this guy anymore. With his kind of gun skills, but with a small critical thinking brain capacity, he was one dangerous moron. He, actually, should be kept away from guns and society, only released in certain necessary conditions. I saw him as a seasoned war veteran, a gun – down anybody fanatic, but one whose wars have no size or matter.

He would happily pull that trigger without thinking at anything that angered him off.

Well he didn't, but I heard the other car door open and then in a moment he walked around the back of the car, and we came face to face again. He stared at the crippled man on the ground between us, and his eyes grew wider, and then he looked up at me again.

"You were talking to someone, huh?" he said, "I thought you were pulling my leg, and that's why I was suspicious at first. Sorry man, but that's how I am. I 've got to see to believe."

Maybe he's not insane, after all, I thought. Just insecure for his reasons.

"Well, now that you know I am no longer in your imagination, can you help get me into the car?" the crippled man intervened, looking up at Mukash with a lot of ferociousness, and at the same time pointing at the car with his left hand; he didn't sound polite either. Oh boy! From my point of view, indiscreet arrogance was now faced to face with unrestrained, raw ruthlessness!

The only problem with this scenario was that one side had a gun, and his counteraction could quickly come with a bang!

Mukash looked at the crippled man at his feet and shook his head slowly. "For a crippled man, you sure seem to have a big mouth," He said, his impatience restrained.

"Excuse me?" the crippled man retorted. "I may be a cripple, but unlike you, big boy, I have a conscious. I know your types. You always have a dark side, evil darkness that does not allow you to see other human beings as equal in life. Disregard for other human lives is deeply engraved in your mind or brain, and it's as simple as blinking for you to end one. Mighty as your defiant self may feel with that gun, Mr., one day, you will meet humiliating defeat, and that weapon will be rendered useless."

Surprisingly, Mukash burst out laughing and pointed at the crippled man with the barrel of his gun, while looking at me. "See I told you, partner, this cripple has a big mouth, and I am about to shut it up for him permanently."

The gun was pointed at the cripple man's head, and his face quickly changed from plain menacing to one of apparent fear. Mukash now had that stupid grin on his face. Both men were staring at each other in some freeze mode, both waiting for something to happen. Knowing very well what could happen, I quickly waved my hands in the air, trying to divert Mukash's attention.

"Alright, guys, let's not get all worked up here," I said quickly.

"Let's focus on the task at hand. Mukash, put that gun away, man. Help me get this man into the car so he can lead us to that B.G Jr. fellow."

Just as I said that I noted the distant sound of a helicopter approaching from somewhere above us and was coming closer and closer, at the same time, Mukash had attracted the locals when he pointed the gun at the crippled man's head. Since this was a crowded place, it didn't take long for a crowd of both curious and scared, onlookers to advance. The crippled fella seemed to be popular around here, and the locals were indeed not about to stand by and watch one of their own get shot in the head. This readily live crowd was abuzz with all kinds of loud mumbling and cursing sounds. A woman suddenly shrieked loudly, clearly a battle cry of some sort.

Here was my thinking: the approaching helicopter and a charged crowd were both recipes for the delay, pure disaster, and only bad news for us. If this crowd suddenly attacks, there would be chaos everywhere, which would attract the helicopter occupants' attention. The helicopter was military, probably part of the ongoing response to the mess we left behind at the monastery grounds. If they decided to take a close look at what was going on below them on the ground, we would be doomed because now the Ethiopian military would be involved. Therefore, we had to act quickly before the status of near chaos erupted into the real havoc.

"Let's get him into the car, now Mukash, "I said quickly, flinging open the back door. I reached down and grabbed hold of the man's arm and then thrust my other arm under his rough bottom. At the same time, I saw the gun in Mukash's hand disappear in a flash into his side pocket, and then he thrust his arms in the same manner as mine, but on the opposite side. The crippled wrapped his powerful arms around ours. Whoosh! I don't know how it happened because it happened so fast, but in the next moment, he was sitting on his butt in the back seat of the range rover, arriving there with a thud, of course. I slammed the door shut after him and turned Mukash.

"Thanks! Now let's get the hell out of here," I said. But then something smashed against the car with a lot of noise, followed by several others. I turned around to face a bunch of locals angrily throwing stuff at us, whatever they could lay their hands on.

Boof! Something hard hit Mukash on the left side head, and I had him growl in pain.

"What the hell! "I heard him curse.

I realized that it was going to be hard on him since he was going to have to go around to the other side. A man jumped at him with a big stick, swiping at his head. I saw Mukash block the stick with his hand, managing to protect his head. At the same time, two more men rushed at him, all armed with some object. It was evident that the crowd was mad at the man who had pointed the gun at their crippled friend. At the same time, another crowd was approaching from the other side of the car. The car was now being pelted with lots of hard stuff from all directions.

This wasn't good at all, because at whatever time this brawl happened to end, someone was going to end up dead, because Mukash was going to lose his patience, pull the gun out of his pocket and use it. So, I decided that this wasn't the time for me to get back into the car. I had to go to his defense against the mass attack and free him before he took his own drastic steps to free himself.

I grabbed the guy with the stick as he raised it again. I took hold of the back of his shirt collar and yanked backward. At the same time, I kicked at the end of his knees, forcing him to stumble backward and fall on the ground. I jumped over and past him and got to the other two attackers. One had something that looked like a machete and was raising it to strike at Mukash. I stepped in and blocked the raised arm with the machete at the wrist level, keeping it up in the air and then swung my clenched left fist fast upwards, slamming him under the chin. He went flying backwards, and his body slammed into the people behind him, taking several of them down with him. Mukash clobbered the other guy hard in the face with his fists twice, before kicking him in the side like some stray dog. The man yelped as he went down, dropping the object in his hand. Another wave of three men jumped in. I ducked under a fist blow and slammed a hard fist into the man's ribs. He went down instantly; another swing at me came in the form of a thick wooden stick held by a pair of hands. I ducked again, this time-bending my upper body all the way backwards. The stick swooshed right past my chest and face. When I came back up, I slightly turned to kick the man hard in the small of his back, which was now fully exposed to me. The force of that blow slammed his skinny body hard against the car with a thud, and then the man hit the ground.

The helicopter was now hovering right above us. It circled for a few minutes and then took off again. They probably took it for a local brawl or, maybe to say, a human stampede.

Mukash now had the gun out and pointing it at the mad crowd. But they kept advancing. Mukash lowered the gun, pulled off the safety catch, raised it again, and fired off a shot into the air. The heavy caliber shot resonated with the resounding effect. The bang scared the crowd back to a safe distance, and even the car pelting ceased momentarily. Some folks took off running in different directions. Still brandishing the gun in the air, he fired another round-off and then managed to quickly make it around the car to his side, open the door, and jump in. I jumped in behind the wheel, and we both slammed the doors shut at the same time. Outside, people were scrambling to their feet after falling over each other while trying to run away from the gun.

"They think you are kidnapping me," the crippled man shouted out from the back seat. "You better get us out of here quickly, man, because they are going to try to stop you again. And we cannot be delayed anymore."

I started the car and raved the engine for a moment. As I looked around us, the crowd was gathering around again, with stones and other stuff in their hands. We were about to be pelted again. Looking up, a series of thick black clouds appeared to be coming together. I could see the thick clumps of thick, dark vapor moving towards each other. It looked like some rainy weather was about to engulf the area, fast.

Mukash turned around and glared at the man. "We? And where do you come in on this, huh?" He growled.

"Calm down, man, "the crippled man replied, this time speaking in low tones. The raspy voice was no longer present, replaced by a smooth, almost a whispering tone. It was like he was talking to someone else, not us, and with the utmost respect. "Because what I am saying is the absolute truth. We are running out of time, and can't be delayed any more. We must get to B.G Fawas's house as quickly as possible."

This strange change in the tone of his voice prompted me to turn around and look at him. He wasn't even looking at us, but upwards at the ceiling of the car, his eyes fixed on the sunroof glass, not blinking. His powerful arms just hung loosely to his side, like a puppet doll. Strange and weird, I instantly started thinking.

"Hey partner, we have company," Mukash said suddenly.

I turned back in my seat and grabbed the steering wheel again. Mukash was pointing at this figure standing right in the middle of our path, in front of the car, but a few yards away. It was a shirtless man, tall and big compared to his peers around him. His pants appeared to be held in place by a brown rope, and he was barefoot. He looked ferocious and angry, with his uncombed mini afro hair and thick, bushy beard, sunken eyes, and thick lips that opened and closed in a snarling manner, his head slightly corked to the right. In his hands was this huge axe; I mean, the blade was massive, and the long handle to which the blade was attached looked metallic. It was very apparent that only a man of his size was capable of wielding such a tool, and he looked like he knew very well how to use.

But it was now obvious that he intended to use it as a weapon and not a tool, on us! As the crowd parted to give him the way, the big man suddenly screamed loudly and then charged, axe raised above his head with both hands, running towards us. I knew then that one blow from that axe could rip through the car's engine hood and break something on the engine, hence messing it up. Then we could be stalled for good, with an angry crowd around us. I had to act fast, deciding instantly that could either save us or doom us. I immediately started the car, engaged drive, and rammed my foot down hard on the pedal. The big car moved, almost jumping forward instantly, its engine roaring with instant power and force...

Boof! Man, and machine collided heavily; both charged up. He didn't even get the chance to bring that axe down. I had the fraction of a second to see the axe fly out of his hands in a different direction as the heavily grilled metallic front of the car hit him, and he went airborne, his body vaulting over and fast past the windshield and car top. I stepped down on the brake pedal, and the car came to an almost instant stop, the action thrusting our bodies forward and back. I looked through the rare view mirror. I could see the man's body behind us, sprawled out on the ground in the middle of the dirt street, motionless. The crowd also appeared to be motionless at the moment. I decided I wasn't going to wait around and see what they were going to do next because I couldn't possibly go back there, whether he was dead or alive. That crowd could butcher me alive. So, I hit the accelerator again, and once again, we were moving, further and further away from them, the vehicle bouncing heavily, but easily through the numerous potholes. I breathed in with a sigh of relief. Even Mukash was wordless for the moment.

"You did the right thing, young man," the same calm voice came from the back seat. "Compared to what might have happened if you didn't take that step, it was better to get him out of the way the best way you can rather than let him stop us."

I didn't respond to him, and Mukash remained quiet on it too. After driving for at least ten minutes, with no one saying anything,

I spotted an old, antic looking petrol station on the side of the road with an older man seated on a stool outside a small brick-walled house. I swerved the car off the road and pulled up right next to the pump. Reaching over Mukash, I flipped open the glove compartment and pulled out a brown paper envelope. It looked all roughed up, and it was hard to tell that it contained money, but Salieya had said to me that she kept emergency roadside money in the compartment, and I had given her a bundle of paper money to add to the stockpile. I opened the envelope, pulled out one bundle, rolled up the envelope, and placed it back into the compartment before closing it. We needed fuel, as I noticed earlier that the fuel meter reader was low. I jumped out of the car. The older man had already gotten up from his seat and was approaching the vehicle. I handed him the whole bundle of money. I saw his eyes widen and he looked at me questioningly. I had probably given him too much money, an amount of cash he has never seen or handled before all at one time in his lifetime.

"Petrol," I said to him, pointing to the car, then walked away from him. Salieya had told me here in this country that the gas attendant pumps the gas into your car for you, but after you pay him. I suddenly felt nauseous and light-headed. There was a small bush nearby, and I went to it. I bent my head into the bush and vomited, at least nonstop for about a full minute. By the time I was done and straightened up, Mukash was standing not far away from me, hands in his trousers' upper pockets, watching me closely.

"What are you staring at?" I asked him as I pulled out a hankie from my pocket and wiped my face, "Stop monitoring me, we are in this to the end …"

"Pull yourself together, man, "Mukash said, shaking his head slowly." We have to get going again."

"Mukash, I just ran down a human being with a car, probably killed him, and you think I can carry on? Are you not bothered by that in any way?" I asked, "Because if you are not, then you must be one heartless son of a bitch! You and your friends must all be evil."

"You can say whatever you have to say, man," Mukash yelled back. "We are soldiers of war, professionals in our own right, battle-tested, and ready. The man that got ran over; he is the enemy, also an apparent casualty of war. He was going to kill you, for god's sake, don't you get it? It was either him or us dead, and that's what war is about. Me and you, we got engaged in a conflict with the village people, and they declared war on us. It would have been stupid for us to stand there and let that man chop us to pieces with his axe. Now I don't know about you, but I am ready to move on. If you don't have the guts to move on, give me the keys, and head out. And you better make sure your crippled friend shuts his mouth because I am getting tired of listening to him telling me what to do."

"What is he saying?" I asked.

"He says we must hasten, that there is no time!" Mukash said. "He is also repeatedly saying that he will destroy everything to get back what is his, to get what he wants. He will not spare us, that the time of destruction is near, there is no time to waste anymore. Then I asked myself: Who and what is this crippled bastard talking about, huh? What is he or anybody else going to destroy? I just don't get it. I think he is sick in the head, deranged, that's it."

Now, I remembered those words very clearly. The very same words were said to me by that boy before he convulsed into a coma. Something must be going on here. The crippled man is likely a part of this whole show, an extension of the mysterious fantasy surrounding the stick. Now I began to realize it was never a coincidental meeting between him and me. He picked on me, particularly for a reason.

But maybe I was overthinking on this, I told myself. Perhaps this was getting to be a little bit too much on me. At the same time, I wouldn't say I liked feeling that I could be going crazy. I decided to get back into the car and ask him a few questions.

"There is probably more to this than what we think, Mukash," I said. I walked past him and headed for the car without saying another word. I could hear him following behind. The old gas pump attendant had finished pumping the fuel and was back on his stool. He smiled at me and waved. I waved back quickly and then opening the car door, I got in behind the wheel and then shut the door again. Mukash did the same thing on the other side. The crippled man was still in the exact spot where we had placed him, yet in that fixed stare trance, this time staring right ahead, he was beyond us.

"Young man, we must leave now …" the crippled man started to say, but I cut him short.

"Listen, man; I am not going anywhere until you tell me who you are, and what your interest is in our business," I said, turning around to face him. "I have a strong feeling there is more to this than just you are guiding us to that B.G Fawas Jr's place."

The crippled man slowly moved his head in my direction until his big, clear white eyes were looking straight into mine, still not blinking. I held on to his stare, with the only difference being that I blinked every other few seconds.

"Very well; I am Sewyew Meliak, Son of Rahel, daughter of Sewyew," he answered. "The people around me keep it simple; they call me Meliak, a name given to me by my mother before birth. I never knew my father, and my mother died when giving birth to me. I was born this way, a disabled person. I was then adopted by a strange older lady that happened to be my Mothers's friend in the village neighborhood. She nursed me and looked after me until old age brought her down, and the good Lord took her. I was twelve years old by then…"

"Alright, man, what has that got to do with all of us, huh?" Mukash asked, sounding very impatient. "We don't want to know your life history. Just answer his question directly, once and for all, to save us time."

"It is relevant that you know about me before you know why I am here with you, "Meliak firmly replied. "After she died, I started having these strange dreams. Dreams of strange people talking to me and then vanishing or others not saying anything at all; of storms and fires, people crying in agony and people dying. Brought up by a woman who lived all her life humbly and believed in our father in heaven, prayer was the answer to almost everything, daily in the morning and nights before going to bed. Amazingly, most of her simple prayers were answered one way or another, so I continued with the tradition. I prayed that the Lord reveal what these strange dreams were about, but nothing happened, and as time went on, the dreams increased in frequency, and their nature became more vivid and fiery. They drove me nuts, insane, and I started living a meaningless life; I became the beggar on the streets, begging for food, money. All the time, I continued seeking for the answers, praying hard every day and night when I returned home to the small house left to me by my adopting parent. The answer finally came to me in one dream while I slept one night not too long ago. The faceless, silent people in my dreams started talking, and the talkative ones became quiet. The often-silent ones, as I call them, told me that our heavenly father was looking for something that belonged to him and that it was here, in this part of the world. An instrument of great deeds, yet one capable of greater destruction of humankind if it landed in the wrong hands of men, but all besought by the devil. It had been released according to the timing of events and changes, and now that timing has come to an end. The instrument itself, given that its awakening is at the end of its time out, is to evolve into something incredible but also preposterously, dangerous to the life around it, because it belongs to the glory of a higher power. That means anything of a lesser glory that's around its powers would destroy it as they unfold due to the instrument's becoming alive and seeking to return to its original home. I was chosen, right from when I was conceived, to find it and return it to its seekers. It is my destiny."

"And what… is this instrument you are talking about?" I asked, for some reason expecting to get back an answer that I was already familiar with. Not so fast, though, for Meliak was still telling his story, totally ignoring my question.

"Over the next few days after this initial revelation, I started receiving special instructions every night while I slept, of what was to come;

Visions of a young human of pure blood to unearth the instrument and expose, or free it, from where it had laid for so long, a process that would allow it to transform and grow stronger. But when the heavens open to reveal a secret, even those who are not meant to know to get to know, and these forces soon activate themselves, implanting and manifesting themselves into susceptible human spirits. And so enters B.G Fawas's son into the process and together with the high priest, who was easily overtaken by the darker side, the forces moved in closer to the boy. But as I watch these scenes unfold, asking myself why the heavens could let this happen, another one of the silent ones takes over, speaks directly to me in the dream and reveals that help was on the way, in the form of a man and a woman; the man being from lands far away, the woman being of an ethnicity familiar to me. The woman is the guide, while the man is an adventurer with a spirit that has the power to challenge the unknown. Together these two will team up to help me fulfill the task allotted to me. I was told when you would appear, the exact day you showed up at that market. It was revealed that despite my ferocious approach, you would still respond favorably. So, it was when I grabbed your leg and held on, and you still didn't do much about it, but instead, I charitably responded that I realized it was you. As for the woman, it was revealed that she would be of a fiery nature, even as we meet. You, my young friend has been chosen to harness the divine instrument from the devil's hands and help me deliver it. And you already know what the instrument is. Anyone else involved is simply interfering with the unknown and having no idea what they are dealing with."

"Then, why am I here, huh?" Mukash said, "Because if what you are saying is all true, then there must be a reason why I am here right now, perhaps the same reason I am involved. I am eager to hear what you have to say about me."

Meliak slowly turned his gaze on Mukash. "Your government was tipped off about this great mystery by someone close to those who were destined to be involved," he said. "But like I said when the heavens open to reveal something, others not meant to hear these secrets, but are capable of doing so, end up part of it. Therefore, your government sent some of its finest soldiers with orders to investigate, secure information, and if true, seize the prize and take it back. But somewhere along the way, your destinies got intertwined. You are a great warrior, but of this world, a soldier dedicated to his country, to his duties, carefully and intensively groomed to fight for your government, and tested and scarred by battles. Yet I see a different destiny right now; you are different from the rest of your group. You have a different goal in mind, a noble goal, but the wrong setting. But let me remind you that it is not the will of your people that matters, but God's will. Your mission is contrary to what the heavens want!"

"And what is my personal mission?" Mukash asked.

"You know what it is, warrior," Meliak replied, his voice now getting louder. "But now I urge you to think twice because what you seek you will not get!"

"Oh really? And how is that so?" Mukash demanded harshly, "This is what we are trained to do, and we have skills to stop at nothing until the task is done, cripple man. I didn't come this far to fail, and no one dare stands in my way, trying to stop me. That's an early warning to both of you!"

"You are indeed a great warrior, one of this world's finest, and you will try to accomplish your mission, and perhaps your objective," Meliak said. "But the price you will pay for that attempt will be high. You will pay the ultimate price."

Mukash's gun went up again, this time being pointed randomly or from me to Meliak, to and fro. It had become his extended warning finger.

"Just stay out of my way, both of you," he hissed, and then looked away, staring out of the window.

But suddenly, the sound of distant thunder erupted.

I looked out of the window and stared up at the sky. Behind us, a very dark, thick cloud was looming at the horizon. So dark was it that it made the lightning against it look so bright and crystal clear.

"Now that you know that much about me, I bid you hurry," Meliak said. "The events I have told you about are unfolding as I speak. It won't be long before things around here change, and many people around here will die. We must hurry to Fawas's place. Go, now, please!"

I looked back at him questioningly.

"Your grandmother, and your little sister, they are longing to see you again," he said, staring straight at me. I could feel his gaze piercing through me like a couple of invisible, dense needles. "They care about you a lot; they love you and want to see you back home in one piece, unlike your mother, who loves you as one of those she gave birth to but has given you up to this world. She doesn't worry much about you anymore. So for the sake of your grandmother and your sister, I bid you please listen to me and get going, or they will never see you again. And that girl that you want, the one you protected in a fight at a party the other day, back in your country, be wary of her for she is for another man now. She has secrets, and she has quickly and effectively changed her mind about you."

"What the hell…" I muttered under my breath, staring at the man in disbelief. There is no way in hell he would have known about me like that! This guy must be way out of this world, I concluded, and I better now listen closely to what he tells me to do.

I turned back to the wheel and started the car. "Which way do I take, mystery man?" I asked.

"Now that you believe, I am confident that we shall all now work together for the common good. Get back on the main road, turn right and head out straight," Meliak answered, and for the first time I saw a faint smile on his face, his eyes blinking slowly, like he was doing so in slow motion.

I did what I was told, still thinking of the outlook of events basing on Meliak 's perspective. Everything he had just told us seemed to fit in well with our own story when linked together. Well, not so well given the extra ordinary circumstances revolving around his own side of it. But his revelations had now helped jumpstart a sense in me that we were not dealing with a simple matter anymore, but something mysterious and perhaps even beyond our human capabilities.

Suddenly, I felt the excitement of adventure into the unknown welling up inside me, the feeling of wanting to get to the bottom of strange, unknown stuff. If God was involved in this, then maybe I will see God today; or one of his winged angels, I told myself. Great, but first, I had to get Salieya back, for I would never forgive myself if anything happened to her.

"Hey man …," Mukash said, breaking into my trail of thoughts.

"Yeah?" I responded, as I drove the big car back on to the road. But his voice was now that of Meliak's, yet it was very apparent that it was him talking to me, facing me and his lips moving concurrently with the speech.

"I am sorry about the bad news about your girlfriend back home, that's cheating on you," he said. There was a big grin on his face too.

I quickly glanced at Meliak, who was looking at Mukash with a fixed stare, but was saying nothing. I cocked my head towards him as my eyes refocused on the road again.

"So, what do I do with my girlfriend, back home, that you said has betrayed me and is going with another man?" I asked.

"Just let her be, she isn't part of your destiny," he replied.

I shook my head but decided to say nothing again. This wasn't the time to discuss, and try to correct, my personal life, I decided.

"So where are you taking us now?" Mukash asked, turning to look at Meliak too. His voice was instantly back, and his facial outlook was passive, like nothing that was just said by Meliak affected him in anyway. "Are you leading us to where the stick is or to someone who knows where the stick is being kept?"

"We're going to where the stick is being kept right now," Meliak replied.

"But we are headed away from the ancient lands," I said, "I thought that this is where the stick is supposed to be, together with the boy and that these two are supposed to be taken care of at same place in the ancient mountains."

"Yes, the lord's instructions are to be carried out within the ancient mountains of Sonomopata on top of the caves of Mejia," Meliak said. "The boy, by this time, is no more. The angels of heaven have already received his spirit; his body destroyed. But the rod itself is not within the ancient land. It has been moved to a place in an area just outside of Addis Ababa. To carry out the lord's instructions, we have to get the stick first and bring it back to the ancient lands, take it to the mountains, and from there I will perform the necessary ceremonies."

"But who in this world would dare to move around such a powerful, sacred, and divine artifact from where it's supposed to be, and why?" I asked.

"Once the high priest got to know of the rod and the facts about it as revealed by the boy, he told the head of the faith, the archbishop, who consulted with other members of the clergy, and some people in government. It was agreed that the lord's instructions were to be carried out immediately. That is why the soldiers were sent out to protect the boy and the monastery. But soon after that, the high priest was contacted by other people who suggested other uses for this instrument of God. The high priest has been corrupted by those with money and other riches in this world. They promised him all the wealth he wanted if he would reveal the stick to them and let them perform a few functions and or tests of their own with it. For a certain amount of money, this weak human soul agreed to have a meeting with these people and expose the rod to them. Yet the instructions from the mighty lord of the heavens permit no exposure, no ceremony, or any other act to be done by those not specially anointed to do so. The people the high priest is meeting with are not anointed by the highest in heaven. I am the only one who can do it. So, it is these humans that we must confront and take the rod away before they taint it with evil, greed, and blasphemy," Meliak concluded.

"But how did the high priest take the stick out of the monastery without being noticed? Isn't it supposed to be guarded by the high priest and other people specially chosen by the archbishop? If he removed it, it should have gone missing by now," I said.

"He fooled them by removing the real rod from its sanctuary and replacing it with a fake one," Meliak said. "He then smuggled the real stick out and is now ready to deliver on his deal with these other people who promised him a reward."

"But if this is all true, why did God allow all this mischief to go on?" Mukash asked. "Surely, he would have sent his angels to prevent all that from happening, protect the rod."

"That I cannot answer, but what I know is that the mighty lord of the heavens acts in mysterious ways," Meliak replied. "And his ways are never questioned. All I can say is that sometimes he will leave behind lessons for his creatures to learn from their disobedience by unleashing his anger at them. Therefore, we must hasten and stop these people from carrying out their acts of defiance against God; that way, we can save this land and its people from divine wrath. We must also try to save the local high priest too, for his very life is in danger. These humans he is dealing with are relentless people. They have plans of their own and plan to kill him and take the stick with them. I hope I have answered your question to the best of my knowledge."

"Indeed, you have," Mukash said, slowly nodding his head. "So, my man, do you know the exact place where these people are meeting with the high priest?"

"Yes. In a big house known as the Villa of Sodgomora," Meliak answered immediately. "It belongs to the richest man in this country. It is where B.G Fawas, the father, hosts all his famous guests who include heads of states, and other very wealthy business friends of his. It's where he conducts most of his dirty business practices, and that is one reason why the son chose it for this particular function. The father is out of the country at the moment. We have to drive faster because it's on the far eastern side of Addis Ababa. We must hasten because I fear the heavens might react before we get there, and all will be lost."

"I am trying my level best, man, "I replied, and stepped down harder on the accelerator. The big car was moving smoothly, responding to the pedal push with the pure power of a well-taken care - of machine. Basing on my calculations, we were past the midafternoon and into the evening hours. I looked out of the window; the black clouds above were gathering all around us, signifying rain and whatever else was in the works for this almost to be forsaken land. Meliak appeared to be reading my very mind like a script and provided the answers to my thinking immediately.

"Yes, you are right, young man," he said. "The Lord's wrath is about to come down upon this land without mercy. Heavy rains are coming that will soak this land until everything is drowned. The extra water will create mudslides, and those hills yonder will collapse. Winds of such high speed and strength will complement these rains, tearing down everything that has defied him. When they stop, the dirty water will breed strange, tiny animals that will cause a bad, skin-blistering disease that will affect both the inside and outside of the human body and every other living animal on the land. This disease will affect the brains of numerous people, which will cause entire communities to wander aimlessly, lost, and performing strange acts like cannibalism and even arson. This disease may start in the dead of night, in the form of an airborne, unseen mist, and will spread rapidly from here to the rest of the world. It will also be spread by contact, and there will be no instant cure for it. It will just go away by itself, but soon the whole world will be distracted and terrified by this disease, as people will be dying in massive numbers. As that goes on, the earth will start burning from beneath its surface, and could cause fires erupting from anywhere at any time. It could be in a big city, airport, or in the sea which will boil, and dams or bridges will melt or break down. That, my friends, is just a hint of what is going to happen if we don't do what the holiest of the holy spirits that reign from above us wants us to do."

As he said these words, he raised both his hands and pointed them upwards.

"And all this is going to happen because of a rod?" I asked, without holding back. "I think God is unfair. What about all the innocent people of this land and the rest of the world that know nothing about all this? Why should they perish for the sins of a few others? Maybe God should send an army of angels straight to this BG Fawas house to retrieve the stick from these people. Maybe he could reach out himself and get it. That way, we don't have to mess with the lives of countless innocent people."

"Well said, my son," Meliak said, but the tone of his voice signaled impatience, yet still with understanding. "My visions also tell me that you are concerned, always asking why things happen the way they do. You fiercely worry about and fight for the good of others, and it is from those two issues that you draw your strength. But my job is to do what I am told to do, and not to question the orders of him the highest and most powerful."

"But all this can be prevented if we make it in time to the Villa and grab the rod from these bad guys, right? "I asked.

"That is correct, son," he answered. "The Lord of the heavens above only wants us to obey his instructions and nothing else. We do what he wants, and we will be spared of his anger. His instructions are in the holy books of this world, and we must take time to read them. It doesn't matter what religious group you belong to, because there is only one God who rules over the heavens, and earth alike, and anywhere else. But equally bad will be the outcome if the angel of darkness, himself banished from heavens, gets to hear of this. He will stop at nothing and try to destroy anyone, anything in his way, to get hold of the divine rod. Judging from the way things are going, I think we are not alone. Evil is already involved."

We approached the steep escarpment route that would take us through the narrow hilly path where I had encountered those outlaws, the Miseges. Meliak started giving me more instructions as to what direction to take. We slowly but steadily started working our way up the steep incline and winding through the narrow path strewed with loose rocks and randomly placed short bushes. After another fifteen minutes or so of driving, we started leveling off; we had reached the topmost escarpment areas, the peaks of the valley wall. In the next few minutes, we were going to start the downward spiral on the other side of the range.

"Hey man, look down at that valley floor. What a spectacular sight," Mukash said suddenly.

I glanced down at the valley below. Now I remembered that this was the area that Salieya had brought me to the day before, where the sunrise had formed a morning glory of fluffy gold. It was the same place we had encountered those guys that Salieya had referred to as the Miseges. And Yes, even now at sundown, it looked spectacular, but this time in the scariest fashion. This time around, big wide valley and its towns had been completely swallowed up by this large, big black ball of smog or thick cloud cover. It was like staring down at a huge, dark-colored piece of cotton wool so dense you could be tempted simply jump into it assuming its real tangible stuff. The scary part is that it had happened so fast and without us even noticing. It looked like the thick, dark cloud was following or chasing us. Added to this view was the distant lightning that flashed brightly at the far edges of the monstrous dark cloud. The lighting had the magnificent blue, red, and yellow lighting, like some Chinese New Year's Day fireworks. The flashes from this lightening display seemed to linger around longer than usual, sometimes so long it appeared to circle around the huge cloud. It was the biggest, most threatening, ugly rain cloud I had ever seen in my life.

As we made the decline on the other side of the slope, we encountered a dense fog, so thick I had to switch on the powerful spotlights on top of the car and the full beam from the headlights to see, and the car shook as we bounced over the rough terrain. But Meliak kept directing me with the expertise of a typical area mountain guide. Faint beams of the evening sunlight were managing to filter through the fog of grey mist, but that was all. I reminded myself that we would soon face sundown and, therefore, the darkness of the night. Mukash told me that one wrong turn or loss of control of the car for even a few seconds would probably send us plummeting over the steep sides of this, loose graveled, treacherous winding descent. Also, this was a narrow two-way path, and chances of colliding head-on with another car were high. I tried not to think of such stuff, though, and entirely focused on driving while catching on Meliak's instructions.

We finally hit a leveled surface, and the car responded smoothly. The engine seemed to pick up and roared forward quickly. The dense fog slowly and strangely cleared up; we seemed to be leaving it behind. Roadsides started becoming visible, an indication that we were approaching the capital city, Addis Ababa. Just as it was when heading out to the ancient city, this was a straight shot to the downtown area. About fifteen minutes later, we came to a T-junction, our route turning into a much wider one.

"Make a right here," Meliak suddenly said to me after a brief moment of silence. "This route is what takes us to the beginning of the eastern region and into the big town where the Villa is. It's about fifty miles out of Addis Ababa. We still have some ways to go; we must move faster."

I made the right turn immediately and stepped on the pedal again. Rolling down the window, I smelled the air. It felt good after being locked up inside the car for some time. There was also that old dust smell that stung my nose with the equal ferocity of Cuban cigar smoke. Another fifteen minutes of breezy driving brought us into Addis Ababa, and I felt the temptation to stop by the hotel and take me a quick birth, a fresh drink, and a change of cloth. But on second thoughts, I gave up the idea, knowing very well that first of all the other two guys wouldn't appreciate it, but secondly, and most important of all, I didn't want to be the guy responsible for the demise of hundreds or thousands of people, not excluding Salieya.

We drove through the streets of Addis Ababa without stopping much, except during a few turns here and there as per Meliak's instructions. The streets were alive with a lot of people; Lots of people gathered around and staring up at the sky. I peered out of my window, looking up at the sky. The strange, black clouds that we had seen back above the ancient township were forming all over the place. That's what the crowds on the streets were observing. I also noticed that the breeze speed had increased, swirling dirt and pieces of trash all around us. I noticed that Mukash was even staring out of his window at the sky. Only Meliak seemed less interested; his only stare was frozen on the path head.

"Are you thinking what I am thinking?" Mukash asked, looking at me briefly, and then getting back to staring at the sky again.

"I don't know. What are you thinking?" I asked.

"Those dark clouds, they seem to be following us," he replied.

"I thought the same a while back, especially when driving on that narrow path up on those hills," I said. "The dark cloud seemed to be moving fast, covering up the valley. I felt like it was competing with us."

"That's why I keep asking you to move us faster," Meliak cut in. "Those clouds should cover up the eastern side before we get there. Just like us, they are moving to where the divine rod is, and as soon as they cover that area, the process will begin. The only way to delay it is if we get to that rod first. We must get to that rod as quickly as possible."

Something beeped from somewhere inside the car. It was a persistent loud beep that grew louder and louder. Mukash looked at me, suspiciously. Meliak asked me what it was.

"It the satellite phone that we use while in remote fields areas like this one, and it's going off," I replied, "There is a call coming through. Mukash, please reach into the glove box and take it out for me."

Mukash responded, and after a brief search inside the carefully stacked glove compartment, he pulled out the satellite phone, which made the beeping even louder. Maintaining one hand on the wheel, I reached over, took it from him, and pressed the receive button.

"This is Kiron."

"Kiron, Jim here," the caller said quickly. "We've been trying to reach you for a long time. It's not your fault, though. Satellite transmission just suddenly went terrible a few hours ago, and we had no reception from that region. National weather satellite Intel says there is a big storm brewing over that part of Africa. How far have you gone with your assignment?"

I told him, in as few words as possible, what we had accomplished so far. He said to me that Eden's communication team had not streamed our visual transmissions to him yet. I also told him that we had other active parties involved and that one of those had taken Salieya captive. I told him that I seemed to have an idea as to where she was being taken, and with assistance from a new special friend of mine, I was on my way to free her from her captors. I didn't tell him, though, that I had a trigger, happy professional soldier, sitting next to me with a gun in his hand, or that this same fellow had earlier tried to kill me.

Jim Holmbeck was instantly worried about the Salieya part of it. He asked me if I was sure I was going to get her out of there safely.

"I think I will be able to do it," I said, looking over at Meliak, who was still looking ahead. "My new buddy is rather… special and will help me get her back."

"Then, when you get her back, I want you to shut it down and come back home immediately," he said. "I have secured a special, temporary visa for Miss Menankala, and she can travel to the U.S anytime she is ready. I am satisfied with what you have so far, so get out of there as soon as possible. In short, Kiron, your assignment is pretty much accomplished, you are entering a dangerous phase, and I don't want you to cross those lines. Just head back home, compile some field notes for us, and create an archive about the case from the material we have. With the visual on the boy, it should suffice."

"Yes, boss, we shall be out of here as soon as possible," I said. "And who knows, we may be able to add a thing or two to the stuff you already have from us, which would make it even more interesting."

"Kiron, just be cautious, ok, man?" Jim said. "You just told me not too long ago that you think the Israelis are involved in all this, right? But only God knows who else is getting involved! It looks like it's becoming dangerous, son, and the whole assignment can easily turn into a hell of a bloody Vendetta. I don't want you, or Miss Menankala hurt or even killed, you hear me? Those are my instructions or orders. Do not pursue that stick more than you should."

"Yes sir, I hear you," I replied. Jim always worried about me and my adventurous spirit. He always felt that I am the type of character that would put myself in the path of danger not only to do an excellent job out of my assignment but also to get the thrill of it. In other words, I wasn't scared of confronting danger. And the assignment was always used as the one great excuse for me to do that. But he had a right to worry about Salieya, for she wasn't my kind. He always told me he felt fully responsible for the agents he sent out to the field.

Mukash questioningly looked at me when I hang up the call.

"That was my boss, people," I said. "He sends greetings to both of you."

We had now left downtown Addis Ababa and entered low key suburbia again. The brighter streetlights were gone, and so were all the other highlights of a major city.

Mukash turned around in his seat and confronted Meliak again.

"Hey, are you sure we are going in the right direction, and are we are going to make it there on time to secure that stick?" he asked.

Meliak's stare slowly converged on Mukash.

"We will soon be in Sodgomora, where the divine rod is being held at the moment," he said. "I can tell that you are very eager to get there, and you will. We shall all get to see it, but whatever happens after that is up to you."

I didn't quite understand what he meant by that last part of his answer, but I left it like that. After all, Mukash seemed to be happy with it, and turned away from Meliak without any further questions. It's all I needed from him, a peaceful entry into this next phase of this mysterious adventure.

Chapter Five

SODGOMORA PROVED TO be quite different from the other parts of this great land. By that, I mean very different from the medieval township from where we had just come. Here, very modern houses lined both sides of the street, all neatly arranged in their respective rows, fenced, and gated. We are talking bigger villas and mansions here, with red-bricked bungalows here and there. Even the main road was smoother to the ride, with barely any potholes. Cars lined the streets, and people were milling around outside what looked bigger flourishing shops or stores. The streets had light poles with lights that illuminated the streets. We drove by a small school complex with a soccer field, a police station with two police pickups trucks parked outside, and a post office block next door. By all standards, this presented a modern suburban affair.

But perhaps the most imposing image in this sprawling suburb affair of Addis Ababa was the huge white villa perched up on top of the single big hill in the area. Most of the houses were below this hill, and were also much smaller compared to the sprawling, all white, walled in villa homestead owned by the country's richest man, Brahim Gawis Fawas, a retired Ethiopian military major general turned businessman.

"Now, that's something to behold, compared to what I have seen so far around this country, "Mukash said, pointing at the sprawling house, illuminated by what appeared to be numerous, very bright, pole and wall lights that made it look similar to a twenty-four-hour public castle; a Taj Mahal sort of deal. It looked like it was designed to stand out as a unique entity always, a symbol of dignity, privilege, and power. "This thing must have cost the owner some fortune to build."

I briefly stopped the car, right in the middle of the roadway, and just stared blankly at the magnificent structure.

"Well, its owned by Ethiopia's wealthiest man, yet nobody knows how Brahim Gawis Fawas made his fortune," Meliak said. "Some say he had sold a lot of elephant tasks after killing a lot of elephants in and around East Africa, others that he smuggled a lot of gold and diamond out of South Africa and or the Congo; it's even rumored that he had participated in the slave trade in Somalia and the Sudan. Regardless of the secret behind his wealth, he is well invested in Ethiopia. He owns miles of land in and around all major towns, and most of the new prominent buildings in the capital city. He has numerous businesses and employs thousands of Ethiopians and non-Ethiopians alike, directly, or indirectly. It is rumored that he controls all or almost all the long-distance transport system and that at least half of the country's foreign trade contracts go through him. As such, Brahim Gawis Fawas, known as Mr. B.G Fawas, owner of B.G Fawas industries, has extensive influence nationally and internationally, and is the most powerful man in Ethiopia today."

"He has a big entourage of bodyguards with guns wherever he goes," Meliak continued. "But he is also rumored to be a quiet man and said to be very generous with his money. It is his oldest son, B.G Fawas Jr that is considered a devil incarnate. This son is known to be very arrogant, harsh, and cruel, and finds himself second to God in this country. He even says that publically, that no one in this country can touch him except God. It is also said that even his father doesn't know what to do with him anymore. Like I said earlier, he is said to be behind several death and or disappearance of many known people. But no one can dare investigate these crimes, prosecute, and or arrest him because he is the son of the most powerful man in the region. I think you now have an idea of the person we are dealing with."

"We will see about that when we meet," Mukash said, biting into his lower lip and widening his eyes like he was about to go nuts suddenly.

I resumed driving and headed for the villa, driving off the road and hitting a smooth road or car trail neatly lined with trees on both sides, behind which was all bushy vegetation. It appeared to be like a mile long and led straight to the big front main gates. We did not encounter anyone along this trail, and it all seemed weirdly quiet.

"Don't be fooled by what you see, my friend," Meliak said, once again reading my mind. "The building is heavily guarded all the time by armed guards with fierce dogs. B.G Jr is extremely nervous about his life."

"So, you are saying we just can't walk in there and claim the stick, because we shall be shot and killed, right?" Mukash asked.

"Yes, his men won't just let you in, and since you are not on the guestlist for today, they will try to stop you," Meliak said. "The main gates are most heavily guarded, and you are greatly outnumbered. Secondly, if you are to get to the stick, you do not want to start any confrontations. We need to go in as quietly as possible. And I do not know of any other route to the inside. This is it."

"We are going to try it out," Mukash said, displaying a lot of enthusiasm, and started corking and uncorking his pistol.

"I am not about to do it, because that would be pure suicide, Mukash," I said. "I came to get my friend back, and also help get the stick back to Meliak if I can, so that we can save thousands, if not millions, of lives, without deliberately destroy myself in the process."

A few yards away from the now visible iron gates, I drove the car off the trail and to the side and switched off the engine.

"We have to somehow sneak into the perimeter," Mukash said. "I say we split up, that way if we meet stiff resistance or get captured, they don't get both of us at the same time."

"No, you will both die!" Meliak said in a sudden outburst. "Your friend is right; it is pure suicide."

I turned around and looked at him. "So, what do you suggest we do now?" I asked.

"Close your eyes, both of you," Meliak said.

"Close my eyes? No way, I am not about to do that!" Mukash responded defiantly. "No one, not even God, can make me do such a stupid thing. Not in a dangerous place like this."

There was a loud boom outside, definitely from the sky above, just right after he said those words. I rolled my window down and stuck my head out, staring up at the sky. We were right, the strange black clouds seemed to be following us, and right now were rapidly gathering above us. It was like watching one of those Steven king horror movies, live. I sat back and looked at Mukash and then Meliak…

"The almighty lord has heard you loud and clear, Mukash," Meliak said, his voice calm and clear. "But now is not the time to deal with your defiant attitude, earthly soldier. A much more important matter has come to hand, and we are almost out of time. Now, if you want to see that stick, do as I say, and please do not waste any more time arguing about it. I ask you again to close your eyes, both of you, and don't open them until I say so."

I turned around in my seat and glared at Mukash. "You heard what he said, Mukash, and you are going to do exactly that, or I will make sure you don't get to see that stick myself, believe it or not," I said menacingly."

"Don't you two start threatening me now, because I can easily kill both of you now without a second thought and move on by myself," Mukash shouted back.

"Just do it, Mukash!" I shouted back, and then instantly, and without warning, I struck him in the face with my left clenched fist. Poof! His head snapped back, banging against the rolled-up windowpane. At the same time, I snatched the pistol out of his hand, and by the time he decided to respond ferociously, I was ready for him. He found himself staring into the barrel of his pistol, again, and safety catch snapped off with a click at the move of my finger. I could tell he was surprised that I could even do that part so fast. "Close your eyes, Mukash, or I will shut them for you permanently. Try to trust another man for once, just this once. I truly believe we shall be ok."

Mukash glared back at me, with the look of a man who is in a state of bewilderment, slowly shook his head, and then suddenly grinned rather sheepishly. "You are one crazy bastard, man. But you really shouldn't have done that, clobbered me that way. For now, I promise you that I will never let you do that again. Just consider yourself dead, my friend. I will kill you the moment I get another chance."

"Yeah, we will see about that later," I replied with a serious, angry face. "Now, I am going to say it one more time. Close your eyes as he asked."

Having said that, the earthly warrior closed his eyes. I half-closed mine, watching him for at least ten seconds, and then slowly wholly closed them.

What followed was a moment of silence that seemed to last for eternity. The sudden still quietness was so intense and abnormal I felt chills immediately run through my body, for it felt like the world had come to a standstill. It was like I had suddenly gone deaf. Nothing moved, not even a whiff of breeze passed by.

It was just … Dead still!

This phase lasted for approximately fifteen seconds. Then a sudden gust of ice-cold wind bust through the moment, so powerful it shook the vehicle. It swept through the car and felt like cold vapor from an icebox. This icy cold gust of moving air swirled around us for about another fifteen seconds, sending chills through my body. Then this noise, not much unlike the sound made by somebody heavily exhaling air, hit the momentum with one big whoosh, and I heard it. That lasted about five seconds and then silenced again. The cold air was gone too. I suddenly could listen to a noisy mosquito buzzing around my head. I opened my eyes, one at a time, and looked around me. I stared at the back seat.

It was empty. Meliak was not there. Meliak had vanished.

"Mukash, you can open your eyes now," I said quickly, my voice tense, and he did so immediately. He, too, stared blankly at the empty back seat.

"What the hell just happened?" he asked, a suspicious look on his face. "Where is the cripple man?"

"I have no idea what happened, but I think Meliak just vanished!" I replied. "He must have vanished with that cold, windy gust, while our eyes were closed. I don't know, man, but this is getting scary, very scary."

"Give me back my gun now!" Mukash said, almost shouting. I quickly handed him the gun, and he checked it immediately. "I don't like this, don't like it at all. The cripple man tricked us with his magic while feeding us all his fake stories about the stick. Yet it's him who is after it. Once we got him here, he tricked us into closing our eyes, did his magic, and took off. He wants to get to the stick before us."

"But ... how? You saw him yourself. The man was crippled," I argued back. "I don't see how he could have done it, and even then, if he used us as his transport, he's going to need us again to take him to whatever place he wants to go after here."

"Well, that's not going to happen," Mukash said, "When I see that bastard again, I am going to bullet right through his head, cut his nonsense out once and for all. And I am getting into that house right now, alone. Don't follow me, because it's now over between you and me, you hear me? You are on your own now. The next time we meet, I will kill you too."

Mukash opened the door, and without closing it behind him, strode off towards the gates. A few yards away from the big metal barriers, he suddenly started running, and then I saw him leap high up into the air, do a vault forward spin, flip over the top of the gates, and disappeared into the darkness beyond. All I heard after that was the sound of a thud, and then silence. What the hell, I marveled. There must have been some high level, intense training behind that action, because not only did it require great strength to do it, but also perfect timing. And he did it without so much hesitation, a matter of making a split decision. But I also hoped that the thud didn't mean he had knocked himself out after underestimating his landing grounds.

Great, now I was alone. And I wasn't about to make myself suddenly vanish, because I didn't know how, and neither was I going to vault my body over a pair of high metallic barriers because I didn't know what was beyond. I was going to take the hard way in. I was going to see if I can sneak through the gates and into the premises without anyone seeing or hearing me, a training drill I had undergone during my time with the Delta cobra Special Forces team. That training manual had emphasized stealth infiltration into enemy lines with as much minimal detection as possible, and they had made sure my team did it so often, repeatedly, that we became rather very good at it. The drill was ended only when we started sneaking up on the trainers and officers undetected, unannounced, and scaring them in their private moments. So now, and maybe, it was time to put that training to use.

The sharp throbbing at the base of my spine, complimented by the strange warmth at the back of my neck, now returned. That was none other than the sign, and symptom, of excitement, the super mood for what I called the feeling for a dangerous adventure. It had kicked in, promptly. Like before, this feeling, driven by a sharp curiosity for the unknown, is that once present, there was never time for looking or turning back, and always useless for me to resist the urge. Therefore, without wasting time, I knew that I had to go in, find my colleague, and get the hell out of place, with or without the stick.

Getting out of the car, I made sure that all the doors are closed, and then I ran around to the back and opened the tailgate. I retrieved a bag, and from a side pocket on this bag, I took out a small, high beam penlight, turning it on. With that light, I was able to see what I was getting out of the bag. I unzipped it and took out a pair of gloves with "lizard specs" technology, a fantastic special pierce-proof hand-wear that lets you cling on to things like walls and poles with incredible ease quickly put them on. Next, I then retrieved from the bag and placed a pair of slip-on shoe covers that provided air rolled sole edges that cut down feet - tread noise to almost zero. All this had been assembled back at EdenCom to allow a field operative to penetrate the worksite more and be able to get a closer look without being easily detected. Everything else I needed for most likely later use was inside my jacket. I shut the tailgate and then looked around me. Lastly, closing my eyes, I quietly muttered a short prayer to myself, asking the almighty God to be with me and continuously guide me in the upcoming phase of this adventure that also seemed to have a particular purpose. Amen.

Because now, my heightened senses seemed to be telling me, this adventure was beginning to be very interesting.

I opened the driver's door and threw the keys at the floorboard below the steering wheel. After closing the door, I headed for the big gates, mindful of my surroundings and the fact that it was drizzling, accompanied by distant lightening and random thunder. The sky was pitch black. The floating dark clouds had finally come together into one big, thick, black blanket, engulfing the entire sky above the area.

To my surprise, the gates were slightly open, the gap wide enough to let a full-sized adult through. I peeped through the hole and scanned the area beyond. There seemed to be no one in sight or anything else moving at all. Neither was there any sound except for the sound made by a whirling light breeze.

This appeared strange to me because, and according to Meliak, this place was supposed to be heavily swooning with the armed guard with dogs. For the same reason now, I found it hard to believe him. I stepped in beyond the gates and noted the guard's small house on the right side. It was dark inside it. Making my way past the guardhouse, and staying on the side of the winding, paved driveway, I made it to the vast green compound with well-maintained flowerbeds lined on the sides. The grass appeared well cut, and short trees randomly spaced the area above wooden bench seats, just like in a public park. There was a full parking row filled with cars in the front of the house, yet I still could not see any human being around. Or a dog to welcome me with its loud, warning bark. The front of the house was marked by wide concrete steps leading upwards to a double door set. This, likely, was the front or main entrance to the house. These double doors, too, were not locked and were slightly open, wide enough for a man to walk through easily—still, no one in sight.

Something was not right.

There were two big doorknobs on both sides of the doors. I grabbed the one on the right and pulled on it. The cold iron felt smooth in my hands, as the heavy, oak wood door yielded back towards me. I stepped back as I pulled it further outwards and then peered inside. Night vision capability picked up nothing, could not detect any movement anywhere. I stepped inside and quietly closed the door behind me. Moving quickly and keeping to the walls hence away from the center, I ended up in what appeared to be a formal dining room with a big dining room set in the middle, and chandeliers hanging from the ceiling. The area had a massive, or fresh, polished wood smell, the unmistakable scent of new furniture. Yet my nostrils also picked up something else— the smell of fresh cigar smoke.

Someone in the place was either smoking or had just smoked, a cigar in this area. My sense of environmental awareness peaked, and the feeling of being trapped set in. Somewhere in this room, or close by, were people, quietly doing something. I could now hear the gentle humming of a generator from somewhere beyond. Apart from this, it was all strangely dark and quiet.

So, why is it all dark and so quiet, I asked myself? There was supposed to be activity going on in this house, and the cars outside suggested the presence of more than one human being inside the house. But maybe I was over expecting things, because this being a huge house, they could be somewhere else in another room doing their thing. On the other side of the big dining area, I could make out a widened spiral staircase. Tiptoeing, I made my way across the big dining room and started making my way upwards. Reaching the next level of the house didn't take long as the winding steps abruptly came to an end, leading me into what appeared to be a big plush living room with several sofa sets and coffee tables, a big Television and several paintings on the wall. I also noted numerous stuffed animal heads lining the walls. I could see the light ahead, through the sides of a closed door. I had the feeling that this is where all the activity was going on. And, I hoped, that is where

Salieya could be. I now headed for that door, which was to the other side of the living room. I was halfway to it when the place was suddenly flooded with bright yellow light. This sudden change in illumination made me jump as if I had witnessed a devious apparition. I hit the floor in a crotch. At the same time, the action was followed by a lot of metallic clicks not unfamiliar to me. It was the sound of safety catch mechanisms coming off guns. I looked around me to see that in every corner of this room was a man with a gun of some type, and all were pointed at me. I slowly raised my hands up and above my head, retaining my crouching posture and position.

"Keep your hands up, man, and I am warning you, make one wrong move, you die," someone growled at me in English with a heavy vernacularized accent. Then something cold and hard, a gun barrel, was roughly shoved into the small of my back, while another poked into my ribs, and another on the back of my neck. Three guns on my body and they expect me to fight back? Hell no! I wasn't that stupid. I was also surrounded by about eight other men, all with guns.

I was suddenly yanked back upright and then roughly shoved forward or herded towards the door with the light behind it. A man opened the door as we came to it, and I was around ushered into this big, brightly illuminated plush living room, all carpeted from wall to wall, and full of leather-backed sofa seats and rocking chairs. A big, oval glass coffee table was the centerpiece of the room. The walls were lined with oil paintings, clocks, stuffed animal heads, and big windows on the sides were heavily camouflaged withdrawn gold curtains. I ended up on one side of the room. My eyes lit up when I saw Salieya seated in a chair in one corner of the room, a man with a gun standing behind her. She was now very close to me. She too, looked thrilled to see me.

"I finally found you," I said, grinning widely.

"I can see that," she replied, looking up at me. "And what took you so long?"

"It's not been very easy trying to track you down," I replied. "And now I have to find a way of getting us out of here. Where are those men who took you?"

"My Hebrew captors cut me loose once I showed them the location of this house, and then took off," she said. "They were pretty civil with me and said they didn't need me anymore. So, I hang around the area till late evening and then decided to check the place out myself. I was approaching the gates when suddenly some men appeared and abducted me at gunpoint, bringing me here. See, I have been abducted twice today. But wait a minute, wasn't that man supposed to kill you? For some reason, and I don't know why I felt that nothing like that was going to happen to you. At least, not yet."

"Yeah, not yet. It's a long story, Salieya. I will tell you when we are free," I said.

Someone behind me said something at us in a low but menacing voice. Salieya whispered to me that he was telling us to shut the hell up.

Then someone else laughed loudly from across the big room, beyond the big coffee table. Speaking in clear, crisp, word by word English, clearly a British accent prototype, he said, "I was told that a bunch of Israeli soldiers were in town looking for us. But now, when I look closely, all I see is one simple man and woman. Bring them closer, boys, let's take a closer look."

We were roughly ushered forward to the center of the room, making us stand at one side of the coffee table, but side by side.

I was now able to see the speaker very well. He was a tall, skinny, brown-skinned man, beardless but with a big afro. He was dressed in what looked to be an expensive suit, complemented by dark-colored snakeskin shoes. From my take, he probably weighed about one hundred fifty pounds. He had a round potbelly visibly sticking out of his loosened coat front.

"That's B.G's son, Jr." Salieya whispered to me. "His father is not here."

Around him, seated back in the luxurious leather sofas and rocking chairs, were several men dressed in different styles. Of interest were two distinct figures. One side was this heavily bearded man dressed in the pure white flowing garments of an Arab prince, complete with a keffiyeh on his head. I recognize him as the sheik from the Middle East that I had seen on a television program back in my room at the hotel. A bunch of men dressed in similar but less luxurious attire surrounded him, and they all were armed with guns.

The other man, and perhaps the most fascinating of the people in the room, was this stocky, also heavily bearded man with a round, wide, bald spot in the middle of his head. Dressed distinctively in a purple robe draped around his body, he also had several thick necklaces hanging around his neck, but with one long, glittering gold chain that dazzled the rest of the pale silvered one. The end of this gold chain bore a big golden cross that dangled on his big, cloaked potbelly. He was barefoot, just like the sheik, and sat upward, hands folded in front of him and across his tummy. His eyes were closed.

I didn't think I had to be told that this heavyset character, looking well-fed and so holy, is the high priest. He sat at one end of the glass coffee table. On the table, in front of him, was a strange-looking object wrapped in a piece of white cloth, about one and a half meters long. This object appeared to be the focus of all in the room. This object then had to be, I quickly concluded, the mysterious stick, or rod.

"On a closer look, I see a boy and a girl, huh! Identify yourselves immediately and tell me what you are doing in my town. On my property, without proper authorization," B.G Jr commanded in a deep cracking voice, characteristic of someone who smokes, and drinks liquor a lot. He stood there in front of us, hands in his trouser pockets.

"We are just simple journalists out to take a peek at your famous farmhouse, sir," Salieya said quickly. "We thought that maybe we could just sneak in and look at the interior since there appeared to be no guards at the gates."

"No guards? Nonsense!" B.G Jr shouted back, sounding angry. "This property is supposed to be guarded day and night. You, Korzei, go find out what's going on. I am telling you right now, a woman that if my guards are found at their posts, it means you sneaked in. It also means that you are spying on me. Now Know this, I hate trespassers, intruders, and spies, and I will kill both of you myself."

One of the men snapped a quick salute and then left the room with his gun. I think that was Korzei responding to an order from his boss.

"I don't like intruders on my property," B.G Jr continued saying menacingly. "It is private, very private. I don't believe you are just journalists either. Someone sent you here. Someone sent you here to spoil today's events, or you are most likely Interpol spies meddling in my private business. Those Interpol fools have been after me for some time. Copa, Chelengele, I want you to take these two people outside and shoot them. Bury their bodies in the woods, and make sure there is no evidence of them ever being on this property, do you understand? Do it now!"

Two men stepped forward immediately, and one roughly grabbed Salieya by the arm and started dragging her towards the door. Salieya started screaming, loudly. She kicked at her captor but to no effect. The burly, scraggly guy holding her was too strong for her feeble feminist, antic sort of moves. As for my captor, he grabbed me by the back of my neck and shoved me forward. I faked a stumble, but neither did I resist his rough urges. I didn't want him to have the slightest hint that I was capable of vigorous animosity when fully provoked. We just made a few steps towards the door when another voice cut through the air.

It was the high priest talking. He surprisingly spoke softly for a heavy set, burly man, his words more of spitting out than said. He spoke in the local dialect. B.G Jr listened to the high priest's dribble for a short while, then suddenly pulled his hands out of his pockets and angrily waved them in the air, gesturing at his men. According to Salieya, who explained later, the orders to have us killed had just been halted at the request of the high priest.

"Sit them down there and watch them very carefully," B.G yelled.

"And if they escape, you will be answerable with your lives. I shall deal with them after we are done here. Sit them down and have them facing the priest, because he wants them to watch the ceremony. The rest of you, get out of here and get back to your posts. Make sure nobody comes to or leaves the premises. Shoot them if they resist, do you understand?"

The men acknowledged quietly and then one by one filed out of the room. Only four armed men remained in the room, with two maintaining a close watch over us. The other two, I presumed, were there to guard their boss. Our two captors then forcefully pushed us down to our knees, facing the high priest on the other side. The object in the white cloth lay on the table between him and us.

"Now, can we begin the ceremony?" B.G almost snapped at the priest. "I have had enough of these interferences, and I think sheik agrees with me."

"Salieya, fall sideways against me like you are fainting," I quickly whispered into her ear by slightly turning my head towards hers.

Salieya suddenly tipped sideways, and her body slammed against mine. My hands dropped from above my head, and I grabbed hold of her body before it hit the floor. The guards jumped back, obviously in panic, and once again, I thought we were going to be shot.

"Someone gets us some water. She's fainting," I shouted.

"No! Let her die!" that harsh command came from B.G Jr. "We are not here to save lives. And if that two moves again, shoot them."

The guards fell back in position, nodding their heads quickly and raising their guns at us again. Salieya was breathing heavily now, and her eyes were closed. What everyone else, including Salieya, didn't know was that I had just created enough time and diversion to press the little button on my belt, which activates the satellite-linked transmission into visual communication mode. A tiny red light flashed three times on the upper left frame of my eyes shades. About five seconds later, it turned to green, flashing three times again. That meant, ladies and gentlemen, that we had now started "viewing live "at the B.G mansion. The two sunglass lenses were now transmitting, and so was the small oval, round pendant attached to my necklace hanging outside my jacket front.

The sheik suddenly spoke. His was a heavy, deep-set gruff voice of a man used to giving orders, not taking them. He spoke in Arabic, some of the words of which I recognized from my time when my commando unit held joint training sessions with the Saudis. But an interpreter repeated the message in English.

"His highness the Emir wishes to know if all the troubles are over so the ceremony can begin. His highness is tired of waiting."

B.G Jr looked around him and was about to say something when the door suddenly opened and Korzei, the man who had been sent out to confirm Salieya's report that the guards were missing, walked in. He looked kind of confused. He saluted his boss quickly.

"What is it, Korzei?" B.G Jr asked, frowning.

Korzei answered back quickly but in the local dialect.

"He says that he just found all the guards on the outside asleep at their posts," Salieya whispered to me. "He tried to wake them up, but they seem to be completely knocked out like they are in a drugged stupor or coma."

B.G Jr 's face now developed a much deeper, and grooved frown.

"Well, do something about it, Korzei. I say shoot those that are sleeping and replace them with those that are awake", he said.

"They don't want to do their job; then we don't need them, they are good for nothing and not worth living. Those are my orders, Korzei."

The sheik's interpreter ranted off quickly into his boss's ear as B.G Jr spoke.

"Sir, I don't know if that is possible," Korzei replied, now speaking in simple, broken English. "It's all over the compound, sir. Every guard is knocked out, including all the dogs. In addition to that, there is a very thick fog outside. And the sky, it is so dark because of this big black cloud. It's getting hard to see out there. I think we should call in reinforcements, sir."

"I don't have time for calling in extra guards, Korzei," B.G Jr exploded, shouting. "And it would take ages for them to get here. Take these two here with you and find out what's happening out there. One of you, give me a gun. I will make sure these two meddlers don't escape."

One of the men handed over his rifle, a ragged looking Kalashnikov with magazines rubber banded to it. And it looked like B.G Jr knew well how to use it just by the way he handled the weapon. Meanwhile, the Sheik's translator continued the exchange to his boss. The Emir shook his head slowly and then spoke.

"His highness thinks that these two people have something to do with your men falling asleep on the job. They probably used to sleep or nerve gas on the guards. They are spies, and need to be executed immediately," the interpreter reported back promptly.

B.G Jr's face now turned towards us. The long, bony face suddenly turned ash grey, his front upper teeth showing dominantly over the lower ones. I realized the killer look when he gripped the gun tightly and corked it rapidly. I had never seen so much sudden anger in someone in my whole life, and it clearly showed on this guy's face. This man was a cold-blooded killer and was about to shoot us dead. I put my arms around Salieya and held her tightly against me, hiding her face below my shoulder and totally shielding her with my body. I didn't even want her to see the evil look on B.G Jr's face, because if she did, and then happened to survive this by any of God's last-minute miracles, the chance was that she could have nightmares over its memory. I was now also worried that my end had come. Nevertheless, my eyes never left his face at all. The cold bloody eyes slowly turned icy, glassy, and transparent like a killer snake, as B.G Jr started leveling the weapon …

There was a sudden booming, thunderous sound, so heavy and loud it shook the house. I heard glass breaking somewhere, possibly from the windowpanes, broken by the impact of the massive thunder stroke. The house lights flickered, dimmed, and then totally went out. A very bright bolt of lightning suddenly flashed through the curtained window, illuminating the room for at least five seconds before disappearing.

But then the house lights came back on. Everybody remained transfixed in their positions. The package on top of the coffee table had been ripped to shreds, and its contents had vanished.

"The rod, where is the rod? It's gone! Find the rod!" the priest suddenly shouted, sounding extremely hysterical, when he finally realized that there was no sight of his golden prize.

"It's right there on the floor, old fool," B.G Jr snapped relentlessly. "Pick it up and make sure you don't lose it again."

The priest scrambled to his feet, almost tripping over his long garments. Salieya and I turned around, and we both stared at this long, thin stick. About one hundred and fifty centimeters long, the browned relic had twisted notches all over its length, like points where twigs had been chopped off, giving the object a weird twisted outlook. Both ends of the stick had smooth rounded surfaces, but one end was bigger than the other and was rounded like a bulb. I think that's where the hand holding the stick rested when using it.

The priest stopped short of reaching down for the stick and instead stared at it for a moment. And for that moment, it looked like he did not recognize the object before him. His face had a look of total surprise, an amazing look that slowly transformed his mouth into a gaping hole, and his eyes into brown, oval spheres with no blinking function. He stood still, with his arms spread outwards in front of him, which made him look like a giant preying-mantis about to seize its prey.

"Lord almighty, behold, the holy stick has transformed itself again," he said, his voice maniacally high pitched and trembling.

"All of you, I command all of you to bow your heads before the Lord; BOW YOUR HEADS NOW! Bowwwwwww..."

The last part of his little, haunting speech was the scariest one, for it made us realize that the man had suddenly gone nuts, and his face was glistering with beads of sweat.

No one moved or said anything as he bent his body down to pick up the stick. But before he could lay his fingers on it, the stick suddenly moved. The bigger, oval bulb end swooped upwards and in a lightening reflex vaulted three times into the space above it before vaulting downwards and then whacked the priest hard on his forehead. I saw the priest's eyes roll upwards, and then his bulky frame toppled backward and hit the floor with a thud. His head crashed into the chair behind him, forcing it to split into two halves. Then the stick vaulted backward back into the air, like an acrobat on a steel bar, went spinning over our heads with a swishing sound, almost hit the ceiling, and then came vaulting downwards again. It's rounded, bulb end once again struck, this time whacking B.G Jr on the back of his head. The impact of the strike sent B.G Jr crushing down to the floor, onto his stomach. The gun fell out of his hands and to the floor, ending up underneath the coffee table. Both men remained still in their fallen positions, unconscious.

We all covered our heads with our hands as the stick went spinning again in midair like a shuttle, and then suddenly dropped itself down on top of the coffee table, into the tattered clothing material that it had previously been wrapped with, and with a loud bang. There it remained still.

Everyone in the room who had witnessed this drama seemed to be completely stunned, and for at least the next five minutes or so, nobody moved or said anything. The only noise around us now was the angry noise of the thundering rain outside. I could see the raging lightning against its dark background of thick black clouds through the transparent curtains in front of one of the big windows, whose glass had been shattered to pieces by the previous thunder boom. The curtains were actively flowing inwards due to the strong whirling wind coming from the outside.

Then I saw the sheik, or Emir, for what his interpreter called him, sit forward in his seat. His bodyguards also rose to their feet. He said something in Arabic, his sentences prolonged and harsh. He pointed to one of his men, and then to the stick on the table. The man fearfully shook his head and stepped further away from the table. He ordered and pointed to another man, but that man too backed off. He then literally barked orders at two more men, and then at his interpreter, but they all stood their ground, refusing to do what he was asking them to do.

"He's ordering them to wrap the stick up in its tattered wrapping material so that he can take it back home with him, but all the men are refusing to do so," Salieya interpreted for me.

The Sheik decided to take matters in his own hands. We watched silently as he slowly rose from his chair, got down on his knees, and slowly crawled over to the glass coffee table. He then reached over it to pick up the stick. Once again, there was this loud, and heavy, booming noise as another round of heavy thunder rocked the building, though less menacing than the first one. The lights dimmed, but this time they did not go off.

"It is true," the Sheik said, the excitement very clear in his voice. "It is indeed the divine stick, the one that Prophet Moses used to part the waters of the sea for those poor people fleeing from Egypt and its soldiers. And now it is mine to claim, to take and use. I am about to be the most powerful man in this world."

The most surprising part of this was that the Sheik was suddenly speaking in English clearly, though still with a heavy accent. He suddenly didn't need his interpreter, who was looking at him with the utmost shock and surprise on his face. How possibly can his boss speaks English now. Unknown to the bewildered interpreter, we were also exactly wondering about the same thing, even if we knew nothing about the Sheik. It was just simply, and truly, bizarre!

But with those words, the heavy-set Sheik suddenly started laughing, starting with a childish giggle, and then progressed into a nonstop adult bellow. For the next three minutes or so, he laughed so hard that his men also slowly started imitating their boss. He laughed until he started coughing, a cough that suddenly started sounding rather unfortunate, and before we realized what was going on, the Sheik was grabbing at his throat like he was choking. And yes, he was being choked by something, for he started gasping, evidently out of breath, and his face started turning pale. Then his whole face took on a nasty, pale blue skin color as his eyes rolled upwards, inwards until only the pale whites were visible. He collapsed over to his side, fell on the floor, and remained still.

Everything, once again, had happened so fast and to the surprise of everybody. The interpreter jumped forward to help his boss, but it was too late. After shaking his boss's body several times and getting no response, he checked for the pulses at the base of the neck. He finally but slowly stood up and shook his head.

"My Emir is no more; he is dead," the interpreter said, sounding shocked. It was yet another shock for everybody present. What the hell was going on here? Nobody seemed to have a clue.

And for the next two minutes or so, the dead sheik's interpreter stared at the stick, his mouth gaping open. We all looked at him like we expected him to take the next step on behalf of all of us. Then slowly, and without turning around, his eyes still fixed on the stick, he gestured to the other men while saying something in his dialect. Right after he spoke, the sheik's entire bodyguard group laid down their guns on the floor, fell to their knees behind and around their boss's still body, and lowered their foreheads to the floor, in front of the stick on the table. They did this three times.

"We wish to leave at once, and without the stick," the interpreter said, now in his heavily accented English, and as he got back up on to his feet. "This stick is divine and not of this world, not meant for humans. We do not want to insult God anymore."

After saying that, he nodded to the rest of his colleagues—a signal to leave.

"We are coming with you … we are not staying here," one of B.G Jr's men stated nervously, quickly harnessing his gun to his shoulder. "I don't want to die here."

"I don't want to die in this evil place too," yet another of B.G Jr's men said quickly and started moving towards the door. The other two men followed without a word. Unlike the Sheik's men, these guys appeared to be deliberately oblivious of their own boss's fate. They didn't seem to care at all about what's next for him.

Two heavy set guys picked up the dead Sheik's body, and slowly the whole group headed for the exit. But then, just as they got to the doors, it burst open, and four men walked into the room. They were all dressed in dusty green military fatigues and berets, and all had pistols, drawn and ready to shoot. And in just a matter of seconds, they were spread out into every corner of the big living room, making sure their guns covered everyone. Their sudden appearance on the scene jolted some notable fright into those of us already in the room. Even the sheik's men tried to take off into different directions, dropping and abandoning their dead boss's body. Salieya turned away and clung to me tightly, frightened like the rest of us by the dramatic entrance.

I recognized the four men immediately. It was the four Israeli men who had hijacked our visit at the monastery, ordered Mukash to kill me, and kidnapped Salieya. Their leader, the same man who talked for everybody else, looked even meaner than at the monastery. He had black artificial feline streaks on his face like those applied by commandos in silent jungle warfare. He said something, which by now I knew was some form of Hebrew dialect.

"He just said nobody is leaving yet," Salieya said, turning her head up and around and looking up at the man.

With his gun still pointed out with a stretched hand, he took a few quick strides forward, and in a flush moment, the mouth of his pistol 's barrel was touching the sheik's interpreter's forehead. I felt Salieya's head sink into my shoulder again. We both were convinced that he was going to blow the man's brains out of his head.

However, he did not. Instead, he shouted something at the Sheik's interpreter. On the other hand, the interpreter did not appear to be bothered at all by the gun pointed directly at his head. He did not even flinch.

The sheik's interpreter answered back calmly and gracefully turned slightly to point at the stick on the table.

"What are they saying, Salieya?" I whispered into her ear as we clung tightly to each other. I could hear the heart pounding in her chest.

"The man with the gun wants to know the whereabouts of the stick," she replied, still not looking up. "He claims it's the property of the Israeli government, and that he is here to claim it on his government's behalf. He is taking it back home with him and no one should dare to stop him at this moment unless they want to die. The Sheik's man has just told him where it is, on the table, and also told him that he absolutely wants nothing to do with that stick, and so they can have it, do whatever they want with it. The sheik's man is also saying that he just wants the Israelis, and everybody else, out of his way so he can get out of this cursed house and go home."

With the gun still pointed at the interpreter's head, the Israeli lead man gestured to one of his own men with his other hand and, at the same time said something.

"That's an order to one of his men to secure the stick immediately," Salieya said. I saw one of the men stick his pistol into his pants belt, his eyes focused on the object on top of the coffee table, and then move towards it.

But his movement was halted by yet another dramatic interference.

There was a loud bang as a gun suddenly went off. I saw the Israeli lead man's body stiffen, a look of surprise coming upon his face, and his left hand grasped at his chest. There was blood on it when he lifted it up again and looked at it. His knees crumbled under him, and his upper body pitched forward, hitting the floor with a thud. His hand still clutched his pistol as he lay still on the floor, eyes wide open.

The stick saga had just claimed yet another victim, and just like the other incidents, it happened so suddenly and in a matter of seconds.

We all looked up at the shooter, definitely terrified!

Standing right in the middle of the doorway was Mukash, his pistol held with both hands and pointed at everyone in the room. The controversial Israeli operative had just shot his boss dead.

He now started waving the gun randomly at all of us and shouting in Hebrew.

Salieya quickly interpreted back to me what Mukash was saying. Surprisingly, she sounded less frantic, though fearful, than before. I think she was getting used to all this. "He's saying there is a change in plans. He says that his government is wrong; it cannot claim the stick anymore. He says the stick belongs to his tribe, the Levites, who are the true descendants of Moses. He was going to take it back to his tribal leader, and nobody would stop him.

One of the other Israeli operatives, obviously shocked by what had just happened, shouted "no way" in English and aimed his gun at Mukash. But Mukash proved to be efficiently much faster, and in one quick turn of his body he had his gun pointed in the direction of the opposing operative, and as his body hit the floor sideways, he fired off several shots just as the other guy managed to fire off just one round only. The opposing operative was dead before his body hit the floor. Mukash was back on his feet in a matter of seconds.

"Anybody else cares to join them, huh?" he taunted menacingly, in English. "Come on, show yourself. Hey, American, perhaps you can lead the way now and step up, try to stop me. Why not? You have succeeded in the past, you know. This time you will not, you son of a bitch. This time around, I will kill you. I am going to kill you."

Those comments were jeeringly directed at me, and he was now staring at me. He wasn't even pointing the gun at me, or even at anybody else anymore. Instead, he held the gun next to his right hip, barrel pointing down at the floor. I knew, and I think everyone had now figured this out by this time, that one unapproved move from any of us and that barrel would swing up in fractions of a second, blazing its deadly bullets. He would probably, in my case, kill us both, since Salieya still clung tightly to me. Therefore, I wasn't going to make that mistake, not even try.

Instead, I slowly shook my head in surrender, my eyes connected to his. What instantly bothered me was his last sentence. He just said he was going to kill me. Sounded like this time, he was determined to do it. For the first time, I saw Salieya as a typical liability to my wellbeing.

Being with her now simply turned me into a seated target, a ready to be murdered prospect because I had to protect her as well as myself. Had I been alone, it would be more difficult for him to carry out his intentions. At this moment, chances were that the girl or I could end up dead if I tried.

"Dude, like I told you earlier, I just came in to get my girl," I said carefully. "You can have the stick, its right there on top of that table. Now whether it belongs to your government or you don't concern me. I only care about getting her back and then getting both of us out of here, alive."

"Good boy, good American," he said. "Now for you two remaining Israelis soldiers, you are my homeboys, so I am going to say this once because I have no time to waste anymore. You can either join me on this or die. I promise you, the tribe will honor you much, and you we will embrace you as our own when you help me take the holy rod back home to where it belongs. We shall become brothers forever, not by nationhood, but by acts of faith. This is an act of faith. So please come with me now, and we shall be one forever."

"I shall help you get the rod out of here, out of this country," one of the remaining Israeli operatives said slowly but nervously. "But after that, you are on your own. You very well know that our government will come after you immediately, and might even wipe out your entire tribe, if need be, to get back the rod. I don't want to be part of that, neither do I have a personal interest in the rod, except to see to it that it goes back to Israel, into the hands of the government. We are soldiers, Mukash, and those are our orders. To me, it doesn't matter which sect of Israel has it; we are all one. Your tribe, the people in our government, we are all Israelis. You did not have to kill commander Eridad. He was simply doing his job."

"I said the rod belongs to my tribe, the Levites," Mukash repeated. "We shall build a shrine for the rod, and time honor it until God Sends someone to get it. Commander Eridad was an old, stubborn, adamant fool who was incapable of listening to reason or thinking independently, just there to follow orders.

He was going to stand in my way as usual, and I don't have time to waste explaining myself to him, and indeed to nobody else. Now are you with me, or do I do this alone?"

"We shall support you, brother Mukash," the other operative said quickly and carefully. "But then you will have to explain to our government why you killed commander Eridad and Brother Joseph, and your whole claim story to the rod. We shall not be there to help you with that."

"I shall worry about and deal with that part of it later," Mukash said. "Just help me get the rod out of here. You, there is nothing for you here, therefore get out of here now. And I better not see you around here again."

He was now pointing the finger at the Sheik's men, including B.G Jr's guards. The men responded by walking past him quickly, without a word, and out of the room. This time, none of the sheik's people bothered to take his body. Not that I blamed them for not being considerate this time, because considering the way things were changing around here, there was no time for him anymore, but to get the hell out while you still can.

Now it was Salieya and me, the two standing Israeli operatives, two unconscious men on the floor, and three dead bodies remaining in the posh living room. Still holding the gun to his side, Mukash stepped over his dead commander's body and briskly strolled over to where the stick was on the table. On his way there, he also stepped over B.G Jr's still body, kicking it roughly with his foot to get it out of his way. As he stood next to the table, staring down at the prized object, Mukash's facial outlook changed to that of delight, and to my surprise, he fell to one knee and laid his gun down on the floor, right close to him, definitely where he could reach it quickly if he had to.

"You guys watch over these other people while I wrap the rod up, and then we shall all get out of here," he said. He bowed down twice before the rod, and then quickly got up and reached for his gun. But the gun was no longer in the place he had put it close to him. It was gone.

He looked around him, his face resuming the angry look again. "What … what happened to my gun?" he roared. His right hand now quickly touched a cargo pocket on the side of his military trousers, and a big, double-edged commando knife amazingly appeared in his hand. Wielding the big knife viciously, he turned his back to the stick on the coffee table and fully faced us, crouched and ready to strike. None of us answered his question, but he still got his answer instantly. Only one person said something to him after the next few seconds of silence, and that person had his gun and was now pointing it at him.

B.G Jr!

B.G Jr had suddenly awakened from his knockout coma. I think the jolt from that heavy prodding from Mukash's booted foot made his way to the stick had awakened him

"Get out of my house, all of you," B.G Jr shouted. "I will give you one minute, and then I will start shooting, starting with you, Pig." He did not sound like his old self, so I suspected that he had not yet fully recovered from the blow to his head.

"And who the hell is this?" Mukash asked with a bemused look on his face.

"I am Mr. B.G Jr, and this is my house, pig," B.G Jr retorted. "Now, you either get your dirty, bruised, stinking self and all these people out of my house right now or I will kill all of you. And I mean exactly that!"

"Now you listen to me carefully, whoever you are," Mukash hissed, brandishing the knife dangerously. "I don't care who you are, and I don't have time for your rhetoric. Now you either hand over that gun to me, or I shall be forced to take it from you, and you will be dead by the time I do so."

Meanwhile, the lights started flickering and dimming again, continuously. The wind, heavy thunder, and the lightning increased in frequency, more than we had witnessed earlier, causing the curtains to flap inconsistently against the window noisily, and the walls to shake.

The lights seemed to dim for a more extended period, before coming up to full bright again. I whispered my observations to Salieya, who agreed with a nod of her head. As the two men continued to exchange the rhetoric, the lights dimmed so low I could only see shadows of both. The brief, wild, and random illumination from the lightning were now brighter than the house lights. It was now also raining vigorously outside, and we could hear the raindrops pelting the walls out, likely with hailstones.

B.G Jr hoisted himself up from the floor, sitting up straight, and pointed the gun straight at Mukash's face.

"No, you now listen to me, your foreign bastard," he shouted with a lot of anger in his voice. "This is my house, in my country, and you will not tell me what to do…"

He did not finish that sentence. There was a sudden bright spark of lightning that brightened the place up, lingering around for longer than usual and then followed by, in a few seconds, a massive boom of thunder, so loud we all grabbed at our heads. The building shook so violently we felt it through the floor. I saw both two Israeli operatives lose their balance and hit the floor. There was more glass breaking from somewhere, and the chandelier that hung from the ceiling threatened to come falling on us but stayed put, attached to an extra piece of chain firmly holding on to a ceiling panel. The lights dimmed further, and then went completely out.

A stunning silence followed, and for the next minute or so, even the rain and wind outside seemed to have stopped. No lightning, or thunder, either. It appeared like we had hit a time freeze of some kind, for nothing moved, everything seemed to be so still. Then someone started chanting a prayer, some nerve-wracking lullaby. It sounded like the priest. He, too, seemed to have suddenly recovered from his knockout coma.

"Well, someone better switch the generator on," B.G Jr suddenly said from somewhere out of the darkness.

As if in reply to his demands, the lights came back on, fully bright. Surprisingly enough, Mukash was standing up, still in his crouched stance, and the only one in the room still on his feet. B.G Jr was still in his half sit-up position; gun pointed at Mukash's face. Everyone and everything else, including chairs, flowerpots, the glass-topped coffee side tables now all shattered, the wall paintings, the stuffed animal heads, gold-tinted clock, every ornament, was on the floor. Even the center coffee table with the rod had vaulted over to its side and smashed up into pieces. I didn't know what had it happened to the stick at that time, but I wasn't thinking about it either, maybe because I was reeling from the impact of the massive thunderbolt and wondering why the two men were the only ones still upright in their previous positions.

That is until I saw this thing …

Chapter Six

I T ROSE STRAIGHT out of the broken, shattered pile of debris that had been the coffee table a few minutes ago, and Mukash had his back turned to it. It rose, parallel to his body until it was at the same level as the back of his head. I saw B.G Jr 's eyes grow wide until it looked like they were about to pop out of their sockets. His extended, gun-wielding hand started shaking as he tried to point at the thing with his other hand. Mukash, totally unaware of the thing that was behind, and so close to him, probably thought B.G Jr's fearful reactions were directed at him and that the man was vigorously threatening to shoot him. Mukash braced himself, flexing the knife in what could be his next deadly move to ward off the threat. I also realized why the man with a gun was suddenly looking so terrified in front of a man with a knife.

What had risen out of that pile of debris that had been a coffee table, and was now upright behind Mukash, was a full-grown king cobra with its distinctive hood already fully flared out, ready to strike! The animal was about four meters long, all black except for the bright, golden cross bands down the length of its body. At the top of the back of its massive head were two little horn-like structures pointing in the opposite direction, while a pair of small holes, which looked like a pair of flattened nostrils, flared outward repeatedly. Its eyes were like a pair of shiny golden sapphires. We were also able to note, a little bit later, that the false eyes spot on the back of its extended hood made the animal look like it indeed had another pair of eyes. Right now, it was emitting a low sound that mimicked that made by a yowling feline, instead of the usual traditional snake hiss. Its forked tongue kept jumping in and out of its mouth like it was under tremendous pressure. The creature slightly swayed or rocked sideways, though utmost steady. During my tour of military special ops training in India's homeland jungles, I saw my share of terrifying snakes, but never anything like this. Compared to this one, those snakes in India were like rubber jokes.

Mukash was about to lunge forward and probably swipe the big knife at B.G Jr's gun-wielding hand when one of the other Israeli operatives shouted a warning at him, perhaps about the imminent danger behind him. Mukash managed to turn around half and probably made eye contact with the creature, but that was it. The big snake snarled, revealing a pair of massive, shiny white, metallic-looking fangs, and then suddenly lunged forward. The target was his left carotid artery. The massive fangs hit home in one strike, and when the snake pulled back, it had pieces of his skin and tissue hanging from its fangs. The strike had probably torn up the blood vessels and surrounding tissue. There was also white creamy stuff dripping from its hollowed fangs. Apart from damage to his neck, Mukash had also received a dose of the snake's lethal venom. Dropping the knife, he clutched tightly at his neck with both of his hands, his mouth opening widely, like choking and fell to his knees. Before our eyes, his mouth rapidly started frothing thick, green-colored stuff and his tongue came out of his mouth almost in its entirety. Then his neck started swelling like someone was blowing air in it until it looked like it was going to burst. The veins in his face also swelled up and so did his eyes. He finally pitched forward and hit the floor, his legs curling up behind his thighs as his body coiled itself inwards as if it was trying to shrink itself. At the same time, his body now started to jerk itself as if he was having a grand mal seizure. His neck didn't burst, but it remained twisted in a grotesque position, while his tongue never went back into his mouth.

It now dawned to me that Mukash had, in just a matter of approximately two or three minutes, suffered a very horrible death!

The animal now turned to B.G Jr, who was just a few yards away from it. The terrified man, still brandishing the gun, was trying to scramble to his feet, trying to get away from the monster that was now fully confronting him. The animal suddenly emitted a prolonged, high pitched, bone-chilling sound not known from snakes. It sounded like the roar of a cornered, wounded leopard faced with several of its hunters threatening to end its life. The noise was horrifying, but what happened next was even worse. As it made the terrifying vocal emission, its mouth snapping open again, a stream of bright red and blue liquid stuff streamed out of its mouth and fully hit B.G Jr. The man let out a blood-curdling scream that pierced every corner of the room and sent everyone scrambling for their lives, before collapsing on the floor, dropping the gun as his hands started clawing and tearing up his face! Everyone for themselves now, even Salieya let go of me and took off in one direction while I took off in another. I mean, everyone in the room took off in all directions except towards the snake.

Terrified by the horrible death of their ...well ... former fellow operative and the sight of B.G Jr's writhing body on the floor as he struggled with the pain of his scorched face, the two Israeli commandos sprang into action. Once they were within safety range, away from the terrifying animal, they both came up armed with a pistol in each hand, and then guns started blazing nonstop, all aimed at the serpent. I also realized that these guns were small machine gun pistols with extremely rapid firepower, and so intense and loud was the shoot-out that I quickly covered my ears again with my hands. I looked up to see streams of hot bullets fly across the room amidst blue smoke and red fire sparks. The two commandos loudly cried foul in their native language as they ran back and forth in the room, trying to get a better shot at the horrifying animal, at the same time trying to corner it. The serpent itself, still upright, kept making that horrible, high pitched, wounded feline sound as it twisted and danced amidst the stream of bullets and smoke. It suddenly dropped to the floor. I saw its slithering black form briefly, and then it disappeared near one of the couches. A minute of bullet riddling of that couch followed before the shooting stopped. One of the guys shouted something at the other, who answered back quickly. They both still sounded terrified.

"It went underneath that big sofa," I shouted, pointing at one of the big and long leather chairs.

There was another burst of communication between the two operatives, and then with guns still aimed, their eyes focused on that chair, they slowly walked towards it. A few yards from it, they stopped and hesitated. They were listening and watching carefully for any slight sound, movement. The smoke was clearing up to reveal the four bodies of the high priest who, for some reason, had blacked out again, the Sheik, Mukash, and B.G Jr. The bodies of the two other Israeli guys, shot by one of their own, were a few yards away from this site.

B.G Jr made some noise, sounding like someone in a lot of pain, a low-pitched breathtaking groan. Then, he slowly started getting up from the floor, in a weird way, like some of those demonized zombies we see in movies. The moaning got louder as he slowly and unsteadily tried to rise to his feet. What I saw in his face almost made me puke. His eyes were gone, and in their place was a mess of charred flesh. The bridge of his nose was now part of this mess, all now flattened, while his cheeks completely collapsed, showing pure, bloody bone. He managed to get to his feet, only to stumble forward and was about end up on the floor again when one of the operatives jumped ahead and grabbed his tumbling body, managing to block the fall with left arm and shoulder. As he did this, he lowered both his hands and so both guns, turning around to bear the full weight of the injured man's body on his back. Most of the burden was on his left arm and shoulder.

Suddenly, the long, dark form of the king cobra appeared from behind B.G Jr's wobbling body, and swaying slightly to the right, the terrifying serpent lunged forward and struck again. Its big fangs sunk into the Israeli operative's body, right between the shoulder blades. It pulled back, and the struck again in another spot, then swayed back and quickly recoiled again. These strikes were so fast, maybe in a matter of three or four seconds, and were complemented by another bone-chilling, deadly wild cat cry, a defiant feline snarling so loud it made me instantly shudder!

The Israeli warrior cried out in pain as the intense force of the deadly strikes made him lose his balance and tumble forward, hitting the floor with a thud, sprawling down on his stomach. Both guns fell out of his hands as his body started going through the massive seizure action as Mukash did.

Meanwhile, the big cobra snake coiled its upper body around B.G Jr's, its massive, hooded head resting on top of his afro haired head. It was obvious that it was holding his body upwards, on his feet, and I do not have the slightest idea how it did that. In that split minute, Salieya screamed out at the other guy, sounding so terrified, making me now remember that she was part of this whole thing. The other operative, who had been looking down at the back of the sofa, now looked up, saw the snake, and instantly aimed and released a barrage of shots at B.G Jr's snake coiled body, focusing at the snake's head. B.G Jr's head exploded like a ripe watermelon, a splutter of blood and tissue, as several heavy-caliber bullets slammed into it. His body slammed to the floor with a thud, lifeless.

It was then that the commando realized that he used his last rounds, that the guns were empty. At the same time, the deadly serpent rose again, gracefully as if it already knew his predicament, and faced its adversary again. This time, it hissed loudly when it looked at him, and then started bleating like a goat, loudly and repeatedly, moving forward towards him. He kept aiming the guns and pulling the triggers, but both guns only gave him clicks. At the same time, he started backing away from it.

I instantly realized that this guy was either going to be hit by a stream of fire, drenched liquid, or the ferocious creature was about to lunge forward and strike him with its deadly fangs. Either way, something had to be quickly done to prevent yet another death.

I quickly looked around me. Near me was the body of the Israeli lead man with his two guns. Reaching over, I yanked one gun out of his dead hand and raising it up, I fired off a single shot, not at the snake, but at the ceiling. I wanted to divert its attention from the commando so he could make a getaway, at the same time without turning its wrath on me instead. The way I saw it, the animal was attacking and killing, everyone who appeared to be threatening it or trying to stop it in any way or form.

"I am trying to divert its attention away from you so you can get away from it before it attacks you," I shouted out at him and fired off another round. "It's useless to fight this thing. It's not a normal animal. So, run when you get a chance to do so."

The commando heeded to my warning. He made a move to the left, but the serpent hissed loudly and swayed to the left, so he quickly changed and immediately took off to the right, but it quickly changed its course too. It was quite evident that it was trying to corner him off. Aiming at the ceiling right above it, I fired off another round. Some debris fell out of the ceiling and down to the floor all around the animal, and this time I caught its attention. Its head swayed towards me. In one leap, the commando leaped to his left and scrambled away from the snake's direct focus.

Realizing that it had lost its kill, the animal let out another born chilling feline cry, turned its attention fully on me and spat out a stream of golden flame liquid, but I was quite out of range for it to reach me, at least for the moment. Still maintaining its upright posture, it started making its way towards me, spitting out short bursts of golden, fiery liquid stuff every time it bleated.

As the deadly creature swayed its way towards me, an idea hit me. Aiming the gun at the ceiling again, I fired off a few shots, but this time is aiming at the piece of chain wiring holding the big, silver chandelier in place. The piece went loose, suddenly detached itself from the ceiling, and down came the big, heavy, metallic, jingling chandelier, crushing smack down on top of the animal!

The chandelier's silver glory broke up into thousands of pieces, spreading everywhere. The heavy frame remained intact, but now it developed a crazy spin around, clattering up and down motion as the snake vigorously writhed underneath it. It was like the heavy frame did not weight its own at all! And then, to my surprise, the animal started writhing its way upwards out of the mess, sideways from the frame, until it was back fully upright again, facing me. Then it stopped moving and maintaining its upright position; its upper body swayed forward towards me. The deadly snake then emitted a loud, bone-chilling cry that was much like the angry, menacing growl of a big dog! It sounded like it was telling me that I had just made it even more upset by doing what I did, snarling and daring me to try again and see what happens. It slowly then swayed back, closing its mouth, and then rolled forward again, getting much closer this time. Much closer now, it stopped moving and opened its mouth again, snarling menacingly.

Without taking my eyes off the deadly creature, I slowly lowered the gun down until I placed it on the floor, in front of my feet, between me and the creature. But this time around, I took my stand, still staring back at it. I decided it was useless for me to try running away, because there was nowhere to run or hide anymore from this beast. After all, the creature had made its point clear, that no matter what, it will not be defeated. Then, suddenly, Salieya joined my frontline, by returning to where I was, standing next to me on my right side and wrapping her hand around mine, she too now facing the beast. Then, to my surprise too, the Israeli operative came up on my left, grabbed my left hand, and also stood his ground. We all stood still, holding hands, facing and staring back at the deadly creature while breathing in deeply, trying to catch our breath, no doubt terrified by the creature and not knowing, but scared of what would happen next. It opened its mouth wide again, menacingly snarling at us. We were now up close and personal!

But as deadly as it had proved to be, I couldn't help wondering how awesomely magnificent this creature looked. It's shiny, jagged black skin and the golden cross bands that lined its body, plus the line of tiny pointed scales that run from the back of its head down to its tail made it look unique from anything I had ever seen before, even though it physically exhibited all attributes of a fully grown king cobra. Its open mouth revealed the pair of massive, metallically shiny fangs, a couple at the top, and a pair at the bottom, the upper set longer than the bottom. Its forked tongue, a long, black leather-like strip of thin, jagged flesh kept constantly darting out of its mouth, entirely sticking out in intervals of seconds. The inside of its mouth was the unusual, filled with a multi-colored vapor that also steamed out at the side of its mouth each time the creature snarled. It was then, too, that I realized that the creature's eyes had no pupils. They were just brightly burning, golden yellow, oval sapphires! Its hood was still fully flared out, a sign that it was perhaps not done with us yet and could strike any moment from now.

"You cannot fight, and expect to win, a battle against God," Someone with a deep-throated, but very clear voice, said from somewhere behind us. "It's enough evidence that even amongst you was one of this world's finest, well-trained, noble human beings extremely skilled in the art of ground battle, warfare. Yet he is, demised with one strike from one of the almighty God's arsenals of deadly weaponry! No human will ever fight a battle, whether in defiance or not, against God and win! Certainly not even his angels can try, even as they live with him in the heavens and know of his being. But that, my friends, whether knowingly or not, is exactly what you've been trying to do."

We all turned around and looked at the person behind the voice. I heard Salieya exhale heavily, and I swore quietly to myself, my mouth falling open. Standing upright before us, in the doorway, dressed in pure white robes, was Meliak. His hair no longer looked dirty or shabby, he looked clean shaved, but most of all, the man was no longer a cripple! In place of the shriveled and contracted, all scratched up, bruised, lower limbs were now a pair of powerful legs. He wore a pair of what looked like hand-woven sandals. His skin was an amazing coffee brown glow, and there was a floral scent around him. Even though it was raining outside, his entire outfit looked dry. The only things not new on him right now were the shining twinkles in his eyes.

"The serpent before you are an instrument of God, not an earthly creature," he continued saying. "It is very deadly, and no human weapon can stop it. In the next few moments, it was going to turn itself into a flying reptile and destroy everything and everyone in its path. Now I bid you stand aside and let me deal with it myself."

We all gave way, moving to the right, our hands still linked together. The serpent closed its mouth but didn't move, still watching us. The menacing growling and snarling stopped, and now all we could hear was loud, frequent hissing. Meliak slowly and gracefully walked towards the creature, which stood its ground, still upright, swaying slightly right and left, like an upright pendulum, forked tongue still darting in and out of its mouth. Its mouth suddenly opened, and once again, we saw the mighty fangs, and the inside of its mouth, which was filled with a multi-colored vapor. But this time around, the creature made no bone-chilling, feline snarling sounds, although its hood remained flared out like it was bracing itself to strike at him. Meliak gracefully continued moving towards it. All the while, he was mumbling some words that none of us had a clue of what they meant. A few feet away from it, he stopped and raised his left hand, the palm facing the animal, and he uttered more strange words, this time louder and sounding stern. As he said these new words, the deadly creature hissed loudly, again swaying left and right menacingly, and then moved towards him until it was within his arm's reach. Right at that very point, the loud hissing stopped, and its jaws closed. To our utmost surprise, the animal started meowing, just like a domesticated cat and began lowering itself to the floor, its base gracefully coiling up into balanced coils on top of each other. Meliak reached out, and his fingers curled around the section right below the serpent's throat.

And then it was no longer there. The change happened so fast, perhaps in a second or so, before our own eyes. There, in Meliak's hand, was the same stick, with its curved notches and rounded ends, was last seen on top of the tattered cloth material on top of the glass coffee table before it got shattered by the massive, grinding thunder. It was now as clear as day that the stick had manifested itself into the deadly serpent once the embattled Mukash had tried to claim it.

"It is time to return this instrument to the one highest, the lord of all life, the spirit of all spirits," Meliak said, slowly turning around and facing us. But he had a grave look on his face. "I still need you, two great friends of mine, to help me do it. You must get me to the inception place. The place is now sacred enough to handle the holy reception, but we must hurry, for the time for the ceremony is very near. This means that the time for the great destruction is also very close, and if we do not deliver on time, the fiery changes will commence."

After a moment of dumbfounded silence from the three of us, Salieya stepped forward and faced Meliak. "You are holy, no doubt about that now. But innocent people have died in this place, and we cannot leave them like this. It is against the tradition of this land to abandon the dead unceremoniously not buried. We can't leave yet."

"It is not my doing that humans have perished in this place today, woman," Meliak said to her grimly. "Evil has a great part in this, but so has one of God's mighty angels, who came down here with thunder and lighting, to represent his lord's will. It is now very clear that the lord's will has indeed prevailed, and therefore those who perished at the hands of evil shall rise again, but those who perished by way of the serpent shall remain so, for the will of the almighty lord of the heavens cannot be altered."

Wow! Even as he spoke these words, the two Israeli operatives gunned down by Mukash started rising from their fallen position. The pools of blood around their bodies had disappeared. As this happened, a fast, warm, breeze blew into the room through the windows, forcing the curtains to flap gently up and down like they were jet-propelled.

The two men quietly got up to their feet and dusted themselves off, like nothing had happened to them before. Although they said nothing at this very moment, they stood there, right in front of us, staring back at us and smiling.

"We must leave now!" Meliak said, appearing not concerned with what had just happened.

But one of the Israeli men stepped forward and grabbed hold of Meliak's arm. It was the sole survivor of the serpent attack. "Sir, my brother was the last person to die from the bite of the serpent, and he was trying to help someone when he was attacked. I beg of you, bring back my brother. He was a good man with good intentions. I cannot go back home without him. My parents would die of total grief if I went back home without him …"

"Enough!" Meliak suddenly shouted, and with one vigorous upward thrust of his arm, he freed himself from the operative's grasp. At that moment, the Israeli commando now went down to his knees, tears streaming down his eyes.

"Your younger brother was a fool to defend a bad person who deserved to be punished, "Meliak stated, sounding angry. "The serpent intended to destroy the man it held, but your brother got in the way. Nevertheless, his intentions were good and not for himself. Now stand back, all of you, and close your eyes. Only open them when I say so."

Well, I closed mine quickly and tightly, and I am sure everyone else did the same. Meliak started chanting, raising his voice until it was comparable to the sound of the light thunder outside. I then heard the tapping noise as he repeatedly hit the floor with the bottom of the stick, seven times to be exact. Then silence followed, except for the thunder and rain outside.

"We must leave now, we must!" Meliak said but sounding exhausted. "We are running out of time, and I cannot hold it back any longer, any… longer…"

Then I heard a flopping thud on the floor and instantly opened my eyes. I blinked twice or more times, for yet another hard to believe, but the true incident had just evolved before our very eyes. The Israeli operative struck down earlier by the fierce serpent while trying to help B.G Jr, was on his feet and walking towards us.

But Meliak had collapsed onto the floor. He now looked very pale, almost all color drained out of his face, and after I quickly checked him out, I determined that though we still had a pulse, the divine man was suddenly very unresponsive and or unconscious on the floor.

Chapter Seven

T HERE WAS NO time for rejoicing those who were happy to see their friends and brothers up and walking again. A single bolt of lightning flashed through the window, and the next thing we saw was real fire flying around us. It died out, leaving a burning smell behind, but then the thunder followed, and it felt like the building was going crumble. More stuff fell from the ceiling, and every remaining thing on the walls fell to the floor. Everyone scrambled for the door, but the reawakened men moved slowly, rather sluggishly, and a grateful brother was assisting one. That left Salieya and me, and we had to figure out how to get Meliak out of the building between the two of us. Salieya, already over-concerned about the miracle man, quickly verbalized my concerns.

"We cannot leave him in here like that. The others are dead, but he is still alive," she said. "Where did you leave the car? Is it close by?"

I told her the car was outside the gates but within the perimeter, near the bushes. It still wasn't exactly very close, I told her, to which she responded by asking me what we were going to do. I looked at Meliak's still form. Even with his transformation, he was not exactly the low weight skinny type, so carrying him by myself was not something I felt I could do. Salieya looked exhausted, and even if she wasn't, I still didn't think she was capable of helping carry a full-grown man for such a long distance. I looked at the Israelis, now congregated near the door, and appears to be conducting a prayer gathering of some kind, their hands joined together in a group circle. I did not know the physical capabilities of those who had just been brought back from the dead, because, as I said, they looked strangely weak for now, like someone just coming out of a deep sleep.

But as if to answer my concerns, the doors to the room suddenly swung open, and the man who had been interpreting for now-deceased sheik stepped into the room, looking around.

"Hey, I need some help to get him out of here," I shouted at him, pointing down at Meliak. "We can't leave him behind. Not like this."

"Sure, I can help you with that," he immediately responded, and then sticking his head out of the doorway, he shouted out something. The rest of the Emir's bodyguards came rushing back in.

The group had not left the house yet. The four men spread out and took hold of the three weak Israeli commandos, assisting them to the door and out of the room, while the interpreter and the remaining commando grabbed hold of the unconscious Meliak and hauled him out too. Surprisingly, his fingers still held on to the stick. As he was carried out of the room, Meliak made moaning sounds, and his eyes rolled back and forth, but that was all. The two men carried him down the short steps, and then to the outside of the building, the rest of the group tagging along ahead. I grabbed hold of Salieya's hand, and we did the same. Meanwhile, the lightning and the thunder had now dramatically increased again, with the lightning remarkably vivid. The strange thing was that we could see the lightning bolts stream through the windows in their live form before dying out inside the room, and each time they seemed to come closer and closer into the interior, making strange swirling motions all over the place, up and down, like live, colorful electric currents. We had to get the hell out of here, or risk being struck down.

Once out of the house, we found the environment, not unlike the one inside that living room, but perhaps less hostile. Despite the fact that it was late in the night, it was dark grey outside and almost as bright as early, sunless morning. The lightning was persistent, and the wind was gusting at breakneck speed, blowing all kinds of things around and into the air. The rain, which seemed to have strangely calmed down to a light drizzle, was nonetheless the source of the stinging raindrops that kept pelting our bodies due to the wind force. The huge, thick, black cloud that now loomed over the entire area told me things were not over yet. For the first time, I realized the house sat on top of a slope, giving the esteemed owner the advantage of an almost total aerial view over his plush estate plus those beyond.

"Do you guys need a ride?" the operative helping with Meliak asked me after they placed Meliak on the wet grass near a flower bed. "We have a Landrover with us that will make it back to the capital in this weather, and I think we can all try to fit in it."

"Thanks, but we have our vehicle not too far away from here. We need to get to it, and then we will be fine, "I replied.

"Sure thing, boss," he said. "Just stay put right here, and I will go get the Landrover closer. He looked over at Salieya, who was shivering and smiling. Taking off his military jacket, he quickly placed it around her shoulders and arms. "I hope that will help warm you up a little bit, miss. And I will be right back."

As Salieya said thank you, the commando turned away from us and shouted something at the other men, who then faded into the dark environment, ghostly. As for us, we stayed put, in the semi-darkness, Salieya standing very close to me, using my body as a shield against the strong wind.

"I wonder what in the world is going on in there," she said, looking up at the big house, which now appeared dark and solitary. From where we stood, we could hear the doors inside the house, and see the windows on the outside, opening and slamming repeatedly. Things seemed to be moving about inside, and we could see strange flashing lights in the interior behind every window and curtains in the big house.

"I have no clue, but I am sure glad we are no longer in there," I said, putting my arms around her and holding her close to me. About two minutes later, we were made quite visible by a pair of strong headlights as the Land Rover came roaring towards us from around the corner. Once it stopped, the commando helped me pick up Meliak and placed him in between me and the driver's seat. Salieya somehow got into the back seat with four me, while the rest of the men hung on to the side of the vehicle. In a moment, we were making our way down the winding driveway, towards the gates. And as we exited the big compound, the rain abruptly changed into a steady unidirectional spray, progressively to the tune of the wind gusts.

Suddenly, a long, bright, streak of blue and yellow lightning lit the sky, coming down straight from the black cloud and connecting to the top of the big house. As it touched the top of the house, it broke out into three branches, like a pitchfork with a long handle. Our driver stopped the car, reversed it to a sideways position, and pointed at the house, making it possible for all of us to witness the unusual phenomenon. The forked streak lingered around long enough to light up the top of the roof into a fiery show of fireworks, and in three different sections, all about at least two seconds apart. It all looked like lighting up three gas channels on top of a stove, the stove being the big B.G mansion. Then, as if that was not enough, another bright streak of lightning, this one bright white, solid and single, hit the center of the top of the roof in one loud whack! I mean, this streak of lightning came down together with the heavy thunder, and as we watched, the whole mansion burst into flames, from top to bottom, and collapsed, but not before visibly breaking into two distinct halves.

And then, as we looked on, a strange upright thing came running out of the burning house, all on flames. It was a human being, engulfed in flames. The person was so lit up; there was no way going to be able to make it back to save him.

"That's the priest, the fat man in the robes," the Sheik's interpreter mumbled, sounding frightened, shaken to the core.

The flaming figure appeared to suddenly stumble and collapse to the ground, remaining still, continuing to burn a few yards away from the inferno that was again engulfing the remains of the mansion. It was a sight never to be forgotten!

Nobody said anything as our driver turned the Vehicle back on to the path and drove further away from the cursed site. I kept looking back at the mansion's burning remains through the rearview mirrors, all now totally engulfed in flames. For some reason that I could not understand, the whole event saddened me. It was like the end of a horrible chapter, of a place in time, a place where people had died horrible, gruesome, deaths not commonly, and if ever, witnessed amongst us, humans.

We found the Range rover where I had left it, in the brushy spot off the road, which appeared to be part of a woody, brushy, vegetation that surrounded the walls of the mansion. The Israeli operative helped me transfer Meliak from their Landrover to our Rangerover. He was semi-conscious now, making much louder moaning sounds. We placed him in the back seat, the same place where he sat as the dirty, crippled beggar man.

"You sure you are going to be ok, my friend?" the commando asked, a big smile on his face. "I suggest we all go back to the city and seek shelter from this storm until it's over."

"I think we shall be fine," I replied, though I wasn't sure what was coming up next. I had bad feelings about that ugly black cloud. I think it had everything to do with our misery right now, plus whatever had just transpired. "You guys can go back to the city and find a place to chill. I have to go somewhere with the girl and the old man."

The commando acknowledged with a nod of his head, and then gave me a big hug, clinging on for a moment longer. "Thank you for saving my life, my friend. I will always remember that and will always be grateful. I really and sincerely do owe you my life. I hope we do meet again, under better, favorable circumstances, so that I can show you my gratitude."

"You are most welcome, my friend," I replied, shaking his hand,

"You never know; we may meet again in someplace. This world is too small, so somewhere on this planet, we may meet again. I work for a company called EdenCom, in Texas, United States. Look me up when and if you can."

I patted him on the back, and he did the same, but before I turned around to get into the car, the Emir's interpreter came forward too and shook my hand with both of his.

"My friend, I must tell you that inside that evil house, you looked brave, stronger than the rest of us," he said. "I think it was because of you that the rest of us did not get killed in there. That is why we came back to help. Please take care of yourself and take care of that stick. Whatever it is, it needs to be returned to where it belongs, and I think you are the man for that job."

"Well, I didn't realize I was brave or strong while in there," I replied. "All I can say is that whatever happened, there was disturbing and horrifying, never to be forgotten. But thank you for coming back and helping us out. It was great to see Arabs and Israelis come together and help each other out, during, and in the face of, a common danger. I wish it can be the same out there in our open worlds. There are many dangerous forces out there that have menacingly and blatantly manifested themselves into clear and present dangers, threatening humanity as a whole today. We need to help each other face and clear, instead of hostilities."

"Well spoken, and yes indeed, my friend, it should be like that, always," the man said, laughing. I grinned, gave him a big hug, and turned around again to get into the range rover. Salieya was already inside, behind the wheel.

That's when I heard a grunt behind me, followed by a thud. I turned around again and found myself staring into the barrel of a revolver. I even knew the gun by just looking at it, an army-issue special handgun used by operatives for its effective destructive capability. Its bullet could split a skull like a watermelon, even from ten yards away. Now imagine what could happen if it was fired into your head at point-blank range, just like right now. Pointing the gun at me was the Israeli lead guy, referred to as commander Eridad, the man who had been dead only a few minutes ago after being shot by Mukash, one of his people. It was the same gun he had pointed at me at the monastery. He had just clobbered the Arab interpreter on the back of the head with the heavy pistol, knocking him out cold. That blow had made his victim grunt, and the thud as his body falling on the ground. I felt the quick surge of warm blood run through my body as survival instincts kicked in. I clenched my fist tightly, and my jaws tightened. Yet I knew right now that one single motion and this man could blow my head apart. I could see it, and for the second time, not too long ago, in his eyes.

"Now, what's your problem, man?" I asked, staring into his cold, reddened unblinking eyes.

"Hand over the stick right now, young man, and I will spare your life and the girls," he said. "I have to take it back to Israel. Those are my orders from my government."

"Are you crazy? This thing is not going anywhere except with him," I said, not believing my ears, pointing at Meliak. "Men have lost their lives in that burning house, because of this relic. You will not get far with it. It will kill you, and that's a fact. I suggest you forget about it if you truly want to live. You have already died once, my friend, shot by one of your very own, over the same thing, the rod, but unlike some others in that house, you've received a second chance to come back to life again. Don't blow it again, man. I suggest that you go back home and tell your superiors, your government, that the mission was impossible."

"He's right, colonel," one of his men, who had himself experienced resurrection, said. "You have died once, don't die again so soon. We all have experienced the miracle of being alive again. Let's just let it be. Let the stick go."

"Shut up!" the Israeli lead man snapped back at his subordinate.

"You work for the CIA, and you are taking back the stick to your superiors, the American government. That's not going to happen, because it belongs to our government, the government of Israel. So, like I said, handover the stick right now or kill you, and I will kill the girl too."

"I don't work for the CIA, and all I am trying to do right now is prevent a catastrophe from hitting us all," I replied. "But I can see that you don't seem to get it. From what I have seen or witnessed, from what I know now, the stick is not just a regular piece of wood or dead plant twig. It's a divine instrument from the heavens and needs to be returned back to wherever it came from. Otherwise, wrath from the heavens will be upon us all, starting with this country. This is very real, colonel; That this nation, and the world over, will face the consequences if we do not do what God wants us to do. That guy right there, in our car, has been chosen to take care of that matter before things go wrong. He is no ordinary man; he's an angel from heaven. He has already proven that fact by bringing you back to life. We have angels among us colonel, open your eyes, and you will see. But now I must help get him to the place where the pick-up of the rod will happen, and we have no time left. So tell you what colonel, you and your government, or any other government or institution for that matter, or some self-gratifying individuals, are not worth an entire nation or the whole world. I am not going to let you sacrifice us all for a few people out there with personal agendas full of selfish intentions. I will not let you take the rod anywhere away from that man in our car. You will have to get it over my dead body, colonel!" I hissed.

"Now, you hold on right there!" Salieya shouted suddenly from behind me, stepping out of the range rover. The Israeli colonel took a few steps back, waving the gun at both of us. My eyes widened in disbelief as I noticed that she had the stick in her right hand. "You want the stick, huh? Here, you can have it, and good luck. At least I get to go back home to bed and sleep without the burden of worrying about how to deal with this thing because I am so tired and exhausted. So here, you idiots can take over now."

And with those words, she threw the stick at the Israeli colonel, who stretched out his free hand to grab it. However, right before he could do so, one of his men stepped forward and, in one quick tackle, knocked the colonel's gun-wielding hand upwards. The stick fell on the ground, and a shot went off into the air, forcing me to instinctively duck, and so did Salieya with a loud scream.

Springing into action, I leaped forward and did my tackle on the colonel, spinning around and sweeping him off his feet with one of my own. He hit the ground with a thud and lost grip of the gun. As I came up again and at him, his left leg shot outwards, and a heavy boot smashed into my face with the force of a sledgehammer, forcing me to retreat backwards in a stumble. In one quick flip, he was up and coming at me with the ferociousness of a hungry, preying tiger. I blocked a fist, only to be slammed in the back of the knee with a kick. That was a hard one, and I bulked down on one knee. A fist slammed into my head, and I felt like a concrete brick had hit me. My head exploded in pain, and I hit the ground instantly. I managed to roll clear of a foot stamp that could have mashed my head up had I stayed in the same position for a second or so longer, and then was able to pally off a foot blow aimed at my ribs. Another left leg came at me, and I grabbed at the foot before it hit home. I pulled hard and bum! Down came the relentless colonel man to the ground. I rolled away and got up; fists clenched. Blood was dripping from my nose, and my head hurt like hell. He came up again and faced me.

"I am going to kill you, man …" he snarled and came at me again. I stopped his advance when, and suddenly, I lashed with a right punch, clubbing him on the left side of his face. His head snapped to the right, followed by stumbling in the same direction. Then I was in the air, spinning around and landing a foot punch on the same side I had just punched. The flying kick blow had the pressured force of kicking at a two-hundred-pound bag of sand. I ended back on my two feet on the ground to his right, firmly upright. At least temporarily, that fixed him up as the blow sent him to the ground again with a big thud, grunting.

He sat up but flopped down again. He shook his head vigorously several times, and then I saw him reach for his jacket's side pocket. I also noticed the bulge. He was reaching for another gun.

"Boss, I ask you to stop, or I will be forced to shoot you myself," someone shouted. It was the operative who had been struck down by the serpent when trying to help B.G Jr. The colonel quickly turned around to stare at his gun, pointed at him by one of his men, just a few yards away. "I swear to God, Colonel, I will pull the trigger and send you back to your death if you don't calm down."

"Put that gun down, soldier or I will have you court marshaled for insubordination and interference with duties assigned by the state," the colonel warned, sounding like a deranged person. At the same time, his hand came out of his pocket with a small black pistol and aiming straight at me.

The operative stepped forward, slowly, and faced his commander. "Colonel, please listen to me," he said, his voice calm. "If we let you take, or even touch, that stick, you will be killed, most likely instantly. You got shot dead by Mukash, who wanted the stick for his reasons. Mukash, in turn, got killed by the stick, which had turned itself into a deadly creature. And while you were dead, you missed seeing what truly happened next. Now I wish you had because then you would easily and quickly change your mind about all this."

"This, sir, is no ordinary stick," another one of his men said, stepping forward. "It's a sacred object, an instrument that truly belongs to God and only that older guy right there, in that car, has the authority to handle it. We don't want you to die again, sir. We are all here because I am told, the old man brought us back to life.

I am now pleading with you to listen to reason. The stick is not for us, colonel. We will never make it back to Israel with it. It will destroy us all, and I don't want to die again. I don't want to be part of this anymore, so please just let it go."

The Situation now looked bleak. I had a gun pointed at me, but my assailant had one pointed at him too. Now he had to make a choice, to shoot me down first or quickly swing around and attempt to take down his imminent threat first. Either way, he was faced with a window of downed luck in case he miscalculated his move. The way it looked like to me, the other guy would shoot first before the colonel got to him, but neither would I stay in place if he moved that gun away from me. He had to think carefully before he decided on his next move. He had to make a quick choice for about his own life too.

He made a choice, quicker than I had expected to. He lowered his gun down, away from me, and then dropped it down to the ground in front of his feet.

The other man sighed in big relief and lowered his gun down too. He then stepped forward and offered it back to his commander. The Israeli lead slowly got up and wiped the blood off his face. It was dripping from his nose, though not profusely like mine. He stared at his operative angrily as he snatched the gun from his hand and expertly checked it out. The safety catch was off. He slowly turned around and faced me; gun pointed down. I, too, sighed in relief when I heard a familiar sound of the safety catch clicking in place on that gun.

"My men speak with good reason and wisdom, and I have decided to listen," he said. "So, take the rod, and your people, and get out of my sight before I change my mind."

Without thinking, I reached down and picked up the stick, but realizing what I had just done, I quickly dropped it down again, stepping back.

"It's all ok now, young man," a voice said behind me. "It will not harm you. Just pick it up and hand it over to me."

It was Meliak, and he was sitting up straight in the back seat of the range rover. Once again, I scooped up the stick and walking over to the car; I handed it to him. I did not feel any difference when handling it. It just felt like a regular stick, though surprisingly solid.

"Let's get out of here," I said quickly, not looking back at the Israelis. Salieya was already behind the steering wheel. I told her where to find the keys. I got into the passenger seat next to her and closed the heavy door behind me.

"Do you have a rug or something I can use to stop, and also clean up this blood?" I asked her.

"You do not need that. Just turn around and look at me," Meliak said before Salieya, who had now started the car and was trying to turn it around, responded. I did as I was told, turning around in my seat and facing him. Reaching out, he gently covered my blood-drenched face with the palm of his right hand. It felt hot, and I felt this warmth sip into the front of my head. His hand remained in this position for at least half a minute, and then he slowly withdrew it. I touched my nose. It no longer hurt, and neither did it feel puffy anymore. There was no blood dripping from it anymore, either. It just felt dry and clear. And the throbbing headache completely, and suddenly, stopped. But I still felt weak from all the beating and fighting.

"Thanks, Meliak," I said, no longer surprised by what he was capable of doing. "So now, where do we go next?"

"Hold it there, Day!" another voice cut in before I could get word back from Meliak. It was closer to my side. It was the Israeli colonel, and he was briskly walking towards me.

"What is it now, colonel?" I asked reluctantly. I was tired of these guys, him and everybody else out there. I didn't even care anymore to wonder how he came to know my last name. These people seemed to know everything about us while we knew less about them, even though he was wrong about the CIA part.

"Good luck, son," he said, now standing next to my window, outside the car. He was smiling as he said this, the same smile I had seen on his face the first time we met in the hotel lobby when he introduced himself, right after my first encounter with Mukash, except that this time his face was bruised, swollen, and bloody.

"I apologize for acting foolish earlier and thank you for saving my men's lives. I hope my apologies are accepted."

I nodded quickly in affirmation.

The colonel smiled briefly, and then his face went grim as he suddenly stood at ease and flipped a quick military salute at me. I had no choice but to salute back, grinning sheepishly. Behind him, I could see his operatives helping with getting up the man he had clobbered down.

"Thanks, colonel, and good luck to you too," I replied, and then looked away. I nodded at Salieya, who stepped on the accelerator, and the big car leaped forward immediately and obediently as if it was so glad to be back on the road. Unlike the drive up to the big house, driving away and down the along the narrow tree-lined strip that formed the driveway proved to be nothing much, and we covered it in no time. We were soon back on the main road, which was filled with people staring at the fiery inferno at the top of the hill behind us despite the threatening weather. As we drove through the crowded street, Salieya managed to glance back at Meliak, and for the first time, I saw her smile, and broadly, at him.

"Thank you for saving us all, for reviving those soldiers, and for putting Kiron back into good shape. I need him to be in good shape to help get us through this last part of our mission," she said.

"It was all by the will of God that these powers were entrusted to me," Meliak replied. "But now I am anxious and concerned that we will not be able to make it to the sacred place."

I turned around in my seat and looked into his grey eyes. The twinkle was no longer there. "Let's try to be optimistic here, Meliak. We are going to get you there. Just a matter of time. So, sit tight and be patient."

"You just don't understand, young man," Meliak said. "The devastation process has already begun evolving, and what lies ahead of us on the path to the sacred place is terrible. It signals impending death for us as we attempt to fulfill the lord's wishes, plus millions of people in the region. It's the price of man's refusal to obey his commands."

"If it's still the same God who's seen us through our assignment and brought us together, so then he should, and will, surely see us through the next phase," Salieya said. "Are you losing your faith in the very God who has empowered you to perform such wonders as we have witnessed earlier? I don't see why he wants us to do one thing yet plans to stop us from doing it. It doesn't make sense."

"I am sorry, but I see it like he is already lost his patience with us," Meliak said. "And every time it happens, his anger is felt all over. His power is so great over everything that no creature on this earth, or beyond, can hide from his wrath. Even man's greatest inventions cannot endure the slightest test from heaven's incumbents. I just tested that power when I revived the last of those men back to life. My own life was almost sucked out of me. And now I am afraid that while I revived these few lives, I see thousands about to perish and nothing I can do about it. Do what you may, my friends and May the almighty God be with all of us."

"Ok. So, where exactly do you want us to go from here?" Salieya asked. "Where is this sacred place that you keep talking about?"

"North from here, and then follow the route to the Amaritatumpa mountain range," he replied. "The sacred place is on one of the range's highest peaks. Get me to the bottom of these mountains, and I will find my way to the peak."

Turning back around to look at me, Salieya lightly touched my arm. "Kiron, we are running out of time, and Meliak has no more answers for us. We are on our own now. We now must do all that is in our human powers to get him there and hence stop the onslaught of an entire civilization, to save everyone and everything on this land."

"Please pull over to the side of the road for a moment," I said, looking straight into her pretty eyes. Looking puzzled, she immediately directed the car to the side of the road and killed the engine.

I smiled at her and then placing my hand on her arm. I closed my eyes, bowing my head. I am sure she did the same, even though I couldn't see her. "Dear God, we come to you one more time to ask that you see us through this. We realize you are angry with us for not always doing what you want us to do, and that is why we constantly come back to you and ask for forgiveness. At this present time, we ask not only for your forgiveness, but that you turn your wrath away and give us the chance to carry out your wishes, and that is to return your instrument to you. We pray that you make our journey possible. Amen."

I took in a deep breath and opened my eyes, just as Salieya did the same.

"Amen!" Salieya said rather loudly, opening her eyes. There was a big smile on her face as she unbuckled her seat belt, reached across to my side, and kissed me thoroughly. "I didn't know you had such faith that you are a true believer in divine intervention."

"Well, welcome to my world, "I replied, grinning. "I never do things like this alone. In other words, there is a point that we humans can't cross, and it is at that moment that we humble ourselves and call for … well … divine intervention."

Salieya sat back in her seat, buckled up again, and started driving again. We were still in the B.G Fawas township, and people were everywhere on the two-way street. We soon realized that the main attraction wasn't the crumbled, burning building on top of the hill anymore. Now people had their faces turned to the sky, at the huge black cloud that now covered the entire area. We observed in silence as we drove through, and soon left, the small town. There was no sign of the Israelis either. Meliak had passed out again and was in a deep slumber, his chin hanging on his chest, hands clutched tightly around the stick. Salieya raced the big car passed eighty miles per hour, and the car was like a beast, eating up the miles. The rough road was now muddy and splashy, and loose stony gravel continuously hit the side of the car. The car's powerful headlight, now switched to full maximum, brightly illuminated the way ahead. All sorts of animals were crossing the road in different directions. It was amazing that Salieya was not running down any of the poor creatures with the car at that speed.

About thirty minutes later, we drove into Addis Ababa, but we did not stop. There was barely any traffic on the roads, both humans and cars, possibly because it was still way too early in the morning.

The dashboard clock showed a few minutes past two in the morning. But the streets were all wet from an earlier flush flood, and now it was beginning to rain again, with the lightning increasing in frequency and brightness. Salieya turned on the radio, hoping to hear something about the weather changes, but nothing came out of it, except static. We soon left the capital city behind, and after another thirty minutes or so of driving, we hit the now muddy and splashy highway that would eventually lead us to the Amarita tumpa mountain range.

Watching Salieya drive, I realized the other side of her. She had that look of resilience on her face. The partial frown and the slightly parted lips, the slow delayed blinking of her tired, sleepless, dry eyes as she focused on the road ahead, the tangled, uncombed hair, all set on a bruised face and neck emphasized that point. Yet, she looked very beautiful, her coffee brown skin clearly golden, bright against the dark, greyish, outlook of the weather outside. Her upper posture erect, legs slightly stretched, and both hands on the steering wheel, Salieya seemed to be as determined as I was to get this thing done with. In all, I now looked at Salieya not just as a simple woman pursuing a complex journalistic career, but as a tough, fearless, unyielding human that knew no boundaries once she decided to go after something. She probably lacked the adventurous spirit that vigorously ruled my realms and set my adrenaline skyrocketing, but the resilience and or determination in her character now made up for that.

I must have fallen asleep because I did not know when we got to or why we had to go to aunt Mumia's. My eyes opened, and we were parked in her yard. Salieya was nowhere in sight, either. I unbuckled myself, stepped out of the car, and ran to the house. I found both women inside the house, talking loudly, face to face. When they saw me, they both burst out laughing I was dripping wet already from the effect of a steady rain downpour outside.

Before I could say anything, Aunt Mumia stepped forward and hugged me tightly.

"Come on inside, my dear, and let's see if we can dry up your cloth for you," She said. "Besides, there is this storm coming up, and we had one last night that had so much thunder and lightning; it got me scared, and worried about everything. The clouds show that it is going to repeat itself, and that is why I also suggest that you all should stay indoors with us until the weather clears up."

I smiled at her, but turned back to look at Salieya, and slowly shook my head, adopting a grim look on my face immediately.

"You didn't have to do it this way, Salieya, because you very well know that we have no time left with what we have to do. We have to move on," I exclaimed.

"I just thought I would come to see my aunt quickly, say some byes in case things changed against us," she replied, sounding very sincere. "I wanted to tell her one more time that I love her, and that I do appreciate everything that she has done for me."

"Ok. Can we leave now?" I said, sounding frustrated.

Hesitantly, Salieya now turned to her aunt. "Aunt Mumia, I am sorry, but he is right, we really must go…"

But aunt Mumia cut her short. "I do not want to hear it, child. Look at you, all beat up, tired, dirty, and probably hungry too. And the weather is bad, very bad. If this man wants to go, let him. He is a man, and maybe he can handle it all. After all, he was supposed to take good care of you, but it doesn't look like he did a good job of it at all," She lamented.

I could not believe what I was hearing. And before I could say anything, aunt Mumia grabbed Salieya's arm and led her away further into the house. To my surprise, she offered little or no resistance at all, and did not even look back at me at all. The two disappeared inside one of the rooms and closed the door.

Great, I thought. I was beginning to believe that everything was working out fine and that we were going to make it through the rain, to deliver Meliak and the stick-on or even in time. Now with this kind of new behavior, it was beginning to seem unlikely. Suddenly, I felt the urge to urinate, realizing that I had not emptied my bladder for over six hours. Without hesitating, I rushed into the narrow corridor and found the small bathroom area. Opening the door quickly, almost kicking it in, I stepped up to the commode. A scuffle followed between me and the buttons, then the zipper, on my pants as I struggled to hold back the pressured outflow while working the two fasteners. I won, but only by a matter of seconds. It was after almost two minutes before I felt better. It was a much welcome relief.

I wanted to get back into my little room and change cloth, shoes and maybe check out other stuff, but something kept nagging me to move on to keep moving. I had this uneasy feeling inside me that was making me quite unsettled, very nervous. I briskly walked past the bedroom and back to the living room. I found Salieya in the dining area, eating something from a bowl. Her eyebrows rose slightly when she saw me, with a look of surprise on her face. I walked up straight to where she sat, smiling wryly.

"Let me, please have the keys to the car, Salieya," I said, stretching out my hand.

"I left them in the car. Why? Aren't you going to grab something to eat before we leave? I am starving," she said.

I didn't answer back but turned away from her and headed for the door. Now, I must have been inside aunt Mumia's house for at least a little over five minutes, right? Nevertheless, that was enough time for things outside the house to change completely, and for the worst. The sky had grown much darker; the rain had changed from a steady downpour to a threatening, wind-driven tempest with lightning scattered all over the sky, and the wind had changed to a much faster and stronger gust, making loud, whirling swishing noises. All sorts of animals, including chicken, goats, sheep, rabbits, big and small rats, dogs, or even wolves, were running all over the place and in all directions. Trees branches were bending and shaking like rubber fibers and all kinds of light things, like leaves, small twigs, and branches; even pebbles were flying all over the place and in the air.

Meliak was now wide awake again, I noted, and was standing outside of the car on his new pair of strong legs, waving the stick in the air like a mad man. When he saw me, he angrily pointed and waved the divine stick at me. He was raving mad, I could tell.

"Calm down, am on my way, man," I shouted, and then sprinted off towards him. "Get back in the car. We are leaving now!"

"What is wrong with you people now, huh?" he growled when I got close to him. "You were not supposed to stop! I went back to sleep again because I trusted in you to go on, not to stop! I trusted you to get me there! Now look, see what's happening? The rage is upon us because you let me down! I should not have trusted you, humans, I should not have!"

And with that, he lashed out with the stick at me. I instantly ducked to avoid the blow, but it was too late. I got whacked right on my back, more on the left shoulder blade. It was like being hit by a big jolt of electric power, and with a big zing! My whole body went into shock, and I must have instantly, though temporarily, blacked out, for I don't remember what happened next except what an eyewitness, Salieya, saw happen. But when I came to, I was lying down on the ground, several yards away from Meliak and the car. Salieya was on my side, shaking my body by the shoulders, screaming my name at the same time.

"What … what happened…?" I asked as water from the rain ran down my face. I was feeling very warm. In fact, hot!

"I don't know, Kiron, I don't know!" She screamed, sounding very frightened. "I followed you after you ran out of the house, and then I saw Meliak shouting at you, and then hit you with the stick. Then came this bright flash of light, and I saw your body tossed into the air like a rag doll and then fall back to the ground, right here. Oh my God, Kiron, he nearly killed you with that stick!"

"It's ok, its ok," I said, coughing repeatedly. My whole mouth was filled with warm fluid, which I decided to spit out. It was blood. "Listen, he's gone crazy, but for a reason. We have to go now!"

I slowly got myself up, shaking my head vigorously, spitting out more blood, and tried to focus myself out of the dark cloud that had been my blackout state in the past few seconds. I could hardly maintain my gait, and I flopped down to the ground again. Yet I got right up, willing up my energy to get going. The cold rainwater in my face helped revive me faster.

As I grabbed hold of her arm and dragged her against the now hard whipping, fast-moving wind towards the car, I could hear aunt Mumia shouting, screaming at me to stop, but I did not stop.

"Where did he go? Where is Meliak?" I asked, not seeing the older man in the spot I had seen him standing outside the car.

"He's inside the car, inside the car …" Salieya shouted back as the wind hit her face while freeing herself from my hold on her hand. "Get in; I will drive."

She made her way to the other side, the driver's side, and managed to pull the car door open, just as I did on my side. That, too, wasn't right on easy, because of wind turbulence and strength, plus the loads of stuff flying in the wind, smashing hard into our bodies from all angles. But it was more stable inside the car, though the heavy car itself was doing its quivering, courtesy of the wind gust outside. Salieya immediately started the car and drove out of aunt Mumia's loose graveled back yard and back to the main road again. I looked at Meliak, who stared back at me with steely gray eyes. The shiny twinkles in the center of his eyes were back and now looked like little live rings of fire.

"I am sorry, my friend, but I warned you, not to take God's wrath for granted," he said gravely. "Now you are seeing and feeling for yourself that anger, and what it can do. And this is just the beginning."

I turned away from him without a word, and focused on the road ahead, clinging on to the dashboard and the armrest. My head hurt like crazy, the side veins throbbing nonstop. I kept closing my eyes intermittently. This time, Salieya didn't care what she ran into as she drove, and so we hit plenty of moving objects out of our way, live or not.

A mile or so down the road, we vied off the main road and made a sharp right turn into a wide, dirt road that was rather rough and appeared to be full of potholes. The car bounced in and out of these rather smoothly, but we still got to be shaken around, bouncing in our seats as Salieya struggled to maneuver the car through the muddy runoff covering the road. I was glad we had good headlights, the strong beams running through the heavy, wind-driven streams of rain and flashing lightning all around us. The car's heavy windshield wipers were running at maximum speed to keep the slamming water off the windshield. The engine growled now and then as it pushed the car against the wind force. There were no houses in this area, just tall shrubs and bushes. We stayed on this road for at least thirty minutes before she turned left into another much narrower one and I felt the car growl more as she suddenly stepped down hard on the accelerator.

"We are now going up one of those steep slopes of the valley," she shouted, and reaching forward, she grabbed one of the extra gear levers on the center panel, behind the main one. She jerked it forward, clutched at another one, and did the same, all with speed and agility. The engine raved with power as it adapted to the new system dimensions, the car eased forward with ease, and the raving stopped.

"That's four times four, off the road, wow!" I shouted excitedly as the car bounced out of potholes and off what felt like rocky hard rocky stuff. "I love it!"

"We are getting into mountain terrain, Kiron," she shouted back, sounding cautious. "These slopes are treacherous, and one bad move could send us rolling over down the stony slopes. As we go higher, it becomes more and more dangerous, even more, dangerous as we get to go down on the other side because of the rain. Only God knows."

We made it up the slope, and leveled off on a narrow, rough path with more random potholes and twisted turns that forced the car to spin and splash. Salieya wrestled with the wheel to keep us going on the nasty terrain covered with chunks of thick muddy runoff coming down from the bordering stony cliff sides. The powerful beams from the car's headlights picked up sight of other debris made of plant material and loose rock all mixed up in the runoff. We smashed through these with great forward thrust force, but I was worried we might experience a mudslide. I experienced at least over thirty minutes of this crazy momentum, and the heavy rain just seemed to get stronger and heavier. And then we started descending.

The winding of the trail seemed not to be any different from when coming up, but now with the rain heavier and stronger, the car was dangerously sliding forward and sideways. The huge, stony chunks of thick runoff slammed against the range rover's tailgate with such force the big vehicle shook. Salieya gripped the steering wheel with both hands, and I could see how tense her body she was as struggled to keep us going. We finally made it onto leveled terrain and swerved dangerously to the right before gaining momentum again. At the same time, this huge muddy wall of water suddenly slammed hard again the car, almost pushing us off the road.

Salieya slammed on the breaks, and the big car stood its ground against the heavy, mud thickened, rock-filled runoff, coming to a halt almost instantly.

"That was close, really close," she said, placing both her hands to her face. "Oh lord, please help us, help us survive this. I don't think I can do this anymore by myself."

Salieya was sobbing.

"Why did you stop? You are headed in the right direction, keep going," Meliak's deep, gruff voice came from behind us. I turned around in my seat and looked at the man. He sat hunched forward in the backseat, staring ahead, both hands rested on top of the stick that was upright between his legs. His face looked gray, and somewhat frightening, clearly illuminated by the scattered lightning that appeared to flash almost every second. His face revealed nothing of his feelings on the situation at hand. It was as if he was oblivious of the volatile, hostile environment around him. I also wondered how he managed to stay upright with no seat belt yet seated in the middle of the bench seat. Then I reminded myself that this was no ordinary human being, and he was capable of doing strange things out of this world. Once again, I turned away from him without saying a word and refocused on the road ahead, as Salieya hit the accelerator pedal again, and the heavy car moved forward. And then I saw it, a bigger than usual object, and longer in size than the usual chunky runoff content, rolling down the sloppy side of our path fast.

It was a large, fallen tree with most of its branches still attached to it. It landed right into our path.

"Watch out, ahead!" I shouted, but it was too late. Salieya applied the brakes, but we skidded forward right into it with a heavy bang. Our bodies were jerked forward by the sudden impact, and had it not been for the thick, leather padded seat belts, we could have gone flying right through the windshield, which, by the way, was still intact. The car once again came to a dead stop.

For a moment, we breathed in heavily as we took in the incident. Salieya put the car in reverse, then stepped on the accelerator again, hard. The heavy vehicle moved slightly, dancing left and right on its wheels, digging and throwing up chunks of mud and rocks, engine raving. It was no match for the massive mountain log, with its branches, wedged across the trail, with some of its long branches now latched to the car.

"Great, we are stuck," I said, banging on the dashboard.

"There could be one way to get out of this mess, but with this kind of weather, I can't guarantee it will work, and it's too risky," Salieya said. "Someone has to go out there, get the front metal tow cable unhooked, and hook in on and around the log. Then I will turn on the special pulley motor attached to the main engine, which in turn rolls the cable, which will hopefully dislodge the tree. I may then be able to move the car forward or backward, and then we unlatch the log, and let it go rolling again down the slope."

"I don't mind doing it, but the possibility of being washed off by the muddy rainwater coming rushing down the slope is very real," I said. I saw her wince, and then shake her head, a sign that she had was not willing to risk losing me that way. We both sat there, looking ahead at the rain-washed, barely visible path whose surface was so active with runoff from above it was difficult to perceive how we were going to make through it all, and that is if we were able to move forward from our current predicament. Salieya suddenly turned around in her seat and faced Meliak.

"Why can't you do something about this, huh?" she snapped, with an edge of impatience in her voice. "I am sure you can see we are not going forward because of this thing at the front of the car, yet you sit there and do nothing about it. But then you were so quick to strike out at Kiron, almost killing him, because we had kept you waiting. Well, now we are stuck, but not out of our own doing. Now, should we blame nature, or maybe blame God, because he owns nature, for bringing in all this heavy, crazy rain before we got you to your destination ..."

"Enough!" Meliak shouted, cutting her short. The menace in his voice forced me to turn around again to look at him instantly. Now both of us stared at him, not so sure what to say or do next at this moment. We saw him raise his right hand, also holding the stick, palm facing upwards, and stretch it between our heads, pointing it at the windshield. He then slowly started raising this hand upwards, bending it at the elbow. We both turned back around in our seats and simultaneously tuned our focus to the windshield, in time to witness another unthinkable thing happening again. As his arm went upwards, so did the big log block the car. It looked like an invisible crane was lifting it. The car shook a little as whatever part of the log attached to it got detached. We stared at the big branch tagged log as it hung suspended in the air in front of the car for at least ten seconds. Then with a sudden twist of his arm to the left, the whole log was tossed off the path to our left and down the dark, almost invisible escarpment. Our path was now clear.

"Nothing is impossible for the almighty lord of the heavens," he growled as he lowered his hand, with the stick, back down again. "Now, please let's get going again. We have but very limited time left to make it."

Without another word, Salieya engaged a gear and then stepped on the accelerator. The big car jumped forward, and once again, we started splashing and bouncing our way through the thick, muddy runoff filled, uneven terrain that now made up the narrow path. The downpour was so heavy and loaded with liter Salieya had the heavy windshield wipers working in full, fast swings. The powerful headlights allowed us to see ahead, although the space in front was mostly filled with flying and rolling objects above and around …

Boof! Shewwwww … Wooovm!

We had just been hit by a huge chunk of rolling stony mud that shattered all the window glass on my side and forced the car into a spin. I saw Salieya pump the breaks continuously as she wrestled with the wheel, spinning it left and right as the car got pulled backward and on to the edge of the escarpment path. Holding on to the steering wheel with one hand, she worked a series of gear levers below the center dashboard area, and I heard the engine screech and groan heavily, and then the range rover made it's mighty pull forward and upward, it's back spinning right and left again and again. Then she twisted the wheel sharply to the right and then to the left, and we suddenly jumped back onto the path again. Just like the car's interior, we were now all mashed with viscous mud and stuff. And then I was being pelted by heavy rain as the wind blew it through the wholly shattered window glass space.

But Salieya didn't stop to think about all this. She stepped hard on the accelerator, and the car rolled forward, engine groaning, bouncing through potholes, humps, and bumps. I held on the arm grip above my door while staring at the path ahead of us.

After experiencing this narrow, winding path for at least another ten minutes, we suddenly started rolling down the slope again, and I could feel and hear the car slamming into lighter rock and stuff. But this didn't last long, though, for the big car suddenly righted itself with a bang as we landed on the horizontal ground again, not stopping.

"There!" Salieya said breathlessly, pointing ahead. As the bright lightning vividly continued to illuminate the area all around and ahead of us, I saw what she was pointing at. It was this sharp peeked range of hills that looked vividly jagged and loomed above or over everything else around it, a magnificent structure that was clear evidence of years of nature's sculpturing habits of the earth. "The Amaritatumpa mountain range, and that's where he wants us to take him."

"And that's where the boy said we should take the stick to," I said. "It was one of the last things he mentioned to me before completely passing out."

We now started driving through bushy, savannah-like terrain as we fast approached the mountain range, with no clear path to really follow. Salieya suddenly vied off a ragged path and took a right turn into nothing but short bushes, shrubs, and other stuff. All around us, all kinds of animals were running in every direction opposite to what we were taking, and I wondered what they were running away from. Then I saw it.

Coming down from above and over the entire front of the mountain range was this huge wall or curtain of something that gleamed like silver. Coming down from the sky, this thing looked so massive and was rapidly obscuring the entire front of the mountain range. And then before our eyes, the entire front of the mountain ranges suddenly and completely disappeared behind this massive silver curtain. At the same time, big, heavy raindrops started pelting the car's windshield and the wind gust seemed to have tripled in force. I now realized that the massive silver curtain was a huge downpour of rain coming out of the sky, and it was this that the animals were running away from. After the next five minutes or so, the big raindrops disappeared; instead, thick sheets of water slammed down on the car with considerable force and deafening roar! Salieya still had the windshield wipers working overtime, set to maximum, but they were no match for this huge downpour of water that completely engulfed the entire car. We were now driving into the massive silver wall or curtain, which was the full wrath of the storm. I heard the Range Rover's engine bellow under pressure from the extremely powerful wind resistance against it, and I thought it was going to explode. The car shook and trembled like a leaf, but it still withstood the force, forcing through the massive storm front. I wondered what could have happened if it had been a smaller car. I found myself clinging on to everything around me, mainly the dashboard and the door armrest as rainwater spewed through my exposed, unshielded door windows side. This influx was a big, incredibly noisy, and painful whiplash that hit me and forced me to learn more inwards towards Salieya as she struggled to hold on to the controls of the big car.

Our headlights suddenly picked up two unusually big antelopes coming straight at us at full gallop. It was happening so fast and without warning, and then one of the big animals suddenly turned sharply to the right and disappeared in the darkness, but the other did not. Salieya slammed on the breaks as impact with the animal became imminent, and I had no choice but to scream too when Salieya threw her arms up in the air and screamed her lungs out. But the big animal suddenly leaped up into the air right before impact with the car, and then I felt and heard the impact of its hooves crash land on top of the car in the form a heavy bang! And then it was off and gone. That antelope had attempted to jump over the entire car and rarely made it. Whew! What a scary moment it was!

But that wasn't it. When we resumed driving, we hit a bunch of animals and heard their brief cry as the impact happened. Then I suddenly found myself face to face with this big, spotted cat, which was either a cheetah or leopard, as it suddenly jumped on to the mu side of the car, on my window ledge clung to it, perhaps wanting to get in. I shouted out loudly and fell back against Salieya. But Salieya did not stop the car this time and was weaving through spaces between small trees and shrubs. The sudden sharp twist of the steering wheel to the left sent the car spinning around and around several times before banging my side against some hard surface, a tree or maybe an anthill, and coming to a stop. I think that threw the animal off, for it disappeared into the darkness, and I never saw it again. Salieya engaged a gear, spun the car around, and we shot forward back.

I was wet now, completely soaked up by the rain that was pouring through my shattered window. Water was dripping down from my head downwards, and I could feel my shoes all covered up in the water as the car floor was now completely submerged in it. The thunder and lightning had not ceased at all, and the wind gust seemed to be at its strongest now, forcing the rain in all directions. We were now being slammed repeatedly with pressurized rainwater from all angles, and it was miraculous that the windshield still held up. The car itself quivered, but it held on steadily. For the next ten minutes or so, we breathlessly endured and drove nonstop through this menacing downpour, with visibility so low I don't think Salieya had a sense of direction anymore. And I believe our terrain angles had changed, from flat to sloppy again.

The car's powerful headlights suddenly picked up something ahead, a big dark object. Salieya must have noted the same, for she suddenly slammed on the breaks and peered forward. We were both trying to figure out what it was. It was a huge boulder rock, and it was rolling towards us. Massive and wide, the rock's height appeared to be more than the car's. That thing would smash us to bits if it cannoned into us.

"Oh my God!" Salieya exclaimed loudly.

"Oh shit! Back up, back up, back up!" I verbally reacted in the next snap second after her reaction, literally shouting at her."

She was like a robot, reacting instantly by throwing the car gear into reverse and jamming the accelerator hard. We shot backward immediately as the tip of the big rock nicked the front of the car and rolled with us for a distance until she suddenly spun the car sharply to the right and out of the way. The big rock rolled past us, scrapping off something from the front of the car as it did, and disappeared into the darkness. The big car went into a spin of its own before stopping. We stopped for a moment, breathless, trying to recover from the terrifying moments, and then Salieya took us forward again, this time slowly as the lightning lit the sky and space around us. I could see more of those boulder rocks, some small some big, rolling down from the slopes in all directions. Even though we seemed to be driving on some natural, rough inclined plane, I figured that we had most likely arrived at the bottom of the mountain ranges.

Now it was as if the skies were pouring down stony material together with the massive downpour of rain, a sudden barrage of lighter, stone-sized material slamming into the car with full force. Hailstones had suddenly made their debut.

And then we got hit!

It was the loudest ripping thud or bang I had ever heard, so sudden and unexpected. The front dashboard area caved inwards, and the entire windshield collapsed on to us. I heard Salieya gasp once and then saw her seat thrust itself backward, with her still in it, and her hands still clinging to the steering wheel. There was also a very loud whirring and then screeching, noise as the engine wound down. We had run the car into another hard object, but this time it wasn't sideways, as in that case with the big cat, but head-on. And at over at least forty miles an hour, I was pretty much surprised that we didn't die. I possibly blacked out, knocked out by this impact, though just briefly, because the rain slamming into my face didn't keep me that way for a long time. I found myself coughing and spluttering, breathing rapidly.

We had now come to a dead stop. The car couldn't take the beating anymore, the engine probably completely damaged. One of its heavy light beams was still on, flashing yellow light all around us.

My first instinct was to check on Salieya, who was lying still in her seat, face turned to the left. The steering column, with the steering wheel still in her hands, had come out of the dashboard, and the stem was hanging between her legs. Once I found out that I was still able to move, and although it took me some minutes, I managed to detach myself from the seatbelt and force myself up and to her side. I managed to get the steering wheel assembly somehow away from her, managing to push most of it outwards through her shattered door window. My hands started shaking as I realized that she could be dead. I shook her still form, yelling and shouting at her to wake up, to please open her eyes and talk to me … to say something. But there was no movement, no response from her.

Oh God, please, she's not dead! She isn't, oh please God she isn't!

This can't be happening to me, why is it this happening to now? No, she isn't dead! And this is not happening to me! These racing, raging thoughts came rushing into my mind, non-stop, despite the pounding headache. Slowly, I lowered the left side of my head to her chest and listened.

Nope! No, she wasn't dead! Not yet, at least, because I could hear the faint but rapid heartbeat. I placed my fingers on the lower left side of her neck. There was a strong pulse, I could feel it! Thank you, God,

Suddenly, she coughed, first lightly, then heavily and nonstop. Warm stuff splashed in my face, and I tested salty stuff in my mouth as she directly cleared her airways right into my face. I spit most of it right out, myself coughing and spluttering.

"Hey, about time you did that," I said, grabbing her and pulling her to me. I held her tightly to me for a moment before realizing that I had to be careful I don't mess up something like an already injured spinal code. Slowly releasing her, I looked at her battered, bloodied face, and I was instead stunned to see this big smile on it. I was instantly speechless.

"We … made it, didn't we?" she whispered to me, and then slowly lifting her arms, she put her hands on both sides of my face and slowly directed my face to the left. What I saw there was even more astounding.

Not too far from where we were, there was this sharp rise in the ground level that developed into a rocky slope with a table like surface that rose several feet into the air. Bigger rocks surrounded it with jagged edges of all kinds and angles, and the tabled rock appeared to be in the center of it all.

Standing on top of this table was a human figure. The human figure, and the surrounding environment, as described above, were illuminated by the constant, unusually bright lightning in the sky. With the thunder roaring and his loose garments blowing frantically all over his body, it was not hard for us, even at this distance, to recognize Meliak. I instantaneously turned my head to the back of the car. The back seat was empty. I looked back again at the figure on the tabled rock.

"It's Meliak," Salieya said, mumbling the words through chattering teeth.

"I can … see that," I said. "But how, and when, in the world, did he get over and up there?"

"If you are asking me, the answer is I don't have a clue on that either," she said. "All I can say, and I hope that it is, is that at least we got him to his destination, and on time to save thousands, if not millions of people from punitive disaster, from the wrath of the divine scepter."

We both stared at the solitary figure standing on the tabled rock, with both his hands holding the rod up above his head. Face raised towards the sky, seemingly defiant against the heavy rain and wind that battered his body even as these now over - heightened forces of nature roared and relentlessly tore up the environment around him.

And then before our very eyes, the sky above him suddenly lit up brightly and the elongated lightning bolt, the same colored, three-way forked bolt last seen on top of BG Jr's house seconds before it got struck down into a massive fiery mess to the ground, lit the sky. This lingered around for about ten to fifteen seconds before another single streak of lightning appeared and diffused it, splitting the sky, suddenly sparking downwards, very similar to a flying comet, for what may have been at least five seconds and connecting with Meliak's body. And then his entire body lit up like a live electric steel rod. Another bright, fiery spark suddenly flashed the area as the lightning streak came into contact with the rock, through Meliak's body, and then the entire rock mass exploded as a missile had hit it. The fiery blaze, its flames bright and clear, lasted for about two minutes and then flashed out, likely because of the heavy rain. Meliak was no longer there, and the flat table-like rock slab he had been standing on, including the entire rocky mass around it, was also gone. Meliak, together with the stick, had been annihilated. The thought of finding burned pieces of flesh in the area gave me a nauseous feeling. That, or total cremation, was the most likely outcome of such a blast. His fate had been sealed with an explosive, fiery conclusion.

We sat there in the car, cold and wet and shivering, our legs submerged in water almost to the knees, for what could have been over twenty or more minutes, huddled together in each other's arms, each in our thoughts as we pondered what had just happened. Salieya had her eyes closed, but I could hear a quiet sob. This time I did not interfere; I just let her do her own thing. It was maybe ten minutes later that I realized there was some change in our current environment. The frequency of the lightning had changed entirely, pretty much distant, and less dramatic, and the powerful wind gust had suddenly changed to a light, breezy temperament. Carefully disentangling myself from Salieya's arms,

I stuck my head out of the window and looked around. The clouds were rapidly breaking up already, and visibility was beginning to filter out. The heavy rain downpour was easing into gentle flush flood mode. What an amazing, instant, or rapid change, I marveled!

Another indication of the way God does things, an example of his mighty power and greatness. In a blink of an eye, things we see as impossibly so messed up just merely returning to normal! That, my friend, is something that man can't do.

After messing with the jammed door for some time, and despite Salieya's objections that I shouldn't go out yet because she envisioned that it was still too dangerous, I opened it and stepped out of the car. Water gushed out of the car to the ground below. I waited for most of it to drain out before I placed both my soaked feet on the soggy ground. When I stood up, water came running down my legs and draining into the already oversaturated socks and shoes. The squishy sound from the soaked shoes as I took a few steps forward did not make it feel any better. It was like strolling in a water filled ditch. And every part of my body was sore, aching painfully, so bad I found myself wincing.

"Come on out Salie, it looks perfectly safe out here," I said to her. "The sky is clearing up fast, the rain is now lighter, and I don't see any live animals around here, except scattered big and small bodies of what looks like dead ones to me."

Then something slithered itself from underneath the car, over my feet, and made its way towards a dense brushy area at breakneck speed.

It was one of the longest snakes I had ever seen, and it disappeared into the dense undergrowth. Its sudden appearance sent a chill through my spine, but so fast was it that I had no time to react. I stood there, feeling dumbfounded.

Salieya stepped out of the car, but after hesitating for some time.

"Well, I guess you are right," she said as she watched the water drain down her body. She was still shivering uncontrollably.

"Am glad that at least we came out of all this alright and well... intact, although I have a lot of chest pain right now. I think the steering wheel rammed into my chest. It's kind of painful to breathe. The question is, how do we now get back home? How do we get back to civilization?"

"I am sorry about your car," I said, looking at the damaged vehicle. I am sure EdenCom will reimburse you for the loss."

She came closer and stood next to me. For some time, we both stood there in the light rain, arms folded in front of our bodies, lost in our thoughts. From where we were, we had a relatively extensive view of the adverse effects of the storm. Bent down or completely uprooted trees and shrubs, wildly patted foliage, steaming holes or areas, lots of scattered large and small stony debris, and a lot of animal bodies scattered randomly everywhere, all these were part of the horrifying scenario. But there were live animals, too.

Occasionally, an animal ran or walked past us and disappeared into the nearby bushy area or shrubs. A few dared to stop and gaze at us for a minute or so and then wandered away. The most spectacular sight was the cheetah. Although the animal was not staring directly at us, she showed up from nowhere and stood in one spot, not too far away from us, for almost five minutes plus, just staring ahead. Not once did he turn his head towards us, although I am sure he could either smell our distinct body odor or hear our breathing. Just as Salieya was suggesting we get back into the car, and while I was trying to figure out how to get both of us on top of the car because inside would be a death trap for both of us if the animal attacked, the cheetah suddenly took off quickly and disappeared into a distant bushy area.

"It's like the beginning of the world," I said, holding her hand, "Genesis, or the creation, with me and you being Adam and Eve."

Salieya burst out laughing, but held on to my hand tightly, squeezing it repeatedly." Yes, it feels like the world has just begun all over again, and I now feel like I don't want to get back to the regular world out there anymore. I wish to stay out here with you. But all good things come to an end, regardless. You know that, right?"

"That's right," I said. "That's why it's important to enjoy every moment as and when it comes."

We quietly stood there for the next fifteen or so minutes, holding each other's hand, the windy rain drizzle blowing onto our bodies. It surprisingly felt good, like having a fresh shower with tepid water. The clouds, quickly breaking up, we're beginning to reveal a clear, blue sky. I was, inwardly, hoping for a ray of sunshine. Then Salieya pointed to something in the distant sky, away from us. It was a rainbow beginning to form.

I turned around and looked at the car. The front was totally messed up, all mashed in and folded up, the engine still hot and steamy. The passenger side, my side, was also banged up and marked with bad scratches, looking like someone had used a big razor to scrap the paint off the sides. The back was intact, and so was the back-passenger area, except for the heavily dented, mangled, glassless, doors. I looked at the place where Meliak had sat. I still couldn't figure out how he had gotten out of there and made it to the top of the cliff, without us even noticing it, or with the vehicle running and reeling.

It was then that I saw the black object in a corner on top of the back seat. I managed to pry open the side door and take the object, one of my leather satchels, out of the car. I opened it to find the satellite phone inside, all intact. I didn't bother to see what else was in it. I was instantly excited that we had a way to call for help, and the probability of sitting out here in the wilderness for hours with no one knowing where we were or coming by to help had been reduced to zero.

"Salieya, look, it's the satellite phone, I found it!" I yelled out. "We can now call for help!"

Salieya immediately came over and stood by me as I excitedly yanked the machine out of the bag and quickly pressed the on the button. A loud beeping sound greeted me, and then a green light came on. That meant we were good to go. I quickly pressed three digits that connected me to one of the preprogrammed numbers, and in a moment, I was talking to Jim. Once I explained what was going on, he told me that they had been closely monitoring the strange Ethiopian storm, where the international weather service stations had labeled a phenomenon because of its nature. The people at EdenCom had a keen interest in it because their agents were on the ground in that country. He hooked me up with his assistant Pam, of course, whose job was to solve problems for agents in the field.

Pam said she would call me back in about fifteen minutes or let me know what to do next. When she called back in precisely fifteen minutes, she told me that everything was going to be alright and that I should sit tight and wait. Yea, like we were going somewhere!

Then she hung up on me before I could ask her some more questions. Salieya then tried to call, and successfully got hold of her Dad, explaining to him what had happened. He was not happy with her and wanted to immediately know what she had been doing in this region that had made her risk her life in what he termed Ethiopia's worst storm. But he promised he was going to act immediately to get us out of the area. As a senior and seasoned international journalist, he knew some people in both the government and private sector relief agencies that would make sure we were located quickly.

And so, we waited, meanwhile salvaging most of our essential stuff from the wrecked vehicle, dry or wet. Some sunshine rays were beginning to filter through the now thin clouds, and it was starting to feel warm, but very muggy. About an hour later, we heard the distant sound of a helicopter, which became louder and louder until we could see the machine hovering around in the sky above us. Salieya was so excited she jumped up from where she was seated and walked out into the open, waving her arms frantically. The helicopter crew soon saw her, and after circling a few times, they landed the helicopter a few yards away from us. But the people on this helicopter told us that they were not on a rescue mission, but to survey the aftermath of the storm, especially its origin, which was around this area. They were not going to evacuate us from here. But they radioed another team about us, and then took off.

It was yet another hour's wait before a red cross helicopter finally arrived and airlifted us to a hospital in Addis Ababa. At the hospital, we were examined, treated, and released. Salieya had a couple of fractured ribs and was ordered to rest for at least a month. I was treated for numerous bumps and bruises and for a severe burn mark on my neck's side. This was the area of contact by the rod when Meliak angrily hit me with it. Yet, for some reason, I decided not to tell the doctor about the cause of the burn, electing to tell them that I was probably hit by lightning. Salieya then called her dad, who came and picked us up, and together we headed over to aunt Mumia's house. Meanwhile, as father and daughter interacted, I got busy on the satellite phone with Jim, who instructed me to immediately secure the satellite-linked communication gear from the house and have it safely locked up at the hotel.

But the bad news was waiting for us at aunt Mumia's. Aunt Mumia had suffered a severe fainting spell and had been taken to the nearest hospital in the area. It was then decided that I pack up the equipment and head back to the hotel while Salieya and her dad stayed at the hospital to check out on her aunt. I could see that Salieya was already very worried, and I think she had all rights to be. Aunt Mumia was pretty much the only mother she had known most of her life, the woman who had practically raised her as her child. I told her that I believed everything was going to be fine and asked that she contacts me immediately if she needed help. Unknowingly, and sadly for me, this could be the last time I saw or heard from Salieya in a long time.

Before we parted, aunt Mumia's husband Enock came back from the hospital to pick up stuff and told us that his wife had suffered a stroke a few hours after we took off in that storm, because she didn't think we could make it through and was so afraid for Salieya's life. He also informed us that things weren't looking good at all for her. She was now in a coma and doctors were still working to bring her back. Then, to my surprise, he pulled me aside and apologized for his conduct on the night we engaged in a scuffle. He explained that he had been under a lot of duress, forced by some men who had followed us to aunt Mumia's house to place a tracking device in our car. They had guns and threatened to kill his family if he didn't do so. I now realized that this was how the Israelis had managed to track us down to the monastery. I had no problem with him anymore and apologized for hurting him. We parted as good friends, sealing it off with a handshake.

* * *

After we dropped the three relatives at the hospital, dad's driver drove me back to the hotel in the center of Addis Ababa. After putting up all the gadgets I had brought back with me, I took a long hot shower, changed into a fresh, clean cloth, and then talked to Jim again via the hotel room telephone. We discussed the assignment's outcome, and he listened with intense interest and wondered as I chronicled it to him. But Jim could not believe what I was telling him at first. Since EdenCom techs had not yet fully processed the satellite feeds from the assignment, he said he would look at it first and then tell me what he thinks. I then asked him to let me rest for a full day before I traveled back to the United States. He granted that and said it would take him that much time to get the satellite streamed data processed and ready for review as on-the-screen material.

Being so exhausted, I slept for what must have been a very long time by my standards, because naturally, I am the type of person who doesn't sleep for long hours. I woke up the next day in the late morning. I ordered hot food, fresh orange juice, and tea. When that food arrived, I devoured it quickly and hungrily, consuming every bit of it and all the drinks. As I did that, I switched on the television and was just in time to catch the morning news bulletin. The news was all about the deadly storm, with pictures of damaged entities due to flash floods, hailstones, some landslides, and yes, fire.

There was also a special broadcast. The country was mourning the death of Mr. B.G Fawas's oldest son, Mr. B.G Fawas Jr. It was being reported that B.G Jr. died in the recent stormy weather, the worst in the country's weather history when his house was struck and burned down by lightning. In a similar case, visiting emirates prince and prominent international businessman Sheik Ahmed Khalid Mosoud Bombaukari was also killed while visiting with Mr. B.G Jr. to discuss business prospects with the B.G Fawas Company, of which B.G Jr was the general manager. The sheik's remains were to be immediately transported back home. The bulletin showed recent pictures of B.G Jr. Working at the ranch house and at charity events.

The other high-profile victim of this tragic storm event was one of the country's major religious figures, the high priest of a sacred Christian following. He was also in the house with B.G and the Sheik, but it was not said what his exact purpose was. The report said he also happened to be visiting at the same time.

It was also being reported, in another segment of the news, that the storm had destroyed an important monastery in the west of the country and several people, mostly security guards on the property, and a few others in the surrounding areas, had been killed. I slowly shook my head, very well knowing the truth of the matter, only to ever be known by the few of us who witnessed the truth behind the horrifying, out of this world, epic events.

Jim's assistant, Pam, called me up a few minutes later, after I had just finished watching the special news bulletin and informed me that she had booked me on a flight out of Ethiopia in the next four hours. My five days of assignment in Ethiopia were finally over.

I spent most of the time sleeping on the flight back to the United States. The rest of the time, when awake, I spent thinking about the assignment, but mostly about Salieya. There was no doubt that this assignment had changed our lives forever. Even with a few days past since we parted unceremoniously, I found myself missing her. I wanted to see her again, perhaps take her out to dinner or something and share thoughts on our joint adventure. I was optimistic that this could happen someday in the future, but also wished it would happen very soon.

It was raining and dreary outside when my plane touched down at DFW airport at eleven o'clock, Saturday night. The same black Tahoe that had dropped me off at the airport for my rushed departure for Ethiopia, was waiting for me outside the airport terminal to take me home. But this time, Pam wasn't in it, just the driver. We talked a lot as he drove. The environment was more relaxed, he told me, for him to speak freely since Pam wasn't in the car. He didn't really like Miss Pam, he confided in me. He also expressed his desire to become a field agent someday. Thirty minutes later, he dropped me off right outside my apartment.

Then I remembered I had no keys. Putting my travel bag at the doorstep, I decided to walk over to Karen's place to retrieve my keys. It was a light but steady rain downpour, enough to give me a light soak by the time I made it around to Karen's apartment, which was several blocks away. But I was one person who never got bothered by walking in the rain. It took me about five minutes to get to her neighborhood and make my way to her apartment on the second floor. At first, I knocked lightly on the door, but after waiting for at least over five minutes, I knocked again, this time much louder. Finally, I heard some noise from within as a chain bolt was rapidly undone, and the door opened widely.

But it wasn't Karen standing in the doorway. It was a tall, bare-chested, Caucasian guy with short-cropped hair, faint mustache linked to a goatee, sprawling arms, and muscles, and dressed in boxers only, nothing else.

"Hey, what do you want?" he growled. He reeked of alcohol and cigarette smoke.

"I am sorry to bother you, but is Karen at home?" I asked.

"Yea, but who the hell are you?" he asked, stepping further out of the house, fully confronting me. He had tattoos all over his body.

"I am a close friend of hers, and I just came back from overseas. She has my car keys, and on the same keychain is my house key, so I came by to pick them up so I can get into the house," I replied politely, but not moving an inch from where I stood.

"Josh, what's going on? Who's at the door? I didn't order pizza," Karen said from inside. Then she appeared, quickly pushing him aside. She was dressed in tight, above the knee, blue shorts, and loose bra only, her hair all loose. She froze when she saw me, and then looking at the man, she nodded her head at him before saying, "It's ok, Josh. Just get back in, I will handle this."

The guy obeyed, rather sluggishly, but not after menacingly glaring at me. I didn't understand what his problem was.

"So, you are back, huh?" She asked, leaning against the doorpost, hands folded over her chest. "How was your trip? You look rather bruised and beat up."

"I Just arrived back home about thirty minutes ago, Karen. My trip, or assignment, was fine but very hectic," I answered, keeping my voice low. "So, who's this guy, Josh? And why is he glaring at me like that?"

"Oh, just a good friend of mine, here to keep me company since you didn't think I was good enough to know about your trip," she replied, staring at me with a grim face. "I got lonely and decided since you kept the whole trip thing a secret, I may as well keep myself busy with another company of my choice. I hope you don't feel the same mental anguish I felt when, after looking for you everywhere, I suddenly got this phone call from outside the country from you. I couldn't believe my ears, not at first, and I thought it was a joke, but then I realized you were really gone when I checked the number. It was unfair, unjustified, Kiron. You acted selfishly, and I hate being taken for granted. I didn't know when, if ever, you were going to come back. So rather than grieve about the issue, I decided to entertain myself. I now suggest that we get together somewhere in the future, and that is if you want to do so and talk about this. Definitely not today, because, as you can see, today is a rather bad day for that."

I slowly shook my head, looked down briefly, and then looked back up at her pretty face again. "That's ok, Karen," I said. "Just please give me my keys if you have them, so I can get inside my place."

"Oh, yes, I do have them. Hold on there for a moment please," She said, and without closing the door in my face, she turned around and walked back into the house. I could now see this guy, Josh, sprawled on top of her sofa, toying with the television remote. She was back in no time and handed me the keys. "Anything else?"

"No, nothing else," I said. And without another word, I turned around and left. After about a moment of a minute or so, I heard the door close behind me. She was wrong if she had expected me to react vigorously to the news of my sudden replacement. I was too tired to engage myself in that. I was glad to be home, and all I now wanted was to wash off again in a hot shower and then crawl into my bed and chill. But I couldn't help remembering that Meliak had warned me about all this. Another positive score on his not being so human.

I woke up late the next day, suddenly awakened by a loud knock on my door. I peeped through the door's peephole, thinking it was perhaps Karen wanting to talk. I wasn't going to open the door to let her in, because as of the previous night, I had no further desire to talk about anything with her, not in the nearest future. But it was Jim Holmbeck knocking on my door. I shouted "coming" and then quickly put on a pair of shorts and a white sleeveless T-shirt, I opened the door.

"Hi, Jim; what a pleasant surprise," I said. It was unusual for him to come around without calling me first.

Jim stepped in and instantly grinned. "Typical bachelor pad you have here, Day, but at least you are clean. I remember those days when I lived alone. I was no way near to being as organized and neat as you are. But first, you are not answering your phone. I wondered why, so I drove over," He said.

I walked to my bedside table and examined my phone. It was dead, having not been charged for over a week.

"Sorry, sir, my bad," I said. "I forgot to charge up my cell last night. I was too exhausted. Let me get ready. Should take me but about five minutes."

"Hmm... trip fatigue, understandable," he said. "You've been sleeping for over twenty fours. Get dressed because Mr. Murphy wants you to come to the office as soon as possible. The clients on your assignment are coming in to pick up their package this morning. It's usually his way of doing things, and that is to have the agent attached to the assignment at the time of delivery of the package to the client, which is also generally known as the handover ceremony. Even the clients themselves totally embrace this technique of receiving what they paid for with the actual person who made it possible."

I left Jim in the living room and quickly brushed my teeth and then put on some fresh cloth. A few minutes later, we were on our way to EdenCom, with Jim driving one of the company cars.

"I must congratulate you on a job well done on this assignment," Jim said to me. "We viewed everything and formatted the recording into sequences that would make sense to the client. Boss is very pleased with the results. Some of those scenes were indeed terrifying to view. That ... thing, whatever it is, was quite something. From the few clear shots, we managed to salvage out of the transmission, it appeared to be vividly complicated. But what was that?"

"An animal, a terrifying animal," I said. "But how come we weren't able to gain full focus on it? That part of the assignment should be clear enough. I had everything fully tuned to capture and record everything within view."

"Everything was reasonably within view, and recognizable in the transmission," Jim acknowledged, "but for this particular ... animal, as you said, something seemed to be obscuring it from full view ... a sort of shiny, bright light. It was mostly noted by two bright fiery spots, which we assumed to be its eyes, and that horrible noise it made."

We arrived at the company headquarters, and then immediately headed for the fourth floor, where the owner's office was. Upon arrival, the secretary informed us that the clients had already arrived and we're already in a meeting with Mr. Murphy. Jim proceeded to join the group, but I was instructed to sit and wait outside the office in the secretary's area. She appeared to be quite busy, typing away on the computer keyboard, and barely looked at me, like I didn't exist. So, I sat down and quietly waited.

About thirty minutes later, the door to the meeting room finally opened, and about six men, all dressed in black suits and white ties, filed out, smiling, and laughing heartily. As each of them walked past me and to the door, each one of them smiled at me broadly and then tapped me lightly on top of my left shoulder. I can never forget those looks. The smiles were so warm and looked so genuine that I was forced rather to grin back stupidly, even though I had never seen any of them before. Inside the office, I could still hear some energetic laughter going on, one of which was that hearty, grinding laugh always presented to customers by Mr. Murphy, plus Jim's light laugh, and then somebody else's rich, deep and booming voice, somebody else I didn't know. Probably one of the clients was still in there. Anyway, they finally all came out, Jim first, stepping aside to let the client through, and Mr. Murphy last.

This man, this client, unlike the others, was dressed in a sparkling white suit, with a matching flower pin neatly stuck to the coat's little front pocket and a sparkling silver tie. The other distinction with this man was that unlike the rest, he wasn't Caucasian, but neither was he black. He seemed to be a mixture of the two, his skin golden coffee brown but his hair of a light black complexion.

"Mr. Wand, I would like to introduce to you the young man who led and successfully concluded the project assignment as you asked," Mr. Murphy said. "You had asked to meet him, so here he is now, our fabulous agent Mr. Kiron Day."

"Aah, I finally get to meet the esteemed gentleman who did such a fine job," the man said, "How are you doing, young man?"

As I stood up and faced the tall, handsome, likely middle-aged gentleman with the rich, booming voice, someone seemed to whisper in my ear, but very clearly, these words.

"It's very important that you don't tell anyone here about us. Never, ever! Keep it our little secret for as long as you can."

It was the same man's rich voice talking in my ear, yet he still stood apart from me. I thought I was going crazy, that I was beginning to hear things. But then, I again realized that what I was experiencing was not a matter of hallucinations, but somewhat very real, basing on my recent experiences.

We faced each other and shook hands.

The man was Meliak.

The End.